FIELD OF HONOUR

FIELD OF HONOUR

MAX AUB

Translated by Gerald Martin

VERSO

London • New York

First published as *Campo Cerrado*, 1943
© Alfaguara 1997
First English edition published by Verso 2009
Translation © Gerald Martin 2009
All rights reserved

1 3 5 7 9 10 8 6 4 2

Verso
UK: 6 Meard Street, London W1F 0EG
US: 20 Jay Street, Suite 1010, Brooklyn, NY 11201
www.versobooks.com

Verso is the imprint of New Left Books

ISBN-13: 978-1-84467-400-8

British Library Cataloguing in Publication Data
A catalogue record for this book is available from the British Library

Library of Congress Cataloging-in-Publication Data
A catalog record for this book is available from the Library of Congress

Typeset by Hewer Text UK Ltd, Edinburgh
Printed in the US by Maple Vail

Contents

Introduction

Max Aub was born in 1903 in Paris to a French mother of German descent and a German Jewish father and died in Mexico in 1972. On the outbreak of the First World War, his father, a commercial traveller, was in Spain and, as an enemy alien, unable to return to France, so his wife and eleven-year-old son joined him in Valencia, and subsequently all took out Spanish nationality. Already bilingual, the young Max quickly picked up Spanish – he always claimed that his accent was atrocious – and wrote his prolific oeuvre solely in his adopted tongue, in which he displayed a mastery akin to Conrad's in English. Although his mother was cultured, Max put financial independence over a university education and followed his father's career in order to pursue his literary interests, which centred on the theatre.

Aub was of the generation that came of age in 1927 and which included Lorca, Buñuel, Dalí, and a long etcetera of poets, playwrights and novelists who formed an artistic renaissance on the eve of the Second Republic's proclamation in 1931. Nonetheless, Aub's literary career did not take off until in exile after the Spanish Civil War and, to his considerable chagrin, he never achieved much recognition during his lifetime even among his adopted compatriots, largely of course because of Franco's long dictatorship. However, since the advent of democracy in the 1970s, his work has become much better known and appreciated in Spain, although it has remained – with the exception of *Jusep Torres Campalans* (1962), and now this edition of his first novel – untranslated into English.

In 1928, Aub joined the Spanish Socialist Workers' Party and throughout his life never wavered from his allegiance to socialism and the Republic. For him, the true Spain, to which he fortuitously belonged, was represented by both; any other Spain, especially Franco's, which he considered an abomination, was an alien land. During the Civil War, the Republican government posted him as cultural attaché to Paris and it was there that he took part in organizing and mounting Picasso's *Guernica* in the Republic's pavilion at the 1937 International Exposition. To those who might protest that the painting was too abstract to portray the Republic's struggle, he retorted: 'If Picasso's picture has any defect it is that it is too real, too terribly true, atrociously true.'

As the Civil War went into its final full year in 1938, the Republic commissioned André Malraux to make a film based on his novel *L'Espoir*, about the first year of the war. Aub became one of Malraux's two assistants, translated the script into Spanish, chose the actors, mostly amateurs and semi-professionals, and the locations for what became the classic *Sierra de Teruel*. Limited by make-shift facilities, the first half of the planned thirty-nine sequences was shot in Barcelona; but Franco's seizure of the Catalan capital in early 1939 obliged the film crew to escape to France, where Malraux, with Aub in tow, was able to complete the rest of the film on location. The film, Aub later wrote, 'expressed the end of a world we had, with a certain hope, dreamt of, though if it would become certain who could say.'

Unlike the great majority of Republicans who fled in a massive exodus before Franco from Catalonia to France, Aub was spared the immediate indignities, the hunger and cold, of the hastily assembled refugee camps on the Mediterranean beaches. But the worst was still to come. In April 1940, Franco's ambassador to Paris complained to the authorities about Aub's presence in France. He was denounced as a 'German Jew, naturalized Spaniard during the Civil War, a notorious communist and active revolutionary'. Aub was not German, was not naturalized during the war and was not a communist, but this did not deter the French from confining him in a series of prisons – internment and concentration camps – until finally deporting him in October 1941, to a concentration camp in the Algerian Atlas Mountains to labour on a railroad the French were building. At the end of the summer of 1942, Aub escaped with the help of a guard. After a series of adventures, he embarked from Casablanca for Mexico where he encountered some of the many Spanish intellectuals of his generation who had fled into exile. He lived in Mexico City for the rest of his life, took out Mexican citizenship, but never felt totally at home there. Nevertheless he was an active member of Mexico's literary community and a close friend of many leading intellectuals, notably Luis Buñuel.

It was in his first exile, while still at liberty in France, that Aub wrote *Field of Honour*, which initiated the cycle of six novels (one in the form of a film script) centred on and around the Civil War, and which is generally considered his most impressive work. He took the manuscript with him to his first concentration camp and entrusted it to a fellow Spaniard who was about to be released, and who succeeded in smuggling it out with him to Mexico, where it was eventually published in 1943. He gave the overall title, *El laberinto mágico* (*The Magic Labyrinth*), to the six 'chronicles' as he called them in preference to novels, for the sense in which they represented 'real', rather than a novelist's imagined, events. Or, as he put it, 'reality's impact on me and mine on reality'. The 'labyrinth' was to him Spain itself. More pertinently than the generic title, each of the novels has a title beginning with the word *campo*, 'countryside', 'field' or 'camp', with its ironic ambiguities: the suggestion of nature's free and open spaces; the field of battle or the enclosed prison-world of labour camps. Whatever he had experienced he used 'to write what I imagine'.

Field of Honour follows the progress of a young village lad of a middling local family as he moves from his home to the provincial capital, Castellón, and then to Barcelona in the years leading up to the start of the Civil War in July 1936. In a sequence of vivid scenes, he witnesses workers and loyal security forces in the streets of the Catalan capital crush the local military uprising and initiate a revolution that in a few days would turn Barcelona into a city run by the working class. As in all the novels, much of the drama is conveyed in participants' conversations – it should be recalled that, by literary inclination, Aub was a dramatist – in which individuals' hopes, doubts, determination and despair are expressed, often with a bitter, ironic thrust. His protagonists are not 'stand-ins' for greater political or social forces in play, but are rounded individuals in their own, often disconcerting, right. Disconcerting because there are no heroes or villains since, depending on circumstances, his characters may at varying times be some of the one or some of the other or neither.

Aub took great pains to ensure the accuracy of his historical detail, but inevitably this did not prevent mistakes. For example, Durruti, the anarchist leader, did not die on the Huesca front, 8 July 1937, as this novel has it, but in the streets of Madrid at the start of the military's assault on the capital in November 1936. Overall, such errors are a minor matter in the vast tapestry which Aub weaves of the war, but they are worth bearing in mind as a caution against reading the novel as 'history'; instead, what the author does superbly is to recreate what no history can adequately achieve: the feelings of 'ordinary' people confronting an event of historic proportions.

As his comment on Malraux's film, *Sierra de Teruel*, which I cited earlier, indicates, Aub had a 'certain hope' that a Republican victory in the war would be the beginning of a new era in Spain. He immediately qualifies this hope, however; 'but who could say for certain?' In his mind – and this is perhaps the dominating theme of *The Magic Labyrinth* – there existed in equal proportions hope and doubt, which helps to explain the ironic edge of his writing. Optimism of the will, pessimism of the intelligence, to adopt Gramsci's adage, was, one could say, Aub's literary leitmotif throughout his life.

Ronald Fraser

Translator's Note

The publication of Max Aub's *Field of Honour* is a significant event in Anglo-Hispanic cultural relations. Aub is by far the most important literary chronicler of the Spanish Civil War but a combination of factors have made his writing relatively unknown, even in Spain itself, not least his exile in Mexico City. Not until the death of Franco in 1975 did his fiction begin to receive some notice; but Aub himself had died, still in exile, three years before; and then – the bitterest irony of all – his books were still not given the attention they deserved because Spain was in transition to a fragile democracy and the majority feeling was that the past should not be dug up any more than the remains of those executed by Franco should be exhumed and identified. This attitude has only changed in the past few years with the unexpected election of a socialist government led by a president, José Luis Rodríguez Zapatero, whose grandfather was an army captain executed by Franco's forces at the beginning of the Civil War for refusing to fight against the legally elected Republican government.

Despite his highly un-Spanish background, explained in Ronald Fraser's biographical introduction, Aub is, unmistakably, a Spanish classic: this can be seen in the stubborn seriousness and complexity of his clipped, telegraphic prose (mixing the Renaissance baroque tradition with that of the 1920s and 1930s avant-garde); in the extraordinary violence of the arguments between his different characters (no book has ever communicated better what political or cultural discussions between Spaniards used to be like); in the severity, or even cruelty of his gaze (one thinks of Quevedo, El Greco, Goya, Picasso's *Guernica*); and finally, in the depth of his extraordinary passion for a country to which he never felt he fully belonged and to which he nevertheless clung, with remarkable tenacity, both in his heart and in his writing, after he was exiled in 1939.

The book has been a challenge for the translator and will be a challenge to the reader; but the rewards are great. Here, in two hundred and forty pages, as a young country boy comes to political consciousness in the twenty years before the Spanish Civil War, the reader will experience, in synthesis: a vision of the relation between the rural and urban sectors, the provinces and a great city (Barcelona), in the most dramatic moments of a unique nation's history; an encapsulation of the national and international politics of the era, pre-Second World War, from extreme Left to extreme Right, including the very significant complication of Catalan nationalism; and a bird's-eye view of the aesthetic debates of the period, from literature through drama to painting, taking in bullfighting, football and even music-hall and burlesque along the way. Readers new to all this will be disorientated at times but I am certain it is one of those occasions when the steepness of the learning curve is more than justified by the results.

Books like this are much easier for the reader to research than they were before the age of Google and Wikipedia. But for his or her convenience, I have prepared a chronology of the period, covering the main events referenced in the novel set against the events of Aub's own life and in Spain, as well as two brief appendices: a list of the *principal political organizations and institutions* mentioned in the text; and a list of the *principal historical characters* depicted.

Chronology

1898   Spain, defeated in Spanish American War, loses Cuba, Puerto Rico and Philippines.

1903   Max Aub born, Paris. Father German Jew (non-practising), mother French. Aub will have, successively, German, French, Spanish and Mexican nationalities.

July
1909   'Tragic Week', defining moment in government-opposition politics in Spain. Troops fire on workers in Barcelona and many executions follow (including that of the revered anarchist Francesc Ferrer).

1913   *Field of Honour* (*Campo cerrado*): Novel's protagonist Rafael López Serrador born in Viver de los Ríos.

1914   Aub's family moves to Valencia, Spain. He quickly learns Spanish and later Catalan.

1920   Aub becomes a travelling salesman.

1923	Primo de Rivera's coup d'état inaugurates a military dictatorship in Spain with the support of King Alfonso XIII.
1926	*Field of Honour*: Rafael López Serrador leaves Viver de los Ríos for Castellón de la Plana.
1928	Aub joins Spanish Socialist Workers' Party (PSOE), lifelong supporter, though sometimes also close to Communist Party.
1929	*Field of Honour*: Rafael López Serrador leaves Castellón de la Plana for Barcelona in May.
26 Jan. 1930	*Field of Honour*: Rafael Serrador sacked from warehouse.
28 Jan. 1930	Primo de Rivera resigns. Military dictatorship continues.
1931	Local elections, Republic declared, 14 April. Alfonso XIII goes into exile.
19 Nov. 1933	Right-wing coalition led by CEDA wins national elections of Republic.

6 Oct.
1934   Socialist revolutionary uprising fails. State of war
        briefly declared.

February
1936   Popular Front wins elections.

17–18 July
1936   Military uprising, Spanish Civil War begins.

July
1936   *Field of Honour*: Rafael Serrador dies of typhoid in
        Barcelona.

1 April
1939   Spanish Civil War ends with General Francisco
        Franco victorious. A ruthless policy of execution and
        imprisonment begins.

May–Aug.
1939   Aub writes *Field of Honour* (*Campo cerrado*) in Paris.

April
1940–
Sept.
1942   Aub interned in prison and concentration camps in
        France, Algeria and Morocco.

October
1942   Aub arrives in Mexico. He will spend the rest of his life there with his wife and three daughters.

1943   *Field of Honour* (*Campo cerrado*) published in Mexico.

1969   Aub returns to Spain briefly. Bitterly disappointed, writes journal *La gallina ciega*.

1972   Aub dies in Mexico after second brief return to Spain.

1975   General Franco dies and the Spanish dictatorship ends. Both the monarchy and parliamentary politics are restored. Aub's writings gradually begin to be published in Spain.

31 Oct.
2007   José Luis Rodríguez Zapatero's PSOE government passes the Law of Historical Memory. This belatedly brings 'symbolic justice' to those defeated by Franco and enables the investigation of crimes and the recovery of disappeared corpses.

2009   *Field of Honour* (*Campo cerrado*) published for the first time in English.

PART ONE

ONE

Viver de las Aguas

Suddenly the lights go out. Ten o'clock, the moon beams down on whitewashed walls; the plaster divides, half white, half grey. Silence runs like a shiver through the streets, from head to toe, from the town square to Quintanar Alto, dark against the hill. Early September, cold air coming down from the Ragudo; higher still, mountain stars, smudges in the wind.

The square, for eight days, turns bullring, its plain façades closed off by barricades of planks and ladders; the last light, at the club, lies low among the scaffolds; out in the middle the small baroque fountain, with its four spouts, becomes a water trough once more. The square, at strike of ten, umbilicus of the world. Fifteen hundred souls perched on the edge of Aragón. Down below, tumbling towards the sea, by way of Jérica and Segorbe, the towns and villages of Valencia; uphill, by Sarrión, the rough, bare road to Teruel.

The church clock takes the moon full on its face. Fear and excitement mingle, with anxious looks over shoulders: everyone moves closer together. Five past ten: a rumour lifts its tail, brave heads peep out past shutters, the more presumptuous start to congregate outside the notary's house and the doctor's next door, all eyes on the eligible daughters leaning over the balconies of those worthy functionaries, dowry up front and suitor close behind, love-lance atilt and invisible hands thanking heaven for the darkness. Old men denying the years, dark faces and dark tunics, slip by against the walls. Any momentary outburst receives immediate correction: a murmur silences it.

In the remotest part of his memory Rafael López Serrador can find no older recollection; it is the most venerable image of his childhood: the moment when, during the September fiesta, the fire bull is about to be unleashed; that, and the sound of living water along the earth: fountains, springs, ditches.

The fire bull has always killed five or six men: a savage and terrifying beast, with bigger horns than 'Favila', who killed eight people in Rubielos de Mora back in '89. His owner, whom the children take to be rich and mysterious, parades the monster through fair and fiesta. Some years, when the pitch has left him half-blind, they turn the great beast over for the young bullfighters to finish off; the devil of a job, even when they escape the horns, because by then the damned brute has learned a thing or two. The cattleman takes coffee in the Maurista Club. The children gather at a prudent distance:

'That's him, that's him!'

The heifers run, the young lads taunt and dodge them; the townsfolk, men and women, go out to greet them along the highway, in search of a fright (oh, what a fright!), a shock (oh, what a shock!), happening upon and pausing, pre-planned, at the grilles of each friend's house, or taking refuge behind fence, wall and hedge along the roadsides. Men with black tunics and sashes, weekenders in shirt-sleeves; some try to execute passes and end up breeches atatter to jeers and guffaws. Dust, beer and scratch races, as the band threads pasodobles.

But the fire bull arrives by night and stands alone on the river bank. No one dares call out to him. Grown-ups and little ones tread paths and walkways, first thing, to spy out and size up the cattle. They are pastured at the edges of the watercourse, half hidden among the reeds, in a dry boulder-strewn bed. Olive and fig trees serve as coverts. Girls give little shouts to animate the crowd. Lovers turn off to right and left to 'get a better look', so they say, and to hitch skirts without risk of surprise. Some take lunch. Down below, completely ignoring the young grazing bulls, three labourers head back to town, sickle on shoulder, dog-end askew, spraying saliva:

'You'd think they'd never seen an animal, for Christ's sake!'

A mule plods round the track of an ancient waterwheel, pounding out the revelry with the rhythm of its blind hooves; a thin stream of water flows. Rafael Serrador moves the little finger of his right hand from his right nostril into his left, stoops to pick up a pebble and tries to throw it to the river, but falls short. Others, bigger than him, hurl volleys of stones at the backs of the heifers. Some of these, a minority, lift their heads and look, indifferently; others, at most, take a step forward, muzzles tracking ahead in search of thin scraps of grass between the ditches.

The river runs in the shelter of a ravine which slashes, from ochre to violet, the greens of the opposite bank. Its water can be smelled and divined behind the canefield; where the cutting dies the waters can be seen swirling. The sky, its own blue; a few crows cut across it, cawing. Those who have been to Mass begin to arrive, making their way between humps and ridges, scorning paths, tramping over alfalfa, tangled pumpkin plants, onions; stealing grapes and melons.

'I hope you all burst, you sons of bitches!' snorts a labourer working at a plot, in the shade of an old half-ruined wall, on the way to the ravine, when each year, after the fiesta, he has to redig vegetable patches and replant fences and stakes. Between the path and the plot runs the irrigation ditch, the clear bright transparent waters ripple weed over moss, coriander shoots grow along the paths. (Two years ago Rafael was in bed with a bad chill and was given an infusion of coriander to cure it.)

His mother is on the flighty side and likes a song and a dance. Some look at Rafael and say he looks like his father. That shocks him: it seems natural enough, but he knows it's not so. What do people mean by it? His father is short and dark. Rafael is glad he's like his mother, who is taller, with her black bodice and black skirt, handkerchief knotted at her throat when she has to go out, and especially when she wears shoes with buttons, a bit of a heel and narrow toe.

So the music plays and gives back to September the warmth it has lost. The deputy and his family have arrived. The recorder, the pharmacist and Don Blas set off to the club each day. It's rumoured that this year there will be an extra day of novice fights. His father continues to curse everything that has happened or ever will: from Monday there is an extra train to and from Valencia, and the yellow omnibus he drives back and forth at a mule's pace will have to make four extra journeys, from the town to the station, rain or shine. The phaeton driver is a republican and an enemy of bullfights, which he thinks a barbarous and backward spectacle, though he never misses one. The flies seem especially agitated just

6

now, and cause more fuss than ever: at siesta time you can hear their whirring buzz on hanging papers and in vinegar jars, with their treacherous sugar lump bait, in desperate super-fly efforts not to come to a sticky end.

Towards the south, along the gorge of Jérica, blue and green distances unfold; towards the north only kermes oaks and scrub, to the snow line: horizon one way, mountain the other.

Fish patties, still hot, come down from the club's kitchen: crisp golden dough, soft underside, smell of best oil, pastry doubled over, imprisoning behind the well-baked edge the green or scarlet strips of roast peppers deliciously married with the rosy pink of minced tuna, the crimson or ruddy colour of fried tomatoes, the yellow of whole pine kernels. Saffron-coloured drips trickle down the cheeks of well-dressed children, leaving a shining trail.

'That's your new suit, José Luis!'

'The peppers are from the estate!'

The word spreads. Don Blas leans back.

'It's the club's treat.'

The village children crowd in the doorway, trying to make themselves stand out.

'The peppers are from the estate, every last one.'

They watch with enthusiasm as those inside sit scoffing away.

'Better than the ones from Martí, Don Blas!'

'No comparison!'

'No chemicals here, nor other concoctions!'

'Call a spade a spade, no messing.'

And Don Blas, crossing his hands like an abbot:

'Good wine needs no bush.'

The fire bull is kept tied with his head covered by a sack, in a cage of wooden stakes in Uncle Cola's shed. On each horn they fix a great ball of tar held up by two iron hoops, then they light them and the balls blaze, and then the dreadful brute is released. A serpent of dread panic zigzags through the black and white streets.

His light announces him. The lime is dyed the faintest pink when he is still fifty metres away from the nearest corner. Immensely long shadows appear, grow smaller as they race away, disappearing to nothing and then growing back again, according to the direction of the basilisk's stampede. From archways, doors, gates, nooks, corners, stairs and posts, from the square itself and the streets, linked in a circle so the bull will chase its own shadow until it fades, shouts and calls, howls and squeals can be heard, each giving rise to the next: 'He's coming! Here he comes! Here he is!' They call him, want him, desire him; and when the light, the flames, the barbarous mass of darkness comes crashing into the street, their desire turns to terror, as after a first, frenzied, furtive coition.

'He's coming! Here he comes! Here he is!' The beast goes flashing by, fleeing from himself, virile burning curse, myth made flesh and blood and smelling of burning horn. He charges headlong uphill. The moon and its light parasol glide down the freshly whitewashed housetops. The bull goes round his enforced circuit; the full roar of the square tells the spectators in the streets that he has completed the lap. 'Here he comes again!' Desperately he looks, five, six, seven times for the unattainable way out. The fire gyrates. He stops outside a house, turns full circle in a blind alley: women scream, even the bravest back off. Finally he stands his ground in a corner of the square. The boldest of them, seeing him exhausted, start to taunt him from a distance, but run for it whenever the brute makes the slightest move. Rafael Serrador hates his neighbours: Mano, Pindongo, Uncle Cuco, Tartanero, Serranet, all rushing off now to challenge the magnificent beast.

'I wish he'd trample the lot of them!'

All the local circles, from the Club to the Radical Party – which now calls itself the Patriotic Union – condemn the cruel custom for 357 days of the year: there is no one, however, when the September fiesta comes around, who does not long for the mythical appearance of the fire bull. Rafael Serrador wishes, with all the might of his eight, nine, ten years, that the bull would set about the whole town and leave no stone standing; and in his darkness he sees the town smouldering and all the people wounded, and a great procession of fire bulls like a rainbow around the sky. He runs through the ruins, on the way to school, burning his feet on the embers. Because the appearance of the fire bull means term will start soon. Go or stay home, it's all the same to Rafael. Don Vicente is harmless and has a beard; he's lost all authority since everyone found out he's had a child by the daughter of Don Blas's gamekeeper. 'Filthy swine!' say Rafael's parents. 'How can he hope to discipline children?' Those who want to study do so. Rafael is not one of the worst. There are two books at home which his father has promised him when he knows how to read properly: a history of the French Revolution, by Don Vicente Blasco Ibáñez, and another, on the Romans, by Don Emilio Castelar. More than one fowl has paid with its life for carelessly crapping on them.

Rafael is usually woken by the clucking of hens above his head. The chicks run back and forth along the edges of his straw mattress. To enter the house you have to go down two steps. The passageway is not paved; earth trodden smooth by generations sees to itself. The mules live on the right, one called Starlight, the other Gabriel. Another, who'd died years before, was called Fraternity. To the dismay of decent folk on their way uphill, the coach driver, raining lashes on the poor nag's back, would wink and pull a face, saying: 'Here, take that, Fraternity, but don't tell Gabriel!' A pig is also fattened up once a year. They usually call him Pete.

'That Pete we had five years ago, when Juana got married, he was really something . . .!'

The whole house reeks of stables and dung; when Rafael looks back on his childhood he remembers the stench of the dungheap, the softness of fresh hay, the ooze of rotting excrement. Behind a big gate was a yard in which they could just about fit, with the bar raised, the shabby yellow omnibus, source of life.

Each year, at grape-harvesting time, a baby is born. Sometimes it dies, sometimes not. Then it grows, dirty, scabby, spotty, with sores and sniffles, never knowing what cold and hunger are, because they are its air and its food. They all grow up blackened, skinny and hard, used to doing much as they please and not giving a damn for anyone else – except, soon enough, the sex of their females, which they prize, and their horses and mules, held in similar esteem, as songs and sayings testify: *zorongos* and *jotas* still abound there, heard in field and on hill.

Olive trees can't survive thereabouts; higher up only kermes oaks, hedge mustard, rosemary and brambles endure. Winters are long and bring snow. After the fire bull, the fields die and fall still. The odd partridge, smarter than hunger, makes off at the slightest sound. The dark shacks' only knowledge of the sky is through the slow smoke of their chimneys. The water keeps flowing true to itself. Each day Rafael Serrador's father drives his yellow covered wagon back and forth through the sleeping fields. Each day the only words they exchange are about buying a second-hand van, a Ford, near new; couldn't ask for better bodywork. Not much traffic, only on Segorbe market day do a few go down, returning at night. Their eyes carry not even the reflection of the big town.

The years keep coming and Rafael passes through them; he grows little by little, measuring himself by enormous leaves which each year, like bark, fall on the highlands adding grey hairs where there's no more room for glory. He has now been through the two books without making much of them; now he is considered grown-up and they send him to Castellón, as a jeweller's apprentice. That year, as chance would have it, there was no fire bull. A new governor had just been appointed and, with the usual array of laudatory adjectives in the local press, prohibited amateur bullfights throughout the province – whilst always ready to grant special permission. Since he demanded more than his predecessors and there wasn't time to haggle or indulge him, the town was left without its bull and the governor was left as a 'new-style' politician and man of integrity.

TWO

Castellón de la Plana

Castellón is a broad, flat town, with no other character than the lack of it. Its houses are white, with two storeys, an attic and a flat roof to dry the clothes; with no other feature than the socle of imitation marble, veined with grey, pink or green. Fascias and cornices undecorated; balconies continuous, in rows; such rails, urns or volleys as the plasterer has seen fit to send the builder; the blinds, green or dirty. Now and then – a dozen in the whole town – a larger house in 'Spanish Renaissance' fashion, with coat of arms and skylights of Portland cement, lintel and branched wainscot, pilasters of uncertain style, large porch, prominent wrought-iron balcony, all rounded off with spherical fleurons, weathervane and lightning conductor. The dark painted wood stands out against the grey and white speckled base of the false stones; across the balustrade, a palm tree bends in a discoloured loop; the plaster looks like cardboard, the wood like paper, the effect is silly, flashy, pompous. Wide streets, sticky heat, many cars; the dust is stirred up, twirled and deposited at the whim of gentle gusts at every corner. It is not the wind that lifts the dust, but the dust itself.

The sea does not exist; there is a harbour in the distance, and its commerce. The traders – dark skin, purple nose, tough wrinkled hands, writing desk with pouncet-box, thrifty with words; throaty, mistrustful, haggling, fond of a bit of cape-play for effect, dragged only on pain of death to the grilles of banks – the traders live for business; all of them sons of the red earth, rich by inheritance, embezzlement or obstinacy. They know no god but their oranges, no Virgin but that of the destitute (their own patron is the Magdalena, but they care less for her than for the Valentina). They go about in black jackets, white shirts, black hats, black trousers, black shoes or white sandals, showing off their cheques, their friends from Hamburg or Liverpool, their hunting dogs. Every one of them has been to Les Halles or Bremen; they bring back from Europe a great contempt for everything which is not theirs.

'It's mighty cold up there, chum!'

To them, food cooked in butter is a personal insult. Some of them have spent months and even years in Paris or London living on boiled eggs and ham, about which they have plenty to say:

'It's called Parma ham and you buy it from Italians.'

Everything lives off the orange, which is sacred – itself, its handling, its price, fertilization, freightage, temperature and phases. Nothing else exists: the land and its cultivation is all that matters; no one would think of building a house down by the sea, only inside the orchard, even though the heat and the mosquitoes oblige them to live in the dark, and to sleep among gauze nets. Baths arrived recently, for show. No one would ever bathe in the sea – at the most, douse their backsides for a day at San Sebastián, after the Valencia fair, in the company of their spouse, to make folks talk. Fish is not a usual meal, unless made respectable by rice. When there's talk of water, it's understood to be for irrigation. No rich man owns a motor launch – cars, yes: Castellón de la Plana is a paradise of Fords and Chevrolets; North America rings loud in their ears and their imagination, and a lot has been heard of 'California' in recent years.

The Club is the Club, very Spanish Renaissance, more Spanish Renaissance than anything, with its games of *julepe*, its dominos and its marksmen – because here, as in Valencia, pigeon-shooting lacks the aristocratic overtones it takes on in Andalusia or Madrid.

Around the orange growers lives the city, growing out of their farms. In the innermost recess sits 'the wife', uncorseted in a rocking chair, dejectedly fanning her underarm odours; the bullrush bends beneath her round flabby weight; a goblet sweats on a table, covered with a cloth.

'Enriqueta, Felisa . . . Doña Perpetua . . . Don Martín . . . Over at Pampló's . . .'

The governor is third-rate; the brothels, few and dirty. The hubbub of cafés can be heard from afar: dominoes is the great game. The only workers to be seen are cart drivers. The factories are on the outskirts, like the station; a land of delivery-men, a quiet, slow town, small, soft and spoiled. An atheneum languishes by an acacia and the odd schoolmaster writes modish verses in Valencian.

A drunkard is an event. Rafael Serrador entered the service of the town soak: the first days he was regarded with pity by the local gossips. It surprised him and he pulled faces at them. They shrugged, turned their backs and left him in peace.

It is not the jeweller – an ugly mug nicknamed Rioja – but his wife that counts. Short and stout, chubby-cheeked, with a shiny nose, mouth and chin together the size of a five-peseta piece; she smells a bit of what might be called bad breath. The chin, split like a peach; foolish eyes, big floppy bosom, swinging hips, high heels and fancy pinafore. It's said they got married without benefit of clergy and she shields herself by blabbing out gossip at the volley: the town knows it, grants her a certain respect in return and comes to her on the quiet, under cover of buying a brooch or pendant, to prospect for whatever nuggets may fall, at the expense of the solicitor or the manager. The shop is on a corner, painted white with gold trim. The counter prevents access to the workshop where the master beats out on the anvil what work disposes and wine permits. Vitrines are piled up, merchandise scattered all about, the novelties attracting dust so fast they can't be distinguished from the junk. The main diversions are the commercial travellers and the servants. The proprietress has a knack for embroiling the former in hope of discounts; the odd simpleton falls for it and the flan-face grows on her heels: she considers herself a great businesswoman, and never fails to remind her truly wedded of it every night. 'If it weren't for me!' Sales are by the piece, though buyers come from time to time on the lookout for a bargain; then the jeweller shambles out into the arena to discuss prices and quantities.

The maid is fifteen and looks twelve, her kneecaps red from going so hard at the floorcloth. Not much flesh on her, big dark eyes, hair like soot, breasts like lemons, joints seemingly dislocated as she carries the water bucket to and from the drain. Rafael rubs up against her just for the fun of it, without knowing why; she pushes him away without embarrassment. She likes to hear what doesn't concern her: they call her 'the

Baggage', and she tries on pendants, bracelets and shawl pins when the masters are otherwise engaged. Rafael feels a certain respect for the saucebox who, moreover, knows the town better than most and always keeps her ears open, because nothing is better for business than knowing about weddings and funerals in good time. 'No weddings this year', they say, to decline an uninteresting offer. The importance of a high-class hitching is measured by the number of sugar basins, cruet stands and boxed sets of six coffee spoons which the happy pair attract. Funerals pay less but there are more of them and they are a speciality of the business; chains for fans, clocks and watches, pendants, fine combs and cufflinks, rosaries and bangles, safety pins and buttons, purses, lockets and necklaces, beads: all black, crystal, corozo, wood or bronzed steel decorated with false agates or jet trinkets, or simply painted brass; respectability is measured by the length of the mourning period.

Rafael was taken on as an errand boy and they had him traipsing back and forth all day. When he wasn't on the run and was tempted – let himself be tempted – by a chair, he would receive a nagging or a cuffing, he could never guess which, an order or a feather duster:

'See to the dust, slowcoach. If I didn't keep my eye on you!'

He would dust away until the jeweller's wife sent him on another errand. She was not usually in the shop, but out back. The customers knew this and hollered for her, receiving a hasty 'I'm coming!' in reply.

She would take some time to appear, out of breath and arranging her bun shining with bandoline. She would then put on her most insolent expression, lifting the half-almonds of her chin as she eyed the intruder and cut him with an incisive:

'Were you wanting something?'

She was short-sighted, but would never admit it. Anyone who dared recommend an optician found himself covered in insults:

'Mind your own business! Your house is short of people and this one's short of air. Me short-sighted! Me wear glasses! What on earth can you mean?'

At any other time she was attentiveness itself, cloying, soft-soaping the most tiresome visitor, whilst criticizing unmercifully those who were absent. Her own delays and absences were due to her brazen randiness. All it took was a taste of something she enjoyed or to knock back a glass of wine, which she wasn't particularly keen on, but which she appreciated as a vehicle for her lust, and then, if business permitted, she would trap the jeweller in a corner, keel him over and entangle him in the most uncomfortable postures. He would get the deed over with as best he could, reflecting that one day death would come to put an end to this. The lady's involuntary haughtiness, when interrupted in her natural frolics, masked her concern less she transmit the jeweller's fetid stench to the customers: she would combat the smell by stuffing herself full of peppermints whose aroma represented, for anyone who might have suspected anything, the tail, the end, the final twirl of love.

The master used to get drunk every night, at home or outside; when the latter occurred the night watchman would bring him home in floods of tears. The woman would undress him without a peep, with the most delicate attention, the only time she showed any tenderness: then she washed and brushed him and put him to bed like a baby. Each moon brought her the illusion of pregnancy; despite certain medical symptoms, imagination was stronger. Rafael could not make out those switchback moods. The proprietress's character would sour menstrually and 'the Baggage' would give him a wink, but he remained totally in the dark. When the jeweller was not drunk, his wife treated him as a doormat and he put up with it.

Another important denizen of the shop was the moggie, a white cat with long fine hair and green almond eyes speckled with bright yellow; vicious towards strangers who tried to stroke him, only too well aware of his prerogatives, and jealous of his domain. He drove his owners to distraction, fretting at every moment about his humour, his health and possible desires; he had a huge collar, name plate, padlock, the whole caboodle. His food was the absolute priority of the jeweller's wife; if someone came in while she was seasoning the morsels destined for the little beast, they would have to wait or come back; nothing in the world, this one or the other, would have made that feline eat at twelve what was due to him at eleven. Unhurried in gait, contemptuous of games without profit, he gazed from the summit of his superiority as trinket salesmen strove to win his friendship with paper balls, fake miaows, scratchings on the counter or other such childish tricks. Lordly he strode across showcases and work benches, among clips, rings, clasps, necklaces and wires, treading on pearls, imitation corundums, earrings and other odds and ends awaiting repair by the jeweller's file and pliers. He was sacred, even when he pushed his whiskers between owner and client, to the latter's discomfiture. Then the chatterbox would say:

'What do you want, my little darling? What do you want, my beauty? What do you say to your tickety-boo?'

She would put him on her shoulder in the hope that such a show of affection would enable her to clinch the deal; but if the cat went back to his wanderings, she would respect his wishes. They treated him as a son, the money-mongers, telling him off quite seriously when, as happened frequently, he went out on the tiles. The search for the puss around the neighbourhood was Rafael's job and an important part of his duties.

Of that entire period, which lasted three years, few memories remain. Above all the area around the store is imprinted on his mind; that time is best represented in the shape of a brass tap. He feels himself asphyxiating in the absence of running water; he misses the gush of springs from below the earth. Water is scarce and hard, they bring it up by force with waterwheels and engines, channel it along ditches and trenches, store it in tanks and distribute it, blind, through lead pipes; they use it with parsimony. It spatters into cans and kettles, buckets and bowls, onto pewter and china, meted out to the taste of the consumer. Rafael sleeps in a cot inside a cubbyhole, by a marble sink fitted into the wall; the tap doesn't fit and the mouth drips. This constant accompaniment is something he will remember always.

Life is flat and Rafael is only troubled or surprised when, from time to time, his willy stands on end. The mistress allows him no friends, robs all of his time. He spends Sundays out at the 'country cottage', helping the bricklayers, who are in no hurry to construct it: because business, despite the odd backward lurch, is prospering, and so the jewellers can build their own country house, give shape to a small garden where they will plant, like everyone else, a bougainvillea – Josefa-Augusta, they say it's really called – along with passion-flowers, geraniums, creepers, hollyhocks, *murcianas* and verbenas. A lemon-tree and a mandarin allow them to imagine a future orchard; to hear them talk, they are already selling oranges at top prices. Every Sunday brings a shrub to plant, a jasmine or a heliotrope; they come and go by trap.

The earth is red and brown, the trees – cypresses and oranges – eternally green, the mountains in the far distance mauve and purple, the sky cloudless, very high and clearest blue. Cicadas and frogs mark time and heat; the channels and ditches are dyed red, they smell of churned-up rainwater, they cease – at times – to be ditches and become parched trenches until the moment of irrigation; freshness waits underground; squashy underfoot, the clay rises to mud, its dark tint chequers the plain; little grass grows along the margins: the exploitation of the land leaves no room for it.

To Rafael, the plain doesn't seem like countryside. For him the country is a place of hills and slopes and scrubland; stony ravines, with ploughed fields rising and falling at the whim of the water: the river and its vales; rosemary, thyme, stones, broom and thickets, the occasional fig tree, some beehives. Distance: glimpsing, far below, the sleeping mist in the valley enveloping his mountain town: cold winds, snow; not even the sky is the same: the stars here seem sparse compared with the stars in his own harsh land.

This soft, easy life neither surprises him nor wins him over; he sees the wealth but is not impressed, he doesn't understand respect for money alone and the land doesn't seem to him more precious because of what it yields. He finds the orange growers – pot-bellied, excitable, greedy – flabby and far too smooth; everything strikes him as bland and dozy in this landscape without slopes. He guesses there must be something out in the world that requires effort, but he doesn't know what. He holds back and keeps mum and takes the first opportunity to give a good hiding to the hare-brained boy next door, who has a stupid face. Then he regrets it: too easy.

Some Sundays he watches the evening fade out of sight, sitting on a concrete block forgotten by the gate. He fidgets with a trowel, unawares, scoring the earth, looking for signs, eyes fixed on he knows not what, without thinking. The atmosphere buoys him up. When something moves in the fading light, he thinks: 'What will I be?' To be a craftsman jeweller has little appeal. Return to the village? Leaving presupposes never going back, except on furlough, should he serve the King.

At the sound of a gasp, at the rustle of a curtain, Rafael discovered love: jeweller and wife in ejaculatory climax surprised him greatly. Until then he had reckoned the mouth was the only cavity favourable for love and natural channel of generation, though it wasn't easy to figure out how it was done. He was cock-a-hoop with his discovery; he felt grown-up, and the family's front and rear took on a whole new meaning.

One of those Sundays at the cottage saw the inauguration, with a special paella and bottles of glowing red Rioja, of the new toilet, with porcelain bowl and polished mahogany seat, and although he was forbidden use of same – plenty of room outside: after all, classes still exist – the young man was tickled by the idea of sitting down to defecate. Astonished by the comfort of the posture, he set to manipulating his penis and soon discovered masturbation, happier than a sandboy; just about then the down on his lip began to darken, dotted with pimples.

To guard the little farm the proprietors took into service a strapping widow of about forty, apron-string for a waist, and a solid eighty kilos. Marieta by name, fisherwoman by trade in former days, she complained bitterly about her rheumatism, the reason for her change of station, though the truth was that work had never been her weakness; she would look for the sun wherever it went and find some way of occupying her hands. Her children roamed where they pleased, brought up by a sister of hers whom they considered more their mother than the real one. On her evenings off she entertained a certain civil guard, a good friend of the previous usufructuary, a braggart, slash-faced and bandy-legged, very self-satisfied, and delighted at the thought of dovetailing with that dark slatternly lump. For it allowed him to bear with a commiserating smile his poor scrap of a sergeant, with his long dry face, straggling moustache, tartar-coated teeth, thin hair and harridan of a wife, her thunderbolts always ready to fire: jealous as a wasp without flowers. The sergeant took refuge in the aura of his stripes and made life difficult for his subordinates, specialists in beating up strikers, petty thieves and bullfight spectators without tickets, unloading on them the free kicks and punches with which he dreamed of blacking and blueing his irresistible consort. He came out of such beatings feeling comforted: there are two types of cop, those who like blood and those who prefer internal contusions; the first tend to carry out their assignments with their bare hands, the second prefer to do their coaxing with the musket butt. The sergeant was of the first kind, Marieta's playmate of the second. He too had a wife: somewhat consumptive, timid and sad, fully committed to the next life, which, being the daughter and granddaughter of civil guards, she imagined as an enormous barracks full of angels with wings and stripes, and God as Commander in Chief. She viewed conjugal copulation with horror, as a sin, and avoided it as much as possible. The guard, Manolo by name, was quite content with that so long as she didn't ask him how and where he compensated. Manolo and Severiano, he of the jealous Aragonese wife, rubbed along as well as could be in the circumstances, given what's been said about the sergeant; they told one another their troubles and were brought together quite often by their enthusiasm for rice, though the one preferred it moist and the other dry, a source of unimpassioned arguments.

One Saturday, in the late afternoon, Rafael took some gear out to the cottage. He had been delayed at the shop polishing a bracelet which had just been repaired. The jewellers had told him to stay over in the country, and they would follow the next day, at the usual time: they were thinking of going to the cinema that evening, as there was a film on with Francesca Bertini. It almost made the shopkeepers feel young again: they had met in a cinema in Valencia, under the auspices of Pina Menichelli, and everything which suggested Italian cinematography had them gazing wistfully at one another. The journey of the King and Primo de Rivera to Italy, which took place around the time of our story, gave added grandeur and weight to this exceptional outing, because they rarely went to shows of any kind.

Rafael arrived at the house as the evening turned sea-blue. There was no feeling of life: the heat had abolished all laws. A cricket stapled the corners of the sky to the earth with saw-like rasping. Marieta was busy with her needles, curled up on the couch.

'Hallo there, laddie!'

The boy left his burden in the room that served for everything and went out to take the air. They dined shortly on rough bread, chops and fried tomatoes, drank a jar of red wine between them, the slattern made coffee and they even had a glass of brandy; then she proffered some tobacco, which he to her amazement refused: he had never smoked.

'Oooh, what a fine young gentleman! The Lord alone knows what you get up to when there's no one looking!'

Rafael was fit to drop and went to bed. The country house, like its neighbours, had on the ground floor a hallway, open to the winds, and two bedrooms. The housekeeper slept up in the garret, by the roof, where they only went to hang out the clothes: no one gives a damn about the landscape. But like it or not, above the orange trees, in the distance, there lies a strip of sea to gladden the heart.

Rafael was in one of the downstairs bedrooms, by a concession only explicable through the impossibility of returning that night to the capital. The bed was new, of lacquered wood with iridescent mother of pearl, beside a table with a red marble top on which stood an aluminium candlestick, with a candle and a cheap box of matches. They had still not installed electric lighting, despite the promises made to the jeweller each Monday by a friend, employed by the Castellón Electric Company some twenty years past. The walls were newly whitewashed and the tile dado gleamed green and red. Rafael got undressed; the clean sheets felt strange. It was hot and he couldn't settle. He pushed back the bedclothes and, to occupy himself and get off to sleep, began to masturbate. At that moment, having been lying in wait, the dark salacious female opened the door and without so much as a by-your-leave climbed on the bed, pulled up her skirts and herself introduced the astonished lad's reason for being into her well-coursed channel.

'Not like that, silly, not like that,' hissed that hulking female.

Rafael lay back silent and still.

'Haven't you done it before?'

And as he just slightly shook his head, the brazen hussy started to twist and turn like some wild bobbin, to the great shock of the beginner who didn't know which saint to commend himself to. The intruder devoured him with kisses and the boy let her go at it. They repeated the performance twice, changing positions; then she wheedled him to let her stay and sleep, but the first-nighter refused categorically. His thwarted bedfellow backed off, snorting, though not without a hundred suggestive remarks, threatening great things for the morning, before the masters arrived, and obliging her irresolute victim to promise likewise. As soon as he heard that she was back upstairs Rafael got up, and putting on his vest and trousers climbed out the window into the tiny garden and over the orchard fence.

Was that all there was to it? He was surprised the pleasure was not greater, different. Love was obviously a chaotic affair, done in any old way. He had imagined something more organized: an ascent to heavenly bliss on the pattern of the catechism, with plenty of time to see the landscape to left and right, and an arrival at the destination rather like landing in New York: Statue of Liberty on one side and skyscrapers on the other, like the pictures. His disillusion was tempered by the sense of having crossed the difficult strait which separated him from manhood; he felt humiliated that it had been so easy, painless, dirty, sticky and smelly. But from now on everything in life would be plain sailing; he was home and dry. 'Well, fancy that!' he told himself, 'just fancy that!' And nothing more. There was a moon and the countryside was perfumed with orange blossom. A train was passing in the distance.

'And now what?' For the first time he thought clearly about the future. He now pictured Barcelona as something which really existed; he realized that the ten-past-ten train really did go there. Until that moment, the Barcelona train was the name of a train that passed through Castellón; now he came to see that those carriages would arrive in a big city, that the people in them kept travelling until they got there, and then lived and worked there. A million inhabitants. When a countryman starts thinking of something more than the local capital, his neighbours look at him with pointed attention. Rafael looked at himself and said: 'Why not?' His lost virginity was turned into geography, and life appeared to him for the first time as a road.

He went back to bed with a great locomotive in his brain, and slept like a rock. When the sun came up, he didn't deliberately ignore the trollop's rapping on the bolted door:

he was fast asleep. When he awoke, the jewellers had arrived. They played hell with him. The boy bowed his head, offering no excuse other than that it was Sunday.

A year went by. The forty-year-old shared herself out between guard and lad, until the day the former sniffed out who knows what and turned up on a Saturday, a day strictly forbidden to him: he drank the bitter dregs and went to mourn his horns on the sergeant's shoulder.

'We'll give *him* a good dusting,' said Severiano, with a certain unaccustomed wit.

Manuel did not catch the allusion and grinned, baring his teeth:

'Blasted kid!'

They waited for him under cover of a canebrake, on the way to the station, and without a word began to set about him, making free with hand and rifle butt. The boy squirmed loose and turned to face them three yards off.

'Why are you hitting me?'

'Come here, thief!'

'You're mistaken, I've stolen nothing from anyone.'

The tricorns looked at one another.

'I suppose you don't go to bed with Marieta?' asked Manolo, with mingled sarcasm and loathing. 'A snotty-nosed kid like that . . .!' he thought.

Rafael was taken aback by the question. He knew nothing of the intrigues of leg-spreading.

'Yes,' he said, backing off.

'Yes, is it, eh?'

They fell upon him together and roughed him up good and proper, egging one another on.

'Careful what you say!' said Manolo, 'there's plenty more where that came from!'

'Just watch your step, smartarse!' added the sergeant.

And they set off cross-country, pilfering oranges to relieve their thirst.

Jeweller and wife were surprised and shocked by the tale. They supposed that Rafael must have been caught stealing something from the orchard, because the boy was naturally careful to conceal the dishonourable reason for the savage beating.

The jeweller had the brass neck to ask if he was a member of some union:

'Because we don't want trouble.'

The boy persisted in not offering an explanation for the thrashing; the jewellers made themselves ill with hypotheses, suppositions, suspicions and gossip, until finally the lad who had caused such vexation was thrown out on the street.

The 'Baggag', who had sussed the whole thing out, spilled the beans the day after Rafael's departure. The mistress was highly indignant, and called the young man indecent:

'It's incredible, bring up crows and they'll peck out your eyes!'

What most upset Rafael was being beaten, yet again, after telling the truth. His parents had never struck him. He was left with a dark, cruel longing to return blow for blow, and a sense of humiliation at not being sufficiently strong to warrant being left in peace. The taste of blood did not bother him, and he had no mirror in which to lament his wretched state – the ditch where he washed had red water anyway and was running steadily. He limped for eight days. The marks lasted longer.

It was May of 1929 when, at 10:10 a.m, he caught the train to Barcelona, with two hundred and forty pesetas in his pocket after paying for his ticket. He was sixteen years old.

THREE

Barcelona

It was hot in the long wooden carriage, and all the windows were lowered. Night air and coal dust blew in. The train was packed full; the luggage racks, jammed: string bags, cardboard boxes tied and double tied with string or twine, sacks, bundles wrapped in shawls; the larger packages and passengers without seats blocked the corridors, resigned and sleepy as if given over irremediably to some fatal destiny; neat orange bunches were interspersed amongst the other luggage.

Rafael, being skinny, found himself a place – six squeezed into a seat for five – between an old woman with a black scarf on her head, on her way back to Viñaroz, and an employee of the Barcelona Telephone Company. He managed to fit his small box under the seat between a bundle of clothing and two tied and patient chickens. 'I'll go straight off to sleep and when I wake up I'll be almost in Barcelona. You sleep, and open your eyes three hundred kilometres away. And you can do it every day, it's unbelievable!' The heat from his neighbours was getting to him. The flat landscape gave off its smell of orange blossom, topped with smoke and ash. 'All like sardines now, yet we'll never see one another again.' The engine? A knife slicing through Spain; a plough tilling a furrow, leaving a trail as if it were the first to make the journey; a discoverer of new worlds, hacking a path by machete through the virgin jungle. Passengers murmuring, axles jolting over the joints of the rails. A few compartments back someone started up a *malagueña*, with two others clapping him on. 'Bar-ce-lo-na-Bar-ce-lo-na-Bar-ce-lo-na.' As though the pounding of the wheels were chanting out the name of his destination. Heads overcome by tiredness or wakefulness nodded in time, from right to left and vice versa. 'Bar-ce-lo-na-Bar-ce-lo-na. I'm going to fall asleep. I want to fall asleep.'

Three people along, a soldier is snoring. His neighbour interrupts his breathing by snapping his fingers. After a pause the blessed fellow starts up again; the trainer gives in before the sleeper. (The funny thing is that after Santa Magdalena, the interrupter drops off and snores in a different key.) Benicásim, Oropesa, Alcalá . . . 'Why can't I sleep?' The violent halts and jolting starts, the racket of chains tightening and loosening, are not sufficient reason. 'I'm tired. This lot around me . . .' Directly opposite a child is sleeping, its head on its mother's lap. A priest muttering away in a corner. 'What have we to do with one another? Have I been asleep? The rocking, lo-na-Bar-ce-lona-Bar – Are the rest thinking the same as me?' Squealing of brakes. Viñaroz. 'My neighbour's getting off, now there's more room.' Rafael follows his journey on the map hanging at Castellón station, in front of which he had stood for half an hour, queuing up waiting for them to open the ticket office; the whole thing crawling with flies, especially the Balearic Islands and the blue of the sea. 'None of these people know I'm going to Barcelona, staying there to live.' He felt with his elbow for the wallet with his money, and the letter from a sales representative to the owner of an ironmonger's warehouse. 'What do all these people know about me? The same as I do about them. They all must have their reasons for travelling. What are they thinking about me? They're not thinking anything about me. What is this guy? What will I do in Barcelona? Will I get lost? What do I want to be? I don't know what I want to be. I can't want to be anything, I have to be what other people want. Do as you please. What a laugh! Rich folks, maybe, the ones who travel with their arses on cushions.'

Rafael takes sleeping cars as a personal affront. 'General? Traveller? Worker?' He doesn't even know the word 'ambition', associated among the people and the petty bourgeoisie with a pejorative definition of lawyers and politicians. 'Will I get lost?' He pictures Barcelona as a latticework of infinite streets with a multitude running through them, their feet barely moving, like in a comedy film he saw – how long ago? Worn out, suitcase in hand, trudging through streets which all looked the same; silent, with rows of locked doors. Suddenly he was alone and the streets were growing longer. Solitude made him aware of his own body. He felt himself. 'Leave me alone. I want to be left alone.' A narrow chest puffed out in the square at Viver. There was a bull of death, then a young, poor bullfighter, shirt-tail flapping, stood in front of the bull and challenged it, pale as death; the brute charged and the matador flew into the air. Several others rushed to help him up, but he pulled away from them. He picked up his sword and cape from the ground and held them up across his chest, shouting: 'Leave me alone! I want to be left alone!' The bullfighter's swarthy, livid face was shadowed with verdigris; his breastpiece was turning red; the young bull in the distance

32

took not the slightest notice. The lad approached and stood straight in front of it. 'Me alone, only me.' Rafael López Serrador. 'Here, bull!' And he pushed out his opposite leg. It bumped his neighbour. The rocking and swaying wears down frontiers. Monotony. 'Bar-ce-lo-na-Bar-ce-lo-na.'

The inspector arrives, like a bucket of cold water. Behind him, for the sake of it, two civil guards. Everyone imagines for a fraction of a second that they are at fault, that they've lost their ticket. 'Bet it's different in first class.' Tickets are shown and the tricorns move off down the train. But in the presence of coercion, Rafael feels united with his travelling companions, as if they were threaded together; he becomes aware of the whole train behind him, like a mass, like heat. 'What unites men? Protest? Fear? The desire to achieve something? Courage is an individual thing, standing alone, defying the bull with your feet close together, imposing order.' Rafael López Serrador overlooks fraternity. Ulldecona, Santa Bárbara. A round tunneled noise, resounding steel. Someone murmurs, half-asleep:

'The Ebro.'

Tortosa. 'I'm tired: worn out. Something must link me to living beings.' When would he return? The bus, his father, his brothers. It can't be right for the truth to result in thrashings. If the whole world lied, there wouldn't be a world. You have to tell the truth and get beaten for it, feet together: not offend father or mother. Always feet together, and thrusting down hard.

He woke up in Rubí. The sun, at the horizon, warmed his right thigh. His hands were dirty and he wanted a pee. He went to queue outside the 'Toilette', as it called itself. He came out on to the plain of Llobregat as if sleep and the night had been a great Garraf Tunnel. The light seemed brighter and thinner than in Castellón. People pointed out Tibidabo, and then Montjuich.

'Never been to Barcelona? Don't forget to see the Park.'

The countryside cloaked in mist. He could make out part of the city perched in the lap of two hills. The other passengers have been dying to see the constructions of the Exposition on the slope opposite. They can just make out the scaffolding. Smoke rises straight up to the sky, right across the plain. They insist on pointing out the fairground of Tibidabo to him.

Sans. Newspaper sellers hawking *La Vanguardia* and *El Día Gráfico* along the platforms. 'Those papers won't be in Castellón till tonight.' A deep siding. Houses with four, five, six storeys, glimpsed from the bottom of a trench.

On to Gracia, all white majolica, narrower, less impressive than he had imagined. They emerge into the morning light again. A bullring of brick and blue-and-white tiles, several level crossings, red double-decker buses, long yellow trams. Above its rooftops the city is tinted as with purple and crimson salts fleeing the blue of a cloudless morning. Dew glistens on thin patches of grass at the edge of empty lots fenced off like football pitches. What most startles Rafael are the honeycombed menhirs of the Sagrada Familia. He promises himself he will take a closer look as soon as he can. The tracks multiply, then separate to be combed between platforms.

So here he is with his little box in Plaza Palacio. He is astonished by the trees. Nobody had told him that there were leafy planes shading the streets, and if he had pictured any they were stunted, like the ones in the squares in Castellón. And the great parks were something else again. Amazing: huge trees in the midst of the city! The palm trees of Paseo de Colón. Plane groves along the Ramblas. Birds, thousands of sparrows. Everything else seems ordinary and small. He soon finds his way to Calle del Hospital and the Bar Estrella, recommended by a railwayman he knows.

They give him a café au lait, he drains it and goes to freshen up at a pink washbasin embossed with gilt. Back to the street. How small and dingy everything is! How many people in such a small space! He is not in the least intimidated, nothing throws him. He is looking for work: he has his whole life to see Barcelona.

He likes the tarmac surface of the Boquería. He has never known a street so soft to walk on, but how narrow and dark it is. Why is everyone so crowded together? Every house is a shop, the doorways serving as display windows. Here, even the doormen are traders. After all that he's heard about these shops . . . Pooh! They're nothing special.

He comes to Baños Nuevos, turns left, locates the number, goes up to the first floor: 'Hardware Store'.

Don Enrique Barberá Comas reads the letter from his representative in Castellón. Rafael will start as an apprentice with a hundred pesetas a month.

'I take it you're a serious boy. I don't put up with layabouts here. I'm taking you because you can't have been led astray yet. And here you'll learn. Do you go to mass? You don't happen to have family in Navarre, by any chance?'

The boy doesn't know what to say.

'Well, it doesn't matter. Going to mass never harmed anyone, never.'

He calls the foreman, an old man in a grey overall.

'Put him in Quimet's place. And keep an eye on him.'

Don Enrique Barberá Comas is a Carlist, belongs to a traditionalist circle and reads *El Correo Catalán*. He has enormous contempt for almost all his fellow Catalans, but that contempt is as nothing compared to his feelings for all other Spaniards, with exception of the Navarrese. His salesmen never step beyond the limits of Greater Catalonia; Don Enrique considers it beneath himself to trade with anyone who doesn't understand Catalan. It is difficult to explain how an absolute monarchist can feel so unilaterally attached to Catalonia, and perhaps he himself could not explain it; he has certainly never tried to explain it to himself. It makes him feel good, and that's that.

Rafael's work is neither enjoyable nor irksome. It consists of making up parcels and taking them to the station or to the delivery men. What are the Catalans like? They are tied like trees, our lad tells himself after the first few days: replanted in their own humus, fertilized by their own humour, watered by their own language. More concerned with money than honour, but very smug about the latter. There is no great discovery, great deed, great metro, great poem, great bridge, religion, painting, battle or miracle which does not have its Catalan around the corner; there's no philosopher like Llull, no poet like Maragall, no general like the Count of Reus, no cable railway like Montserrat, no Exposition like theirs, no salami like Vich's, no sausage like Garriga's, no composer like Albéniz. All this Rafael had learned after eight days in the job through the proselytizing, pedagogical zeal of one of the employees, who was also the secretary of a Catalan tourist organization and the drummer with a leading *sardana* band. He learns that there is no water like Canaletas, nor Vichy like the Catalan version; Enrique Borrás is the greatest actor, Margarita Xirgu the greatest actress and *Terra baixa* the last word in drama. Rafael listens and says nothing. He doesn't quite believe it all, but he's pleased to have fallen on a land of such outstanding qualities.

The other apprentice, thickset and scruffy, talks only of football; Alcántara's goal at Bordeaux, Samitier's transfer, how he had diarrhoea for a week when he heard. He emits a stream of the worst abuse when he refers to the Club Deportivo Español, an anti-Catalan organization kept going by industrialists hungry for baronetcies or marquissships or getting into the Governor's good books. God, meaning Zamora, has ceased to be God, despite being Catalan, since joining that team. Pecuniary motives soften up hearts. Rafael simply can't understand or take any interest in the battle for goals, still less its daily political seasoning. (Primo de Rivera's dictatorship is about to disappear; Barcelona-Español rivalry will never again reach the frenzy of those years.) To Rafael, twenty-two seems a lot of men for one leather ball.

He hit it off with the messenger, an ageless, runty man, flushed and covered in wrinkles, wiry and peppery, quietly foul-mouthed but hard-working, despite the animosity of the owner who suspected the little chap didn't much go for Catholicism; the others all kept him in quarantine so the ironmonger would not suspect their intentions.

'Bad influence!' muttered the warehouse owner, weighed down by God, King and Country, but as there was no reason to sack him he just had to lump it. There were also other factors. Don Enrique had inherited the messenger along with the business from his putative father-in-law, after marrying the former owner's bastard daughter, his only child to boot. She was heir, on her father's death, to several fat current accounts and well-stocked shelves which an immoral life had not prevented the long-since deceased from accumulating. Mariano – as the messenger is called – knew the whole story, having been something of a pimp for the dead man.

In view of the morality defended by the present employer, it was somewhat difficult to explain his marriage. Everyone knew about it, making him a constant source of gossip and the butt of endless and none too pleasant jokes. As may be supposed, that stout supporter of Don Carlos had long since cottoned on, and it gnawed away at his insides. Eventually the worm emerged from his nose, which was very large, and they diagnosed cancer. Famous doctors gave him a cash cure.

'The leading clinic in Saint-Gervais, the finest specialists in Europe!' boasted for ever after, in café and parlour, his musician and tour-guide employee.

Don Enrique Barberá Comas is about forty, and in his prime. His wife deceives him with a young man from the cream of society.

'He's a born cuckold,' says Mariano, 'that's why he does well at business. Just you remember, young fellow, that's the way to do it, because when that scoundrel arrived in Barcelona he started at the bottom, just like you, as an assistant in a shoe-shop, but always with a yen to be "someone". So he becomes secretary of the trade union, and a proper revolutionary, a priest-basher and convent-burner such as you can't imagine.

Then soon as he gets a sniff of this rich man's daughter's cod cave – now there was a real man for you! – he becomes more of a candlesucker than Count Güell. He's a skinflint who only lives for the smell of money. He has a mistress he forces out to work, to redeem herself from the sin of bedding down with him. The old boy would turn in his grave . . .! Not that he was ever taken in, mind you, but the daughter was stubborn. Women, my son, are all bad news.'

Naturally, Rafael preferred the messenger's gossip to the nitwitterings of his other workmates. The said Mariano, tiny and a rascal, was a bit of a skirt-chaser, married to an unfortunate woman disabled after her first confinement. He'd had to mother his son, nurse his wife, and put up with his own mother – an ancient maenad who spent her days spluttering insults at her daughter-in-law and her nights complaining loudly, to prevent them from resting or whatever else they might be up to, because as for the latter she had the nose of a bloodhound. Somehow all this had given the little fellow a certain lecherous air. 'Just like a monkey,' people would say. He was also an inventor. In his youth he had come up with a formula for burnishing iron, and hid it carefully away; but when he went to fetch it, months later, to negotiate with some manufacturers interested in the process, he couldn't find it. Since then he had devoted all his spare time, which was little enough, to rediscovering the formula. Each year, each spring he thinks he's found it.

'Got it! The results of the first tests are brilliant.'

Then, due to some acid or other, that attempt fails too. But he's sure he'll hit on the solution sooner or later:

'Now if I was being cuckolded, like someone I could mention, my luck would be different.'

He adores bullfights, and tells Rafael of all the prodigious things he has seen or heard. As it's all so long ago, he can't tell the one from the other. His ring is the old one at Barcelona; his idols are Mazzantini, Fuentes, El Bomba, Fernando el Gallo, Frascuelo, Freg, from when he was young. He doesn't like a particular style of fighting, or a particular matador, he has no preference for a given phase of the fight; he likes bullfighting in general, the whole thing. He remembers minor events which fill him with satisfaction and delight: when so-and-so planted banderillas in a perfect line, when what-not killed six Miuras in one session. Since the death of his former boss, he hasn't the money to go to the fights.

'Besides, my wife's illness . . .'

But nothing could stop him reading the bullfight reports, and commenting on them at length; at home he has a collection of *La Lidia* through which his son learned to read. Whilst they cut up wrapping paper and measure out string, he tells Rafael about bullfighters from thirty years ago, whom no one remembers.

Three days after he is taken on, Rafael is sent to deliver some goods to the Avenida de la República Argentina.

'You go down to the Ramblas and take the number 22.'

Rafael hauls himself up to the top deck of the tram by a steep winding staircase. He sits at the front. Now this is what you call a city, and brand new! The tram and its trolley pole, the greasy cable and the sparks impose respect, plus the allure of imminent death; the branches along the Ramblas, banging and scraping against the side of the carriage as it bounces on the uneven rails; the whistle of the engine at each stop, its smooth pulling-away. All the cars look small from here; there is no Rolls, however opulent, whose roof cannot be seen. Men seem tiny, insignificant. Rafael, in the prow of his tram, feels like the pilot of a flying ship. The Church of El Carmen with its staggered layers of stone. El Siglo – at last, a big store! The Plaza de Cataluña, surveyed from a height, makes a big impression on him. That's what a city is: breadth. The Paseo de Gracia fills him with pride, as if it were some satisfaction owing to himself alone. He gazes at Tibidabo, blue and straight ahead, and breathes in deeply. He feels triumphant, as if the spoils of his own victories were yoked to the wheels of the tram. Is it the wind? His hair flies away, parted by the breeze. The tramcar pushes into the funnel of Calle de Salmerón. He doesn't like it around Gracia, all stunted, full of comings and goings, crammed with factories, tall chimney-stacks everywhere. Lesseps next, and then his delivery point. After getting off he starts to climb. Hills and ravines are calling, pinewoods line the horizon. Vallcarca. Finally he looks back, thinking it may be getting late. He stops, dumbfounded. He had no idea he'd climbed so far. Height engenders distance. The sea, joined invisibly to the land, shades away into white. From Montjuich to San Andrés, the city climbs like a carpet until it dies of green. The blocks in the new suburbs run from pink to grey, plugged with bursts of emerald. The slope of Montjuich is striped sepia by four great chimneys. Most remarkable of all is the air: over the city, haze; over the harbour, smoke; over the sea, mist, as if the world had been dusted with silver. Sky newly emerged from sea turns gradually blue, hung out to dry, still wet at the horizon.

Rafael keeps on climbing, takes the road to Rabassada. Up he goes. The city shrinks and grows. Rafael is all alone in the countryside. He sits down and gazes around. 'The most beautiful countryside in the world.' He smiles, unbuttons his trouser, and in homage to nature pumps his forearm up and down until he comes. Below, in its vapour, Barcelona.

'I got lost.'

'It's unbelievable, at your age! Aren't you ashamed?'

He wanted to go to the Sagrada Familia on Sunday. He was put off by Mariano and the tubby apprentice, who took him to see a morning football match instead.

'He was crazy,' they said, of Gaudí.

'And it's not finished,' they insisted; about the church.

On the other hand, the touristologist acclaimed Gaudí as a genius. Time passed. Rafael always 'had to see the Sagrada Familia'; it was a sacrosanct weight in his decisions about how to spend his days off. Eight or ten months passed.

In the midst of a cleared space closed off by a sagging partition, surrounded by a few hovels that might as well not be there, rises the façade of the unfinished temple. Rafael was flabbergasted; he had never seen anything like it.

High fretwork towers, obstinate blending of soaring gothic with flowing fin-de-siècle curves, secreting swirling volutes, intricate folds, atlases, medusas, conifers and palms, butterflies, snails and rhinoceroses, with plaster coxcombs by way of spires, frilling, curling, fusing with white majolica; azure, ruby and light green, like glass teeming with iridescent spalls. And all those slabs, archivolts and dolmens of stone, cement and porcelain, in motion; stalagmites of wet sand and faith, moving, growing, soaring up to the skies in difficult equilibrium.

The constructions which Rafael had seen up till then were built for repose; still, measured, angular, dead. Now he saw columns that seemed more vertebral than stylized, trying to twist their way like corkscrews into the clouds, whilst walking a tightrope; and at the same time a morass, still waters, rapids.

A church at cross-purposes, for souls in torment, consciences ultimately disposed to depart none too clean from the temple; a cathedral for Pharisees, a hollow façade. Thus it had remained, enough for the Barcelona capitalists: fame and glory, artistic monographs, and world renown. There were no altars or confessionals, nor, come to that, catacombs. Rafael did not go down to the crypt. He didn't know it existed.

By now he knew Barcelona: the circulatory movement of the Rondas, the great cross of its tunnels; he held it in his hand, like some living creature. The Paseo de Gracia was its breastbone; its ribs curved from Córcega down to Diputación; the Diagonal and Cortes were its humeri; its radii, the Paseo de San Juan and the Parallel, folded and joined by its crossed hands down at the harbour, holding up its heart and intestines; the Ramblas, its arteries and veins, knifed by the Vía Layetana, artfully stabbed by the Portal del Ángel, flowing away into the sea. Its coccyx was the harbour itself; its legs and its motion, the wind and the waves. Barcelona, bleeding and crippled, joyous in sunshine and abundance, anchored but ever ready to sail; dirty and naked, free yet mysteriously bound, tongue-tied and seething with desire.

Rafael Serrador goes to evening classes organized by the Diputación; he is a good student. He is none too struck on the people around him, every one a Catalan nationalist, left-wing to a man and passionate about *sardana* festivals, about which he could not care less.

Primo de Rivera fell, Berenguer took over amidst strikes, demonstrations and amendments to the Constitution. Rafael remembers all this as if it were a dream. He is eighteen, nineteen, twenty years old; all these events – important? insignificant? – wash over him, he notices them, but they leave no mark. He lives, he notes that he is becoming more capable, and that today, faced with yesterday's problems, he would maybe do things differently.

He goes out and about, he eats, drinks coffee, and goes to bed with a girl who earns her living dancing in The Left Hand, a 'taxi-girls' bar. He earns three hundred pesetas a month. Within ten years it'll be six hundred. For him those years are one long night.

On 26 January 1930, he rides back from Plaza España in the Metro; greets a friend who works for one of his boss's competitors; the fellow shows him a newspaper, the communist daily, and gives it him.

'Read it. They go on about your twerp of a boss. You can give it back to me tonight, at the Tostadero.'

Rafael is looking forward to a good laugh with Mariano. He stuffs the paper in his coat pocket, which he hangs, on arrival at the warehouse, on the collective hook. Within the hour Don Enrique summons him, newspaper in hand.

'Read this trash, do you?'

'No, sir.'

'Then what were you doing with it?'

'Someone gave it me.'

'Liar.'

'If you'd been minding your own business . . .!'

'You know where the door is.'

He takes it and goes. He doesn't try to justify himself. 'That's the second time I've told the truth when they've asked me with a straight face, and the second time I've taken a bashing. The third time will be the last, but the loser will not be this mother's son. Eyes open and trap shut from now on. Bastard! I'd like to string them all up with their own ties. I don't know how people who ought to know better can't see it! It makes me sick! All that running around, and for what?' He was standing in the middle of the Rambla de las Flores. People were coming down on his right, and going up on his left. They looked like cartesian divers or roly-polies. 'Wet bugger! If I'd told him I did read it, he'd have likely taken fright and raised my wages!'

He turned Wednesday into Sunday. He went to find the girl and took her out to lunch at the Patria. Her name is Carmen and she's the same age as him. They call her Miss Lovely-Legs; she has taken to Rafael because of his lack of airs, narrow hips and self-assuredness; because he never asks but takes without a word what he knows he can have, without going further, always leaving a slight edge to desire. He has been discovering her with delight. He never imagined, from his previous experiences, that a breast could be so firm, that skin could reach so many roads from nowhere, that flesh was so hard and resistant, like a liquid with no way out; that a hand could float so softly along the tender firmness of a back.

A fellow evening-school pupil soon got him a job in a chromium-plate shop. The workshop was in Hostafranchs, so to save himself a long journey Rafael went to live near the

Plaza España. When the girl learned of his change of job, she soon turned sniffy. To her a shop assistant was a somebody, but not a worker. The outfit made the man: their relationship ended without feeling.

On the same floor of the house where Rafael lived, a workmate was subletting an apartment. Celestino Escobar, from a mining family in Cartagena, had come to Barcelona seven or eight years before, when they closed the mines of La Unión. Now he was the CNT trade-union delegate in the factory.

The whole floor belonged to a married couple, he a navvy, she a former corset-maker, Matilde by name, a bit of a floozie, lazy, always singing, usually dolled up, not bad-looking and free with her tongue. Her mother lived with them, and took her side in everything. The food was all right; she was a good cook, and knew how to time her rice; cleanliness was another story.

Elections were held and the Republic was proclaimed.

PART TWO

ONE

The Parallel

'Yeah, we've always been the same in my family. When we say a thing, we mean it. We're from Rioja.'

'I thought you were from Cartagena?'

'We just followed the smell of the mines there, nothing but shit! Some fiddle to do with papers had left us stony broke. So they tell me, I was only little at the time. My dad stayed on at La Unión, selling monkey-nuts in the empty streets and hoping they'll open the pits again. He'll be under the earth by himself 'fore that day comes! When we say ten, it ain't nine or eleven; ten, come what may. Take my gran. Everyone trying to comfort her and her telling us all to get lost: "I'll die when I'm good and ready!" Seems we had a house, bit of land, the works. Grandma was sitting out front, dying, gasping away; but she wouldn't be put to bed for anything in the world. So then a woman who used to help my mum comes down the back stairs (the house had two floors and all) moaning and snivelling, and grandma, who's breathing her last, starts ranting: "No one cries in this house! I'll die when I please! Shut up, you're like a jelly!" This while she's fading away, in the half-light, and the other woman in floods of tears: "Oh, don't say that!" Well now, up gets grandma, takes hold of a whip and sets about the mourner, who – need I say more . . .!

Family all standing around like the cat got their tongues. When she's given her a good hiding she goes out into the yard, straight as a rod, and throws herself down the well. She died when she felt like it, just to spite God – and my father, who she couldn't abide.'

'Then what happened?'

'Oh, nothing. You got anything to do between now and three?'

The café where they meet is one of those enormous places that line the Parallel between the Ronda de San Antonio and the Teatro Español. At night they go to a bar on the opposite side of the street, right next to the Teatro Victoria.

The avenue they call the Parallel has three faces: day, night and Sunday morning. By day it's dull and peaceful, so broad it looks somehow ridiculous. The papier-mâché façades which front the theatres contrive to disguise their entrances; when the sun shines on them the street is beyond redemption. Montjuich rises away in the background, beyond Pueblo Seco, brown, shabby, dirty, with grey wooden huts; the whole hillside a patchwork of green and yellow ochre. The only tolerable sight, by day, is the electricity works, gleaming coal and four immense chimney-stacks lending dignity to the earth as they rise into the sky. For the rest: pavements, cafés, theatres, music-halls, barrows and stalls selling soft drinks, chestnuts, peanuts, hard roes, salt tuna and pinwheels. Bars with chromium trim and marbled counters, Ron Negrita and Anís del Mono, and outside lanterns courtesy of Sidral; news-stands and puppet-shows also display their woes in the daylight hours. Come evening the tables turn, but by day even ruffians, spivs and pimps can look half-decent here. Only the whores remain true to their trade, unless they have aspirations. The trollops come for coffee and whatever might turn up.

'You're either a revolutionary or a reactionary; the rest is nonsense, artful dodging or waste of time. Liberalism? Come off it, mate! All you care about is the democratic system: corruption, Parliament, the honours game, dirty business. But if you really have a brain and a memory, you can't help but be a revolutionary, not just a man of the left. Left-wingers always smell of shit, somehow. What matters is man, or better said, the universe. You're either for the present state of affairs, or you're with man in all his nakedness. As for improving things bit by bit – shameful, cowardly! Earthquakes, fires, cyclones, natural phenomena don't do things gradually or by halves. Same with social evolution: what's needed is force. And guts.'

At the other end of the table, slightly apart, Rafael Serrador is chatting to a bootblack with a pockmarked face.

'The trouble with me,' says Rafael, ignoring what everyone else is saying, 'is I don't know what I want, that's why I get so bad-tempered. I expect you think I'm daft.'

'No, mate. I used to be the same. Until the day I asked meself, why's that geezer got a car when I don't?'

The Hermit began to speak and, as always, all other conversations were buried alive. Gawky, interminable nose, sparse straggling hair, unshaven jaw, long delicate hands; a stained grey jacket whose too-short sleeves exposed heavy silver cufflinks of Salamanca filigree; ragged trousers over sandalled bare feet. Hoarse voice, elegant gestures, domineering index finger:

'Science, wisdom, nothing but commonplaces! One proverb can tell you more about the people than any statistic. It goes straight to the nub.'

No one takes him seriously, but they all listen with great attention. Ghosts, the dead, madness, strike them as important matters.

'Literature's just a lot of showing off; things are quite simple. Same with music: musicians have to kick up a fuss, it gives them something to do. Opportunists to a man. Like writers, except it's easier to spot it in their case,'cause there are more words than notes. Yet words, if they're used too much they wear out, lose their force, they switch from delights into lights, and we're left dazzled, hypnotized, ready for the wool to be pulled over our eyes.'

'That's enough of your drivel, spare us the philosophy.'

'Belt up, dimwit!'

'Words turn to syrup, like some folks drink before they eat meat.'

He slurped at his glass of water.

'The whole meaning of life today can be summed up in two sayings, or rather slayings. Earning a living, say the poor. Killing time, say the rich. You hear it every day and think nothing of it, because people don't know what they say, only what they mean. God Almighty! . . . and he can shit himself if he's listening!'

He jabbed his finger at heaven, the ceiling, he called it.

'Do you get it? Earn your living! They give you your life and then you have to earn it!'

'Yeah, and we do.'

'Oh, sure you do! Well, I'm no mug.'

'You live on air, I suppose,' someone muttered.

The Hermit ignored him and went on:

'For anyone who's got his own share and the other fellow's

too, earning a living is a waste of time. So they set about earning the next life, by flashing their socks on the terraces of their clubs and social circles.'

'Oh, not your record about those vicious circles again, we've heard that one!'

'We' – he corrected himself – 'you, when you lose, you lose without meaning to, you can't help it. They can afford to. That's what they call luxury. They can afford the luxury of losing. Do you know what I hate most in all the world? The theatre.'

Among the group were an actor and two technicians from the Apollo.

'What are you on about now?'

'Let's understand one another; I am talking in the high sense.'

High sense was part of his system.

'Your work, when it's to "earn your living", has nothing to do with what I'm saying. Shows are a disgrace, sitting down to pass the time watching other people work is absolutely disgusting. Do you suppose cats and birds do the same?'

'So, according to you, then, Hermit, what should we be doing?'

'Nothing. But I object to being called Hermit. I neither do penance nor believe in death. Behold the world and praise the Lord, who is nobody and everything.'

The old boy spent most of his time wandering the slopes of Montjuich, where he'd sit himself down and start endlessly repeating certain 'meaningful' words, like 'never', 'deep', 'always', 'nothing', 'light', 'tomorrow' . . . It was his 'system'. A vegetarian, sodomite and pederast, he inspired, for no very good reason, a certain respect among the locals; he was, moreover, a police informant, and made no bones about it, some said to make ends meet, others so they'd leave him in peace. The anarchists put up with him in their discussion groups because he spoke Esperanto. It was said he'd once been a captain in Cuba.

'The worst of it,' said he, 'is that the workers don't care whether what they make is useful or not. They lack "finality". What's the point of earning your living? That's why I don't work. If everyone followed my example . . .'

He delighted in taking on a prophetic air, Jeremiah-like:

'Can you imagine all this in ruins? Ruined houses, rusty iron, rotting beams, debris, rubble, weeds, garbage, shavings, bare stones just lying in the sun . . .'

Paradise, to him.

'And you've got all that coming to you because you eat meat, and don't measure the value of words.'

This oddball did not belong to any organization.

'I'm an anarchist, but how can I affiliate to something without ceasing to be one?'

And if people started hinting about his relations with the police, he would answer quite seriously:

'It's the only thing that keeps me free.'

Some took him for a great philosopher and sage: he had discovered well-springs, and sometimes wore a chlamys.

'Why has this geezer got a car and not me?' Rafael gave this some thought. Wasn't it the same everywhere? By now he was quite well read. He returned his books punctually and without stains to the Libertarian Atheneum, earning him the confidence of the librarian. He worked his way through Max

Nordau, Eliseo Reclus, Bakhunin, Tolstoy and Eugène Sue without too much difficulty. At first he didn't know which of the last two he preferred. He came to see that people took more account of the Russian, accepted it and eventually understood why. That was how he had got into politics – at least that's what one comrade said to him, a big strong Valencian lad, always joking:

'You'n all, mate?'

Politics consisted of reading the 'Soli' and paying your sub.

The midday meeting was much better attended than the evening one. As well as seven or eight men from the Confederation, their numbers always decimated by the Model Prison, there was every other type: idlers, actors, journalists, one or two teachers, a second-hand bookseller, the odd Italian, a beggar and a smattering of scroungers. The regulars included an old federal Republican with a white beard like Pi y Margall, an out-of-work chauffeur and the cashier from the Sevilla, the night-club next door. They thought Rafael unsociable, but treated him well because he'd come with Celestino Escobar.

'It was decided one day, at home, just like that,' the Italian was saying. '"Fact is," says my father, "you neither love nor respect your parents." I answer, without thinking, "It's true!", and I up and leave, astonished by my discovery. I like many things in this life, but not too many people. I like cats and chip potatoes. I thought I could get on with the communists, but I couldn't. Communism is a serious business, but the communists spoil it. I can't stand slogans and all that rubbish. I like the world, but not how it's organized; I like cities, but barracks and discipline get right up my nose. And I cannot accept that for to put an end to barracks we have to build more barracks.'

'Because what bothers you, like everyone else . . .'

'Shut up, you. Go on, you.'

'It's not that I left the party, they kicked me out.'

'They're like the Jesuits,' said the ticket clerk.

'Right,' joined in a man from the Union of Actors and Technicians, 'Catholicism is Communism in the other world.'

'Do you think it's a small difference?' another remarks.

'I don't know if Communism and Catholicism are serious questions. What I can assure you is that the Party and the Church . . .'

'So serious,' says a man from the Organization, 'that if we don't do for them, they'll do for us. Just a matter of time.'

'It twists up my guts to hear such talk!' roars the federal Republican, Don Félix by name. 'You're all proletarians and workers. Capital punishment is at the root of all our troubles. Lock people up and try to persuade them.'

'And if they persist?'

'We commit suicide!' pipes a musical voice.

'Mankind evolves,' proclaims the white-beard.

'Savvy or no savvy?' banters the mellifluous voice.

'Shut up, you,' snaps the man from Actors and Technicians. 'Here every man-jack says what his balls tell him! The time for fighting will come soon enough.'

'If tomorrow was the day before yesterday . . .' begins the chauffeur, and they smile, mostly inwardly, because enjoyment among them is rarely raucous. The saying had become a catch-phrase, and its author was on his way in the door. He was a ragged young fellow, a tobacco smuggler who had a job to put together the simplest phrases, not because he stuttered but because he simply couldn't come up with the words. He sabotaged the plainest statements with meaningless multiples, like: this, that, the thing, like I told you, you know, thingummy, whatsit, this here story, know what I mean – entrusting to his hands the mission of outlining exactly what it was about. 'If tomorrow was the day before yesterday . . .!' For no apparent reason, the phrase had become famous. Today they were using it to taunt one of their number who'd been promised a pound of Gener tobacco.

To some people, the harbour zone stinks of American tobacco. A great many sailors, waiters, bootblacks, carabineers and policemen live off selling Lucky and Camel, tobacco they all despise, trash fit only for playboys and prostitutes. They smoke the local rough-cut in all its shapes and sizes, which to them smells of men and Overseas.

At night, no more than seven or eight turn up. Trams clank by outside, tow-rails chiming; double-decker buses trailing clouds of gasoline fumes behind them; night-clubs ploughing the darkness with neon signs, from pink to purple, buzzing like crickets; small bands playing, here and there a pianola, radio speakers on different stations. The cafés spill out over the pavements. People flow between two light zones, the road and the bars, lined by vendors of lighters, flints, wicks, pipes, stems, combs, matches and cigarette papers. Here Barcelona's flank is revealed, a shining wound which opens every night, always; and through that bore-hole humours, blood, pus and time all drain away, presided over by advertisements for venereal cures, lest anyone delude themselves.

Rafael took a liking to the Engineer, a bald man of about forty, half-crippled by a bullet wound earned at the entrance to a bank, years before, when the Organization needed funds to sustain a strike. He worked now in the offices of the Marítima Terrestre, thin, pale, stomach pounded to pulp; more time inside than out since he'd been able to think for himself.

'What counts, what really truly counts, is indiscipline, the uncontrolled will of each individual. Of course, every time discipline and indiscipline have clashed up to now, discipline has always triumphed. Wait! ... Not through its intrinsic strength' – the man could talk, even though he tended to preach – 'but because discipline, you know who I mean, had more rifles, more machine guns or more cannon fodder. What I mean to say is: with equal forces indiscipline will always win, always. Bet you anything.'

'It's not a question of betting.'

'Who asked you. Indiscipline is the sum of all the voluntary efforts – voluntary! – of all the people. Discipline's a mechanical sheep shearer. Think of the difference between the man who wants to fight, and the one who's forced to. How can you doubt the result for a moment? Look at Sallent: we beat the Civil Guard there!'

'Yes, but as soon as they sent reinforcements, some took a walk and others took to the hills, and you were left on your own.'

'So? There were more of them by then. Discipline kills the best instincts, the desire to fight, the best in a man, the roots that mean you can always get on with the other fellow. If I have to die, I'll do it in my own way, not to please Tom or Dick just because they've got stripes and want to tell me which bucket to kick. Everyone has to sort his own life out. Me . . . This discipline lark was invented by politicians to get themselves in the papers: it's easy to prepare or direct actions from your bed, we can leave that to your Socialist leaders. If I've got a pistol in my hand I can die where I please, the rest is fairy tales. Our leaders have no choice but to move among us, where the olives are actually picked, black, green or grey; and do the same work as the rest. You tell me if your Socialist or Communist bosses dare as much! Go to jail? Very brave! You can only tell a man when he's got a gun in his hand!'

'That way they'll finish you all off.'

'There'll be others!'

In general everyone agreed about fundamentals, namely that the leaders of workers' parties were all frauds and conmen. To them the prototype of the species was Largo Caballero, whom they considered a traitor and a coward.

'Why all the fuss,' the Engineer went on, 'when things are so simple? This feller's got what the people haven't got, and that's that . . . If you can take it off him, you take it, and if not, hard cheese! Speeches in parliament are for wiping your arse on!'

He had been involved in the attacks at Gijón, and they looked up to him for it.

'Hey you, Serrador,' said González Cantos, a podgy man who was secretary to one of the unions down at the docks. 'Haven't the draft board got on to you yet?'

'I expect so. I don't know.'

'Well, have they ruled you out as unfit?'

'I don't know. I haven't bothered about it.'

'Haven't you heard from back home? Where are you from?'

'No one knows if I'm alive or dead.'

'You could be picked up any day, you know.'

'I know. I won't be a soldier.'

'All well and good, but let me know if things get tough.'

González Cantos was a dirty-looking character who had spent a lot of time abroad, spoke good French and was very close to Durruti. Even his own comrades admitted he was uncouth. He had been one of the deportees to Bata. He always wore short-sleeved shirts and scruffy trousers that kept falling down, whereupon he'd hoist them up with a violent tug from left to right, then scratch himself around the crotch and sniff in noisily, wiping his hand across his prominent nostrils.

'The people,' he said, 'will be saved by the people, and no one but the people. All that claptrap from intellectuals and politicians, especially if it's sincere, has nothing to do with us. If they think we'll pull their chestnuts out of the fire, they're mistaken . . . Right now they're waiting for a military uprising by CEDA, Alcalá Zamora's lot, whatever they call themselves.' (González Cantos is referring to the defeated revolutionary movement of 6 October 1934.) 'Bloody cheek! The best bit is they want us to get our heads smashed in in the streets and leave them sitting pretty in their ministerial armchairs. Armchairs my arse. I'll give them armchairs! Yellow-bellies. Makes no difference to us, we'll have the Guards against us, with Companys or Cambó. They want to ride to safety on the backs of the people. Hah, if salvation was what they were after! What they want is power. And as the banks are busy looking after their own people, well, hey now, let the people carry us! Republican bastards! And as for so-called intellectuals! Ah, the poor dears! Look where the ones in Servicio de la República ended up: as maidservants! Yes, they've shown their backsides quicker than anyone. What they wanted was to water their crops with our blood. Me, a guinea pig! I wasn't born yesterday. Them in their offices, full bellies bulging, warming their tootsies by the electric fire, with the other one waiting in bed, and their heads full of plans . . . And they're just as likely to write to you about the future of humanity, when we'll all be very good and very holy, and won't go on strike, full of trust in the honourable minister of unemployment – a socialist into the bargain – as about the psychology of frogs or flamenco singers. You know how important the psychology of frogs is to the people!'

'What an ignorant bugger you are!'

'Thanks be to God! But you try talking to them. For those dreamers, a picture, a museum, are more important than the life of a worker. Azaña said as much only the other day! Yes, man, that he cared more about the Mininas' – he garbled the word deliberately – 'than anything else! And people sit and read that and don't get angry; but are we going to fight and die for it? Come off it! The people must save themselves with their fists, and they will. And we'll put all those grammarphones and moanergraphs in a stable, so they can wank each other off: what a spunky sight!'

'And what about human intelligence?'

'To put an end to inequality, I don't need much intelligence. My body demands it. Do you hear me? My body. Besides, I don't deny that if we were to go on arguing all day, you'd end up convincing me.'

'Well, then!'

'That's the trouble. I'd let myself be taken in by the letters, the words, by word games. And I'd trudge home to my slum

61

totally convinced that the world is just fine as it is, or that Dencàs is a genius and what I need is to go and light candles to the Virgin of Pilar.'

'I never said that, you prick!'

'It amounts to the same. The point is, you'd convince me of something airy-fairy. And what I want, what my body is demanding, my soul, if you believe I've got one, is what my hands desire, what my fingers, arms, heart and guts' – he pats himself noisily on the belly – 'are longing for, my balls and my head, and the heads, arms and hands of all the workers. And to get that I don't need ideas. What I need is weapons, strength, power. What matters in the struggle is winning, no matter how.'

'We all agree on that!'

'Yes, but you amuse yourselves thinking of a hundred different things, taking this and that into account, just like a bourgeois!'

'All we're like is ourselves.'

'Well, I don't care what I am, only what I want to be! And I want power for the people.'

'And who are the people, according to you?'

'Who the fuck do you think? What kind of damn-fool question is that? The CNT, man, the CNT!'

Then they would get bogged down in endless facts, statistics and grievances against the provincial unions.

'Let's wait and see what the committee says.'

That was how they settled every question. Rafael's intentions were good, but he couldn't get a clear picture. He could see the struggle, he understood it, and he was ready to take part in it. 'But what comes after? Most likely there won't be an after.

And if there is? Fight for a better world, yes, but which world?'
Bakhunin didn't ease his doubts, nor did Celestino Escobar,
whose real name was Celestino Morales. Their friendship
had grown firmer through daily contact. There was a fraternal
honesty in Escobar which somehow anchored him to the here
and now, no messing; a way of concerning himself only with
the moment, a way of doing things properly that made Rafael
feel better in the midst of so many uncertainties. Escobar had
been a bank clerk on arriving in Barcelona:

'There must have been ledgers in my cradle.'

His section head had been a poor scrap with glasses,
tethered like a sheep to the department by his silver-plated
chain and enamel locket with a picture of his late spouse: high
bun, ruffed collar and gold brooch.

'The fish dies not through its mouth but through its tits,'
Celestino insisted, because the man had three daughters, and
none of them with either flavour or fortune; the middle one
fussier than a hen.

The subordinate, highly thought-of in the household, did
what he could, first to liven them up, and then to keep them
happy, but with such poor timing that the tethered pen-pusher,
for ever on his knees in act of prayer – they were all in Acción
Católica, friends of the sacristy – opened the parlour door at
the worst possible moment; not that his offspring's hidden
powder-puff was in any danger, but the poor fellow saw visions
undoubtedly engendered in hell itself, and stratagems only
suspected, let us say, in that crafty, liberal, treacherous and above
all lewd capital of the Gallic republic, which God confound. So
to mouth-rinsing. They tried to persuade him he was imagining
things. He got on his high horse and demanded a wedding.

Celestino was just a kid and promised heaven and earth, then made a run for it. He was broke; did a bit of everything, what he knew and what he didn't, roaming around every quarter of Barcelona: pilfered in the docks, smashed and grabbed in the Calle del Este, sold trinkets on the Ramblas, opened doors and peddled trash in the Tivoli arcades, guarded fields out at Prat, cleaned tramlines for Foronda, and finally washed up in the small factory where Rafael worked, highly regarded both for attitude and performance. He was a man who never said no when precision, good judgment and nerve were required. Despite his occupation, he won the confidence of both the Confederation and the FAI, though he would never accept any post of responsibility in either:

'I just do things. Why think about them? I don't want responsibilities.'

Cheerful and carefree, he laughed at Serrador's misgivings:

'Hunger is on the march. The world is full of swine. When there aren't so many, we can talk about it. In the meantime, just keep going.'

There was a sponger who used to go to the café, a scoundrel and a scribbler who had his moments as a poet, though fonder of booze than of verses, gangling, fidgety, shoulders snowy with dandruff and nits, spots around the mouth from poor eating, married with a stack of children. One died soon after birth and he went about for almost a fortnight with the corpse inside a cardboard box on his back, asking for money for the poor little devil's funeral in cafés and brothels. When he'd been once around the circuit he couldn't be fagged to start again. Besides, the deceased, worm-eaten, stank. He buried it on the slope of Montjuich. Celestino helped with the digging.

'You haven't heard the best bit,' he tells Rafael. 'A few days ago, when he'd not long started hawking the little stiff around on his back, come nightfall he drinks the day's proceeds so's not to lose the habit, and leaves the package in the tavern. That's not all, the very best bit is that next day he couldn't remember where he'd left the damned thing.'

'How did he find it?'

'It wasn't too hard. He was right third time, but not before he'd kicked up a shindig in the first waterhole 'cause he'd got it in his nut that that was where he'd stewed his brains.'

'Hadn't they unwrapped the parcel?'

'What for? They already knew what was in it. Besides, it stank. He begs everywhere he goes, but he drinks it all away again in four or five dives he goes to, where he feels safe. They value him for himself, he says, and it's true. They address him as Don and pin his poems on the walls.'

One Saturday afternoon they went up to the place where the baby was buried. From there they could see the docks and the open sea, and, turning round, the labouring city. Rafael recalled his first vision of Barcelona from the foothills of Tibidabo; now, much higher up, he could feel the city working: he saw the coal, knew where the electricity ran from, noted how the whole thing fits together, fastens, unites and intertwines, joins and connects, buildings meshing with one another like cogwheels. And amid all that vast mechanical motion, he remembered the tiny corpse beneath his feet, with the earth in its bones. It stirred a primitive emotion which was somehow embarrassing, he couldn't have said why. The docile sky bedaubed everything with colours.

Four of them had gone up that afternoon: Don Félix, he of the white beard, a metalworker friend of Serrador's who'd read *Capital* ('No one fools me', 'You can't tell me'), and a Galician, Fernández, who taught history in the Workers Institute. They went on to Miramar, to come back through the Leforestier gardens.

Manicured hedges, tamarinds, exquisite brickwork, Sevillian majolica, roses climbing the green trellis-work of the pergolas, water in pipe and fountain, vines, ivy, flies, solitude; nature and artifice in peaceful ferment. The odd flash of broom added its wilder note. Distance quells the city, overcome by water and trees.

Marx's apprentice gets on Don Félix's nerves.

'The only victory is life!' he bawls. 'Everything that preserves it is good, whatever it is.'

'You confuse life with your own life', retorts the metalworker. 'So long as there's a peseta for your coffee, bring on the deluge, as the king of France once said.'

'Since we're stranded in this blasted world, why not make it bearable? Put an end to war. No man has the right to take another's life. You won't shift me on that.'

'What does having the right mean? Have the rich the right to make me work to eat? It's not their life, it's mine. And if to defend life and breath – everybody's – I have to do away with them, I will.'

'Where does that get you?'

'It simplifies the world. If each one of us killed a traitor or an enemy . . .'

'You can argue, come to an agreement', repeats the bearded republican.

'Arseholes! Any deal they accept or propose will be against the workers: even if they say yes to all we ask for. It's in the blood, and there's no way out but death. Farting about may be all very well for socialists, who want to negotiate with the bosses just so they can get a whiff of the tribunal chairman's mistress. That's where their so-called honour leads them.'

'And their bellies,' adds Rafael.

'Right! You've no idea of the damage that Julián from *La Verbena* has done the Spanish revolutionary movement.'

'Get away, man!'

'Oh, yes! An honest, decent fellow. And his master the godfather to his first littl'un.'

'Yes,' says Fernández, 'and then there's Arniches's plays.'

'You must be joking, there's nothing more reactionary. Yet the people go out and imitate him, for Christ's sake!'

'So there's no alternative to direct action,' concluded the old republican gloomily. 'What a bright lot you are!'

'Have to make the best of a bad job!'

Everyone fell silent.

'You're all barbarians.'

'Anarchism is the opposite of barbarism,' said the Galician, with the air of a peripatetic professor. 'Anarchism and barbarism are like good and evil. You tell me what came first, the chicken or the egg! Well, I believe they were simultaneous. On the one side you have the man who wants to do as he pleases, and on the other the man who wants everyone else to do as he pleases.'

'So what?'

'That's where all the trouble started, that's what!' says the metalworker.

Rafael and Celestino sense that the argument will go on and on, so vague and transcendental is it; they invent an excuse and walk away down Calle Lérida.

Still Rafael insists:

'The old man's right about one thing, what matters is life.'

'No!' protests the other, 'Death! That's what gives quality to life. Life only takes on meaning through the way it's lost or risked.'

'What can you do if you're dead?'

'It's a case of getting things done. Don't matter if it's you or someone else. Death is a private business that has nothing to do with life or work. If that's what you meant, I agree. Your death is a personal matter, the value, the quality of your life; if it's good, then good for you. But it's for you to keep as a personal souvenir, a frame with porcelain flowers around it.'

'But that rubs me out of the world.'

'What's the alternative? Do you want your portrait put in a niche? Until you realize that a man alone is nothing, we shan't understand one another. An anarchist, contrary to what people think, is someone who doesn't know what it is to be alone. Look, the only true individualist is the bourgeois, the Catholic who believes in and seeks his own personal salvation; the fascist is a bourgeois with a mask on. I believe in the fist, the group. The communists think too big, they're kidding themselves; they'll sacrifice the sea for a rivulet, trying to bureaucratize fraternity; equality by numbers. Claptrap! And as for the Party, everyone knows it's the Company of Jesus. There's no smoke without fire . . .'

'I don't know if you're right or not. What I am sure of is that I want to protest, live, do things. If everything's as you say, courage has nothing to do with life, but I believe it does. I'm not capable of doing what you do, and possibly vice versa. You're for launching yourself into the void with your eyes closed. That's no good.'

'We're not going to agree. You want to touch the results. You'd like medals, parades, anthems and your name in the history books. I'm not saying you can't change and work with us, but if you knocked off a boss, you'd want everyone to know it was you. That's not the way.'

'What is the way?'

'For you? Fate will decide.'

On Sunday mornings Rafael would stroll down to the book fair. He used to go with a barber he knew, a great fan of detective stories who lived on the ground floor and was well in with some of the booksellers. The stalls stretched from the corner of the Ronda to the Plaza de España, with no fixed limit at the far end, taking up half the right-hand pavement. People milled about and picked at the volumes laid out on counters or in boxes: odd volumes from sets of two or more, pamphlets, serialized novels, guidebooks, almanacs, bound volumes of extinct magazines, books without covers or with duplicate pages, prayerbooks and occasionally a real find, soiled and weary of being fingered and unrecognized. Most of the dealers had second-hand bookshops in Atarazanas, Tallers or Muntaner, and were there to sell off on Sunday morning what they judged worthless for everyday business. Keen readers of slender means gathered around them, some poking about for a second volume, some, who thought themselves clever, looking for that miraculous bargain; others just breathing in the smell of old books as they took the sun, so as not to lose touch with the printed word; and the odd youngster, anxious to build himself up a library. Boys turned up to swap transfers, and a few small-time stamp collectors would carry out their exchanges there. It had become a sort of literary auction for people who couldn't bear to let a day go by without nosing about in bookshops and thus rejoiced in that Sunday morning bonus. The sun gilded everything and the books grew warm beneath their dust, which was plentiful. The browsers bargained away, haggling in the sunshine over trifling amounts. Their offers and counter-offers varied with the curve of the sun, until fixed prices finally put an end to fun and games. The crowd bustled peacefully back and forth.

'Now where do I know him from? Oh yes, the book fair!' They were a special sect, a masonry. Bibliophiles who loved books with fine covers despised the open air.

'Me, I'm always the same,' one old bookseller told Rafael, wrinkled, bound in parchment, as he himself said, in a hoarse voice which used to crack as though caked in dust. He often passed the time of day with Serrador. 'What changes is time. And as it has to make its mark somehow, it paints grey hairs and clears bald patches; but it can't fool me, I see it coming and I duck. Phooey! I know that if you look at me you'll say I've grown older, but as the same has happened to you, they cancel one another out.'

'But what about death, Don Phooey?'

'Who believes in that? Time's little joke. Not knowing what else to do, it disappears. Phooey, my young friend, phooey! When people say I've died, I'm sure I shall be going on just the same.'

'And birth?'

'Loss of memory, young man, loss of memory.'

He was a spiritualist and an authority on Esperanto. President of the Esperanto Association of the Fifth District, a friend of the Hermit, he sometimes went along to the café, always well informed about his specialities. In his time he had published a grammar book and put on a comic opera.

'It's all the fault of the Tower of Babel. The day we all speak the same language, there'll be no more wars!'

No one argued with him because it was pointless, and besides, most of the company thought the same.

On Sunday afternoons Rafael would go to a bullfight. To Arenas or the Monumental ring, depending on what was on offer. That autumn Domingo Ortega was making his debut in Barcelona, so successfully that he fought three weeks in a row. Rafael was surprised by the Catalan public's liking for the Toledan. Barcelona people go for showiness; they're content with surface brilliance, settle for spectacle and glamour, applaud affectation, the eye-catching flourish rather than the casual mastery that escapes them through its very lightness of touch; in no other arena does cape-work count for so much as in Barcelona. All that's required are a few fancy twirls, a string of swanky passes, a well-executed *larga* or a few moves with back to bull, to redeem a bad performance.

'That *quite* made the whole afternoon.' Yes, that and the overweight, over-horned bull, all show. That's why bullfighters who can't get contracts in the rest of the country can go on working in the Monumental with star matadors like Marcial Lalanda and Vicente Barrera. Marcial alongside mere animal-tamers, dabblers in bullfighting . . . Chicuelo with his *quites* alongside the novices with their great big banderillas . . .

Palha bulls, exposed flesh and the menace of death, against the clowns: Freg, Larita and Llapisera.

What Rafael likes is the bull: specially when it's black, with good horns. Small lively ears, thick matted neck, black hump, bristling tail all the way to the ground, no tongue, stirring the air with its snorts, ridged forehead, steady gaze, dark savage charge, all in one go: divine majesty and light, cutting the air to shreds. And the bullfighter, medium height, motionless, waiting; arms doing what the arms should, leading; fists like the wind, giving grace; waist like water, flowing; legs like stone, imposing stillness.

Rafael had never seen Belmonte fight with Joselito, a myth turned god in the bullfighter's heaven: a paradise of tassels and fans, with posters for walls and tambourines for stars. Ortega had a down-to-earth way of planting himself in front of the bull, as if he wasn't going to let it past – it's me or you! – which excited our man. Then, over time, he lost that tree-like quality. The only thing he perfected was his two-handed pass: rough and uncouth, like the country man he was. Domingo Ortega brought to the bullring the colour of his own earth, which Rafael imagined like the scrubland around Teruel, less green than the area round Barcelona where shrubs, bushes, thistles and weeds conceal the true colour of the earth and branches blot out the sky. The Toledan's way of fighting stirred in Rafael the desire to see himself once more between soil and sky, with nothing before but open country, gorse, stone, the colour of earth; real mountains in the distance, ranges untrammelled by vegetation, naked as God intended. And him alone, ringed by the horizon, with the sky for his cap. If a bull rushed him there he would fight it straight, hand held low, the tip of his cape following the contours of the barren landscape, feeling the earth spin beneath his left leg, planted, axis of the world, standing firm.

The one thing a Spaniard never thinks about when he goes to a bullfight is death. Were this not so, the spectacle would be intolerable, as it is for the parties of foreigners who come in search of bitter tastes, for all the good it does them. There is nothing more joyful or optimistic than a bullfight. It is that difference of attitude in the face of death which sets the Spaniard apart and astounds the rest of the world. We are a superstitious people, and that's a great thing: it's death that is caught unawares. The third bull came out. 'If they like Ortega so much here, maybe he's not as good as I think he is.'

Serrador always sat in the mixed sun and shade section. There wasn't room to fit a razor- blade. The matador's every move raised a cry or a gesture from Rafael. He realized he was gradually transmitting his excitement to his neighbours. A man alone can do wonders. A group, who knows? He felt the arena, he felt he *was* the arena, just as years before he had believed himself to be the Barcelona train. 'We don't know who we are. The same thing would happen listening to a speech. But there's more to a bullfighter: he comes in through the eyes. Can the feeling be used for anything? Its strength lies in its brevity. Then victory goes to those who take action when it matters, as it unfolds. Without them we'd all be worse off.'

He found it hard to sleep; the fights between landlady and husband were endless. He was a slovenly dunderhead, and she was not the one to cure him. He drove cranes in the docks, lazy and feckless, name of Tomás. Each day his better half would shake him out of his precariously achieved equilibrium. Matilde had come to see him not as a husband but as a son-in-law. When he clambered on top of her she took it as an offence to her flesh, as if her body were her child rather than her person, and so rejecting pleasure she remained outside, fixing the man with a pitying stare of disgust and contempt. Add to this the silent presence of her mother, providing more of the same, immensely wrinkled lips pursed in unmistakable expression of the heartache it caused her to see her daughter linked to such a creature, such an intruder upon the ever-mysterious relationship between two women. Matilde had been infected by that contemptuous silence, and would only break her own taciturnity with a desultory 'Yes, yes,' imbued with obscure hidden meanings, in response to any comment from that pathetic character. They often came to blows. The woman was undaunted, returning slap for clout: that brought them closer together. And so it went on. The rice and the proximity to the workshop was all that kept Rafael and Celestino in that house, on the principle that 'better the devil you know . . .'

At the bullring Rafael got to know two brothers from Jaca, Atilio and Jaime Fernández, long-time fugitives from their Aragonese homeland. They'd been back briefly with Galán and García's uprising, then down with the Republican column to Ayerbe; after that reverse they went into hiding, holing up in Barbastro, and from there to Lérida, where they were helped with their expenses to Barcelona. They rarely spoke of the past, but Rafael gathered from the things they said that before '31 they'd been involved, always together, in various strikes that had ended in bloodshed. They'd lost a bit of their enthusiasm since then.

'You can't reach Liberty and Equality along the path of Liberty and Equality,' they said. 'To travel a road you've imagined, you first have to build it; and just when you're taking a break in the shade of an olive tree you'll be woken up with a baton about your skull, and then you can only flail your arms about like a mill without water: your enemies will smash you. To progress to a half-decent humanity, you have to construct it by force, and take no notice of those who want it too but don't know where they're going. To reach democracy, if it can be reached at all, you have to play rough. Nobody stays in a post if they're offered a better one, so you have to crack their heads a bit . . . We've seen enough to know that if everyone goes their own way you don't get anywhere, you just end up flogging yourself to death.'

The brothers were alike physically and in character: on the tall side, pale but with red noses, pointed and slightly upturned, sharp incisors showing beneath a raised upper lip; one with hair sticking up like a brush, the other with long dark locks parted across his narrow forehead. They were flashy dressers, fussy about shining their boots, with broad hands, stubby fingers and clean nails; white buttoned shirts, no tie, light caps, heavy smokers. Being a pair had come in useful; it was natural that one should praise the other in his absence, and they made the most of it; if something didn't suit them, they used the excuse of needing to stick together. They had been active in numerous social conflicts, always in prominent and responsible positions. Atilio was a carpenter; Jaime, a turner.

'What counts in the Confederation is syndicalism,' they said. 'Libertarian communism, if it's just a name, is unimportant. If it's a tactic, it's a disgrace; if it's a moral principle, it's no way to make the revolution. What's needed is iron discipline in the unions.'

They rarely went to the café, though everybody knew them.

'That's all fairy stories!' exclaimed the Teacher, a tall wizened man who tried his best to look the spitting image of Don Quixote – a choice made in heaven by the looks of him, and which gave him a grave voice and circumspect bearing. 'On this side you have those of us who believe that this cup and this spoon are God. And opposite you have those who think that God created them by sneezing.'

Serrador reproached the Fernández brothers for their irregular attendance.

'Why bother? Each one turns up carrying his own world on his back, and ready to die for it. Where does that get us? What's needed is to force them to go along with something that makes sense.'

One night Rafael took them back home for a coffee. Jaime quite fancied Matilde, and she, just to spite her husband, took it into her head to rub his nose in it. Until one day Tomás asked the man from Jaca:

'Do you like the looks of my Matilde?'

Jaime Fernández, poker-faced, hit straight back:

'What do you care?'

'That's just it, I don't,' replied the crane-driver. 'If you want her you can have her.'

The brothers did not go back:

'Why do you put up with those boobies?' they asked Rafael.

'What does it matter?'

'You're right.'

Deep down, Rafael fancied Matilde too. He never actually thought about it, but the set of her breasts and the sway of her arse across a room were things that gave him pleasure. The unexpected outburst from her husband doused things down for a while, to the surprise of their lodgers. Celestino had known the Fernández brothers years before.

'They've turned into toffs. They're brave, but . . .'

'But what?'

'Nothing. I got nothing against them.'

'Do you suspect they're informers?'

'Them? Never!'

About that time, a transport-workers strike was declared in the docks. Tomás went back to work on the second day.

'Aren't you ashamed?' Rafael asked him that night, when he found out.

'Look, don't poke your nose in.' He paused: 'Are you going to pay my wages?'

'What about the others?' said Celestino.

'That's their lookout! I make my bed and I'll lie in it.'

For once, Matilde kept her mouth shut.

'I'll be moving out in the morning,' snapped Rafael, and they went up to bed.

'Don't get mixed in politic,' said the beauty to her man, once they were alone in the dining room, in her strange garbled tongue: born in Alcoy, she'd been brought up in Barcelona, and married a Castilian.

'I ain't mixed up in nuthin'!' replied the henpecked husband.

'Yes, yes! All they are tricksters. You just work and earn youse cash, thas'all. What they do is up to they. It's all the fault of peoples like Celestino and the Fernándezes. But you. Even youse woman . . .'

'All right, that's enough,' the weakling tried to interrupt.

'Yes, yes! I know that behind youse "all right" you always does what you wants. If you don't go to work tomorrow, it's 'cause youse not a man!'

'Have you finished? If I drive the crane it's because I want to, and not because a woman . . . Come on, let's get to bed. Oh, I might have known it, you've forgotten to grind the coffee.'

They killed him two days later as he left the house: one bullet in the chest, two in the stomach, a neat job. That afternoon at work Rafael heard that the widow had accused the Fernández brothers and Celestino Escobar of the crime.

'She says she saw them from the balcony.'

Rafael told Celestino at once, but too late. The police picked him up as he left the workshop. Serrador got through to the Fernández brothers by phone, and they got away.

Celestino had no trouble proving his alibi: he was at work when the murder took place. But the police caught on to his real name, and as a state of war had been declared (we're talking about October 1934) there was a summary hearing and they shot him two days later. Before this they beat his head in.

'We'll respect you as Celestino Escobar, but as for Celestino Morales, we're going to show him what's what!' said the inspector. And they showed him.

Rafael had moved to the end of the Calle de San Pablo. For a time it was as though they'd sawn off his right arm. Blood-lust kept rising up in his throat. 'If every one of us killed a traitor . . .' Matilde and her mother had disappeared; for a time he heard no more of the two Aragonese. Then, two months later, he bumped into Jaime in the Calle del Conde del Asalto.

'We hardly go out. Come to our place tonight.'

They lived in the Calle de Aribau, near the Diagonal. Rafael was surprised by the relative luxury: velvet curtains, imperial decor on the walls, watercolours and prints. They didn't introduce him to the landlady.

'Did you know the squealer came to see us?'

'Matilde?'

'The same. She's gone to pot.'

'Have you done her in?'

'Come off it, man. Do you take us for kids? She must still be in touch with the Specials. Besides, you can never be sure with those tip-offs. It may not have been her. She swears blind . . .'

'How come they haven't arrested you two?'

'They know perfectly well it wasn't us. They've let us alone. It was people from the docks, and they were within their rights.'

'So what's she doing now?'

'She doesn't know whether she's coming or going. If she squeals, she goes down.'

She went down all right, but to whoring. 'If I find her, I'll flatten her,' thought Rafael. He walked straight into her, late one night, by the Café Oriente, amongst other women charging ten, twelve, fifteen and twenty pesetas, according to desire and negotiation, mincing up and down with her handbag between the Pitarra statue and the Boquería.

Rafael made a sign to her and carried on down the street. The night had retained the sun's heat; the half-moon staggered through rapid clouds with silver edges. Dry leaves scratched at the asphalt with each brief gust of wind. Cars turned their lights up and down sooner than use their horns. She caught up with him opposite the Principal. The harbour lay dark and silent in the distance.

'Keep going!' Rafael told her.

'What you want?'

Rafael took her arm:

'Keep walking!'

The solitude begins past Casa Juan; the trees separate and grow smaller as you get closer to the sea. A tram drags its way back, with its yellow rectangles; above, Columbus makes his appearance, depending on the moon and the clouds. A half-open café shines up the cobbles.

'Keep walking, I want to talk to you.'

'You know what, youse really quite good-looking.'

Her voice has changed; his stomach turns. She snuggles close, her right thigh against his left. 'She's not wearing a corset,' thinks the male, and puts his arm round her waist. They were leeward of the last lights of the city, leaning against the railings around the base of Don Cristóbal's column:

'Youse really to blame for everything.'

'Why?' (He finds even the effort of speaking painful now.)

'If you hadn't come to the house . . .'

She doesn't even remember that it was Escobar who brought him.

'I still don't understand.'

His head is whirling. The scapegrace realizes she's on the wrong track. She changes the subject.

'What you doing now? Where d'you live?'

Trams go rumbling past, hanging by a thread and squealing.

'What do you care?'

'I care about you.'

'Don't start that . . .!'

Rafael could not see his way out. 'She's got to tell me the truth!' He took her arm again and pushed her towards the harbour. Three o'clock by the Customs House.

'Where we going?'

'Move!'

'Where we going? We could go back to my house. Is better there.'

('I don't hate her'), Rafael was surprised. ('It's almost as though I had nothing against her. But if she's to blame for Celestino's death, she must die. Or I have no right to live.') They were walking by the water's edge, towards Barceloneta. Rafael turned her face towards him.

'You informed on Celestino and the Fernández brothers.'

'What . . . Youse barmy!'

She said it quite matter-of-factly.

'Everyone says it was you.'

She laughed:

'Youse cracked. Why would I want to . . .?'

The calm water lapped against the gently rocking keels.

'I s'pose that rotten Jaime told you. Just because I wouldn't go to bed with him. He always laying his dirty hands on me in the passageway. Filthy pig! Where have you seen him . . .?'

'He hasn't told me anything.'

'Where does he live?'

'You know.'

'Do I?'

'Yes, you do. You went to see them. Why lie?'

The wail of a train comes from the North Station.

'Come on, is late.'

'It was you!'

'Shut up, dahling, don't be such a pain!'

They are speaking in half-tones, face to face.

'Did you nark on them, yes or no?'

'No!'

With that, Rafael turned and walked away. 'I'm a coward.' Ten paces further the trollop caught him up. The rolling of the buoys was the only sound to be heard.

'Come on, don't be such a misery, take me home.'

On the quayside was a great pile of cement bags; between them and the water, barely two metres; the moon in a grey sky, coating everything below as with dead whitewash. The hussy backed against the massive pile; in the silvery beam he saw her in a different light, greasy patches and covered in spots, chops smeared with crimson.

'Listen, stupid, if you don't tell the truth, you've had it.'

'Stop it, youse scaring me.'

'Good. Talk. Was it you?'

'No. And stop messing about.'

Rafael was tempted to break every bone in her body. Thump her till the blood spurted out of her. Only physical repugnance stopped him. He could almost feel the floozie's soft, oily flesh beneath his fists.

'They say you're a squealer.'

'Which son of a bitch says that?'

'Never you mind. I believe it. You've always liked snooping around poking your nose in other people's business.'

It was nauseating. He would have given an arm and a leg not to be there, to be home in bed asleep.

'Come on, leave me alone. That's enough now.'

'If you don't tell me the truth, I'll throttle you!' And he put his hands around her throat. He did it out of bravado, to force a solution, recklessly. He had her head pressed hard against one of those sacks – grey dust all around, as if death had passed by – with his thumbs against her windpipe. He could feel the Adam's apple give way inside her throat.

'I'll scream!'

He gave a squeeze. She, with the moon in her face, could not see him; otherwise she wouldn't have taken it seriously. Just one push would have got him away; as it was, she didn't dare move, and she talked. The moon was to blame.

'You never had husband killed!'

'Don't speak of the dead!'

Rafael didn't know what to do.

'Youse all sons of bitches. You sell youse own mothers for politic!'

'You prefer to sell people to the police.'

'At least they pay.'

A siren made them jump. A ship making for the sea. She began to arrange her hair.

'Who put you up to this game?'

'You don't know him. No one.'

Rafael breathed in: now he knew. In the sky, below the clouds, the white of the moon striped by topmasts, cables, idle cranes; the boom of a large sailing ship was pointing at them from the sea like a thin index finger; loose ends in the air, black ropes tied to black bollards. The deep smell of salt water. Water and seaweed slopping against stone. And no one; no one else on the land, no one on the sea, no one in the sky. The gentle clucking of the waves. Only them, returning in silence to the city, mute in the approaching dawn, the woman by the water's edge. He counted to three, and with a sudden charge and a shove pushed her into the sea; threw himself in after her. The bare three metres' height of the quay allowed the whore to reappear at once, waving her arms and spluttering. He grabbed her hair and kept her under the water with his right hand, clutching on to a ring embedded in the masonry with his left.

('Struggle all you like, I baptize you and baptize you again. Swirl around. Swallow, swallow. Now you can flow; scream, shake, pull. The uptow buoys you and lifts you; but I am stronger than the eddying currents and the lashing of the helpless sea against the blocks of stone.')

He steadied himself against the side. His victim's hands clawed at his wrist; a last frenzied effort, desperately seeking some way out from the intolerable asphyxiation.

('Stinking pool, what clings against me? As if a hundred currents were scrambling to carry you away.') When she stopped moving, he let her float gently away from his hand. He swam to the steps, climbed up and, choosing a bollard at random, sat and let the sea wind dry him out, until he was cold and hard. His hands ached, he noticed one was bleeding and remembered the rusty iron of the ring; but it was the right hand, and broken finger-nails had done the scratching. Two carabineers pass by, smoking. Trains whistle long and loud. The forgotten clattering of a tram. An hour. Things start to take shape, the warehouses begin to stand out against a puffy purple sky. He did not think. ('I should be thinking of Celestino.') He stood up and set off very slowly for home.

The night was turning into day, whilst yet remaining night. How do forms creep in? What poisonous liquid makes them appear? What false tin smears the sea, soldering it to the sky? What treachery opens all the doors, as death sneaks up on the city lights? The day is born surreptitiously. Even the wind dies in the face of such felony, so much death. Everything falls still. Height and distance dull colour. The cobbled roadway begins to swell with stone. The day comes with the cold and the low, the low and the far. The night backs off in fear, slithers away and hides. The light is timid and hides its face as it advances. All betrayed: these cables, these masts, these boxes, this crane, this clock, this boat, this abandoned propeller, like a metal rose, this bunker, this machinery, the movement of that man. White, red and green can now be made out on that painted funnel. The water again washes against iron, wood, stone. Salt water, sea. From thee cometh the light, my wretched scaffold, shabby hiding-place of the sun, beyond all reach or understanding.

He slumped, fully dressed, on his bed, trembling. He sank straight into sleep as into a swamp.

A clammy silence binds my hands, poisoned fish float without currents, turning the green water white. Brown and black seaweed, green poison. Ferns and moss sink, entangling my feet. The water does not flow, it descends. I shall die drowning in air. The fish begin to graze by me, a shuddering of clouds, a shiver of wounded velvet, my veins begin to tremble like a great fern; my blue veins and red arteries, as in school.

I would have twisted the last vein of water between my hand of crystal and my hand of flesh, but I was bound, completely bound.

The dead hang around until they file them in their box. Then, only then, do they begin to sing. Matilde will keep her beak shut – she's a crow, a wet crow – because she has seaweed for a tongue and when she opens her mouth it will all come spurting out, covered in pus.

I'm cold. I need a blanket.

Shallow water is born to flow with the smell of earth. Still water is scary. Living ditches of Viver, unravel, the stagnant pool is coming, it will envelop you and eat you alive: waggle your mosses and lichens as if they were your own tail!

If a hand is trapped between the tides, the hand is doomed. The weed always hides something: jellyfish, medusas, groupers, octopuses, eels. Lacinias are the hair of drowned women. Hair is made for water: it dances to and fro without asking for directions, softly, wavily, like a *habanera* song, a slow curve lovingly swaying. What does your hair care for your face! The sea sustains it, beats against it, cradles it and lulls it, cuddles and smoothes and combs it.

What fearful taste in my mouth? I've got you held tight by the mane, your open mouth sunk beneath the still water. There are no teeth or slides, cards or combs like the waters of Viver, not even the sea water. Rocks are born in the water, like fish, even though they come flying out of the seaweed. My hand made of water is beginning to hurt me, I can't move my gaping fingers. Ah, the slow swirl of the sea water! (Its long slaps against the paunches of ships as though they were the bellies of black horses, and its constant rise and fall against the wall of the wharf.) My hand stays beneath the water, and I set off along the path to Uncle Quico's. On the path to Uncle Quico's there's a dead snake. If I speak my mouth fills with slime, with lichens, with grey and green seaweed, withered lacinias, green mother of pus and black humours. I'm eight years old and I already have a hand of glass; the snake is dead, in the middle of the path, its head squashed flat, crushed, its eyes bulging. My hand is cold, transparent and numb. Probably because I've left the balcony open.

I shall never go swimming in the sea again.

TWO

The 'Rhine Gold'

They found the body the next day. The police didn't bother much with the investigation. Information is cheap and it's as well to have a change. Three lines in *La Vanguardia*, and the affair was buried.

Rafael lived above a restaurant, The Pearl of the New World. A few travellers from Ampurdán (the owner was from those parts) used to sleep there when they came to do business in Barcelona. Long-term residents, no more than four or five. There was a general instruction, after the events of 6 October 1934, not to go out after dark. Once the overnight guests were in bed, a discussion would get going in the dining room. There would be the proprietor, known as the 'Fat Man', a bit of a fixer and small-time gambler; his wife, Desideria, who hailed from Collbato, a Carlist village on the slopes of Montserrat; a foreman from the local electricity works, who was a communist from Seville, and his wife, Emilia, from Madrid, a shy, retiring woman who stayed at home and sewed for friends. They were joined on around the tenth by a frail, pasty, red-haired lad of about twenty-five, with his arm in a sling thanks to a glancing bullet wound picked up on the morning of the 7th – he was in Alianza Obrera, a separatist organization – which had caused more fright than damage. The communist's name was Agustín Espinosa; the young Dencàs supporter's, José Reverter. Espinosa's wife gave Desideria what help she could. Rafael contrived to make the talk last as long as possible: bedtime was painful to him, because of the memory of Celestino. They talked of everything humanly possible but left divine affairs to the landlord's better half, very given to devotions, the bone of much contention with her sponger of a husband, who was excessively inclined to cursing and blaspheming in God's holy name.

After Companys' defeat and imprisonment, José Reverter no longer dared go down even to the dining room. Rafael kept him company in his tiny room.

'It's your fault,' said the Catalan. 'If the CNT had taken to the streets we'd have won. Batet would have gone over to the Generalitat; he decided against it as soon as he knew you weren't going to budge.'

Rafael felt somewhat uneasy at hearing himself referred to as an active member of the Confederation. Up until then, his coincidence of views with the syndicalists had implied little more than obeying the instructions of the confederal organization, paying his subs, and reading the newspaper. Am I an anarchist? he asked himself and, none too sure, was tempted to answer in the negative. It seemed to him presumptuous to express his disagreements, especially when he had nothing but doubts with which to confront them. 'Doubts give rise to calamities. I can't stop doubting: the calamity is me.'

He replied airily:

'The days are gone when we'd let ourselves be smashed to pieces in the streets so that Joe Soap can enjoy power on the proceeds of our bloodshed. We'll only take to the streets when power can be harvested by the CNT. Why should we have risked death the other day? Who for? For old whiskers Companys, or some incompetent coward like Dencàs, or Badía? Hadn't you made our ears ring with your boasts about how strong you were? You said you didn't need anyone. Now we've seen. So what if you lost? It's nothing to us.'

'That way you play into the reactionaries' hands.'

'Look, matey: to us, reactionaries can as well be called Anguera de Sojo as Martínez de Velasco; both will machine-gun us as soon as look at us. Besides, you don't even know what you want. Let's see now, what are you: communist, fascist, anarchist?'

'You can't put the question like that. I think that any policy, if it's to triumph, needs to mobilize youth, offer it a mystique, discipline, action.'

'Fine, but what mystique? Action in the interests of what?'

'We want a young, passionate political movement, to promote two basic principles: nationalism and socialism.'

'In theory I might want something similar, though we probably mean two quite different things by "nationalist". But do you realize that what you're formulating is a national-socialist profession of faith, in other words, a fascist one?'

'Get away!'

'Like it or not, you are. I'm not the CNT, nor the FAI, but I have to agree with them: they were right to leave you on your own. Or do you think we can gaily hand back power to people who support what was done at Figols, Arnedo, Casas Viejas and Castilblanco? If by some miracle you'd won, who would be in power now? Azaña, Reverter. Azaña and the socialists. And us on our way to the penal colony. We anarchists want to bring in libertarian communism, and so long as there's no chance of our bloodshed helping to bring it in, don't count on us.'

'But then the Republic will go to the wall!'

'It can go where it pleases, for all we care. The liberals have thumped us just like the conservatives did. And we'd rather have Lerroux than Largo Caballero.'

Lerroux was the touchstone. The Fat Man had been a 'Young Barbarian', knew Ferrer and even today remained the stalwart of a Radical circle. With his broad face and saffron-coloured cheeks lent extra virility by long mutton-chop whiskers, profligate and bombastic, ever ready to play the bogey-man, he dressed always in a shiny grey alpaca jacket, over dark trousers in winter and beige ones in summer. He dealt in cocaine and had an arrangement with a number of local bawds, who would concede the blusterer certain favours relating to their persons or their merchandise. Traditionalism, authoritarianism, anti-Catalanism and anti-clericalism were the fellow's four hobby-horses, in discourses well seasoned with oaths and steeped in a cosmic contempt for mankind from which even he was not excluded. He could not accept that anyone would ever act disinterestedly: he truly believed that all human beings were swine, that there is no virtue without price and no functionary who is not for sale.

'It all comes down to bidding, or for-bidding,' he would say. 'I've been told that in one of them so-called holy books it says there are three things that push a man on: persecution, madness and poverty; all to end up recommending, naturally, greater veneration of our holy father, or how's your father, as I prefer to call him. (He winked.) I've never forgotten that, and as I don't want to be pushed anywhere, not even to heaven, I'm neither persecuted, nor mad, nor poor. The world is badly shared out, but if it had a divine origin, as my missus believes, I reckon we should all of us commit suicide as a sign of protest, just to annoy God. The fact is that no one believes it, and it's the priests who profit from all the humbug. In this damned life there's nothing but the scramble; and if you don't watch out they'll leave you as your mother bore you, in the twinkling of an eye. But not if I see them first!'

'The road to perdition . . .' muttered his wife.

'Shut your mouth!' retorted the idle rogue. 'What business have you to be a Christian? If you are, it's out of selfishness and for peace of mind. To insure tomorrow. You don't give a damn about anyone else! And if I'm mistaken, why don't you go down right now and hand out your jewellery to the passers-by, and your clothes to anyone who's shivering. Go on, you have my permission! (Laughter bubbled out of him and his belly heaved.) And they'll burn your arse for all eternity. I wouldn't trust those devils for a moment!'

The socialists were his bugbear. 'That rabble should be thumped and clubbed to death. They live off the backs of the workers.'

He had no truck with firearms, though: 'They're for cowards,' he said. 'To have a man's life at the end of a trigger: it's indecent! Now giving it to someone straight in the face, that's another story. At a pinch, if necessary, with a knife, that's a fair fight, too. Lerroux knows what he's about. I laugh when people talk to me about Catalan anarchism and its traditions. The anarchists have a father, and he's still a fine figure of a man: Don Alejandro Lerroux!'

'You've got a point,' said Espinosa, who usually kept quiet when the Fat Man was present. 'People do tend to confuse anarchism with individualism.'

'If you say so!' said Fatso, with a sneer.

'We all speak our minds here, but that's just bloody arrogance, and shameful,' observed the man from Seville.

There was a shocked silence.

'In the elections,' persisted that porcine personage, 'the socialists won; the anarchists and Lerroux were against, with no need to gang up. And the other day, when Dencàs, Companys and company bungled things, it was the same.'

'Dencàs,' Rafael butted in, 'put the CNT leaders in jail on the morning of the 6th, in case you hadn't noticed. No doubt he was counting on Señor Maurín's forces . . .'

Serrador used to chat with Espinosa on Saturday afternoons.

'I can't understand why you hate us,' said the Sevillian. 'Aren't we all workers? Don't we all want the same thing, a fairer world?'

'When you're in power, you'll kill us.'

'First of all, it's not us; and second, there aren't just socialists in the government.'

'Dead men tell tales! We have to answer! And hit harder, if possible . . .'

'That way we'll get nowhere. The bourgeoisie just profits from our divisions.'

'Yes, but if we were united, you'd want to give the orders, and that's not on. There are more of us.'

'But we're right. Your actions – leaving your theories aside for the moment – lead to a dead end.'

'It's because you think that way that we're in the mess we are. And the people are with us.'

'And you'll settle for that. But suppose you win and take power: how are you going to make the state disappear? With what? You have to crush your opponents. For that you need an apparatus, a dictatorial machine, whatever direction you take. Or they'll be back inside your house in no time. Because, as for picking off your enemies individually! . . . Imagine where that will get you! Do you really think that's a solution? Do you really have the right to kill everybody who makes you sick? Everyone betrays someone. There'd be nobody left, it would cancel itself out.'

'And then a new world could begin.'

'The fact is, you're afraid of us. You know that on the ground of reality we're stronger. Your consciences aren't clear, by which I don't mean to say that you have anything to reproach yourselves with, other than your own sense of insecurity.'

'I don't know. The truth is that deep down, you despise us anarchists. And in spite of all your promises, we can see it. You're not sincere. And your tactics are obvious: you want to finish us off around the corner, at the first opportunity. It wouldn't be the first time!'

'Would you rather the bourgeoisie went on winning?'

'At least that way we stay alive!' Rafael smiled.

They had just finished two beers which Espinosa's silent companion had brought up from the bar.

'Personally,' Rafael went on, 'I feel sick at having to accept moulds that other people have shaped as containers for my thought. Something rises up inside me . . .'

'What did you expect, you bloody fool: that you were somehow going to extract from the world, through the power of your own brain cells, some new conception of humanity? We can only think things insofar as others have thought about them before us. You pick up the world, when you're born, in the state in which you find it, and you move among the forms that others have created; and you can no more change the layout of those thoughts than the layout of the streets. You can choose, but even then not much. And your progress and glory depend on how you leave humanity when you die. To start from zero is either outrageous naivety, or something worse. I know individual rebellion is a fine thing, but that's all.'

'Streets, institutions, churches can be burned.'

'Yes, and there are earthquakes, too. But the reconstructed streets, if it's private individuals who rebuild them, will show a fatal resemblance to the ones destroyed. Styles are mere fripperies, their differences a lot of fuss about nothing. What counts is the structure, that the buildings should be of stone, not cardboard like today. That we should know who lives in them, and what exactly needs to be done. Feelings belong to you, but ideas come ready-made, whether you like it or not, through language. Language is a serious matter. The only way of understanding one another, according to you anarchists, would be for each of you to be taught a different language: an Esperantist panacea, say what you like. Your politics is sentimental and full of hot air, which comes to the same thing.'

'Stop right there! What we want is freedom and equality for all. With the dictatorship of the proletariat – of the Communist Party, in other words – you reduce freedom to nothing.'

'You're mixing up your words! For a communist the problem of freedom doesn't exist, because it's resolved from the moment you become one. To be a communist is to forget yourself. Whereas you represent the individual, the basis of the bourgeoisie. You're united by the same sense of what you call freedom, which is really just a free-for-all: all for me and to hell with the last in the queue! You, in the middle of the night, all on your own, look down from the clouds and feel sufficiently virtuous to judge everyone else. We don't: we feel the weight of the world on our shoulders, and we obey it. That's why being a communist would require more strength than you can muster.'

'I see you coming, snake in the grass! You won't fool me with soft soap! If I was going to believe in God the father and Trotsky the devil I'd have been a Catholic like my village priest wanted, which would have saved me no end of bother, by the way! And he had different methods from yours . . . but he still hit stony ground.'

'If you were in power you'd be far more intransigent and sectarian than us. You don't know where to go, where to aim. You accept absurdity as feasible. You proclaim the discipline of indiscipline. It's either one thing or the other: one minus one equals zero; one divided by zero, zero; or, if you like, the discipline of indiscipline equals indiscipline. You're a negative force. That way all power is personal, be it that of an individual, or, if it makes you feel better, that of a group.'

'Can you assure me, at this point, that in the USSR the dictatorship is that of a class and not a person, or, if it makes you feel better, of a soviet?'

'Yes, I maintain it, even though the bourgeoisie won't accept it for its own reasons, and you for . . . sentimental ones. In the USSR there is the dictatorship of the proletariat – got that? – of the proletariat. The bourgeoisie just weeps for its own. Now what would you have, if you won? Anarchy? That died years ago. Old gentlemen with long white beards are busy burying it, completely gaga. So you've come up with the bright idea of libertarian communism: all that would mean is living off the rotting corpse of the bourgeoisie. Then what? Peasant revolution, right? And after that – showing your true colours – fascism. Yes, mate, fascism! Straight up: I, if I was a sincere syndicalist, would join the Falange; it's the closest thing to you. Don't lose your temper, you know I'm only talking with the frankness you deserve. And pardon the sermon. But I'm sick of always hearing, "We'll organize in the streets!" Improvization is a Spanish virtue, but not that much. Your objective? Bring down the government! Whichever it is. And you kid yourselves you won't be used to bring down what interferes with certain other interests I shan't mention. Anyone can find his way into an organization as open as yours . . .'

Rafael could see how much the party line was imprinted on these last paragraphs; but they increased his doubts and uncertainties. He ate his supper in silence that evening and went straight to bed. On Sunday morning he gave the book fair a miss; sat down at the table, took a sheet of paper and began to write:

I want to start from zero.

I

I think, therefore I am incomplete.
My body, water, don't they also exist?

What am I?

A	B
For others	For myself
1	1
What I do	What I think
2	2
My physical presence	My feelings

I: a spring. Some water inside, some given away. As you discourse, so you are. Currents differ, people know them. Personality, me: zero. He that hath, giveth. Covetousness is not a vice of the soul, but of the body. Likewise: gluttony, anger, sloth. Vices of the soul: lust and envy. And hatred? Hatred is a virtue. To hate you need passion. I don't hate, I despise. Example: Matilde.

I'm lost

I am, therefore I think, therefore I am
I exist, therefore I live, therefore I exist

II

Who am I with?

On the one hand:
People with nothing,
the poor, those who
turn their efforts
into bare bread; those
without even that, nor
shoes nor coat;
people with nowhere to
wash, who dread
the winter, who have
grime and lice; the
dirty, the illiterate,
those who work from
the age of seven,
eight, nine, ten, day
labourers, yes, wage-
earners, carriers,
drudges, those whose
palms have turned to
stone, machinists,
ploughmen, tramps,
whores, those who
stink. People who've
never seen the
country,
who've never seen
the sea. Who
live in direct
contact with matter,
water, fire and earth.

In between:
Book-keepers, clerks,
shopkeepers, office
workers, newspaper-
men, actors, tailors
and hatters without
staff. Those who've
achieved their
ambition in life.
Bureaucrats, second-
and third-level
officials, I don't
know. Hermaphrodites,
hybrids. People
content with
what they have.
Pensioners, invalids,
intellectuals, saints,
the wise and the just.
Above all, grocers'
assistants, travel-
ling salesmen and
peasants. Beggars.

On the other hand:
People with bath-
rooms, more than two
towels and clean wives
waiting for them in
fine linen underwear
or lying back on
couches in negligés
and embroidered
petticoats. Women who
paint their nails with
varnish brought from
New York in luxury
cabins with sun decks
and ping-pong tables.
People who pay with the
work of others. The
police, generals,
the kind who ride in
taxis. Toffs with
leather-bound
libraries. With
two toilets.
With boxes at the
theatre. Those who
get bored. Those with
soft hands. Those who
despise us.

If I were dictator, the first group would be clean-shaven, the last would have moustaches, and the ones in between would have beards. I am and I exist with the first group. I know it and I re-know it, but it's as well to remind oneself every now and then, just as you look and look again at something that pleases you.

III

What have I been?

1	2
To others	To myself
Nothing	Nothing

What is there to show, what remains of my work?
Have I been, am I just the dust I swept in the jeweller's store
at Castellón?
The packets I delivered here in Barcelona?
The shine on the rails I coat with chromium?
Am I living out the drowned life of Matilde?

IV

What should I do?

a) Create.
What? No idea. Then un-create.
b) Construct.

Phooey! as the old fellow would say. Then de-struct.
The only way I can leave a mark: kill or burn.
They say that being born and dying are the same thing. We
shall find out, by making
and unmaking. If I destroy a thing it has to be reborn;
therefore if I crush, I create.

Who should I kill?   What should I burn?

Is suicide a solution?   Revolution? For the moment we
Matilde.   haven't the means to carry it
So much twisting and   out. Recent proof, the 6th of
turning simply to   October. Work for unity? I am
justify myself again!   nobody. Obey? If it means
I think less of myself.   ceasing to be myself, a bullet is better.

Am I lying? I believe in my uselessness. I feel I'm lying. I believe
I'm lying. I'm up against a wall. A wall of solid concrete. As
Celestino would have said, you can't even climb up the walls.

Rafael read over what he'd written, screwed it up and slumped
on his bed. He tried to read beyond page two of the *Discourse
on Method*, which the bookseller had recommended, and fell
back upon himself.

'What matters is the truth. Not what I'm living for, but
what I should be living for. I can't choose. Rubbish! You can
always choose. You always do choose. Like it or not. To live
is to make choices. You can always do what you don't do. You
don't do what you want, but what you choose. You choose

between what they offer you. To choose is to win or to give in. If I choose by overcoming myself, then I've won. He who doubts, dies; he who chooses, wins. I doubt, therefore I'm beaten. Not true. I know where truth lies, and I'm for it. What I don't know is the way. The paths of providence, etcetera, but all roads lead to Rome, for goodness sake! Yes, laddie, but sometimes by a roundabout route! And what if you realize you've taken the wrong road half-way along? It doesn't matter! That's the road! And if you turn back, that's the road too!

'Injustice is the truth. I wish for justice. The way to truth and justice is injustice. To justice via injustice. How's that for a road lined with precipices! If you don't fall to the right you topple to the left. The question is not to know what is or isn't right, but to be in the right yourself. And above all, not to be a spectator. That'll be some theatre the day there's no audience, only actors! To be part of the truth! To fight and see. Do you understand what I'm saying: it's important that the thing be right and true, but also that I don't see it, that I be the thing itself.'

He fell asleep. He woke up at midnight and went back to the mania of his papers.

I

What justifies my life?
The idea, the presence, of my body in the world.

II

What is worth sacrificing it for?
The life of others, including my own.

Writing can take a hike. He slumps back again. Life is a spinning mill. We untangle the skein without losing the thread. The world's as small as a handkerchief. Life is as it is and not as it has been. It's not your father that matters, but your brother, the shoemaker on the corner. The memory of Matilde like a sour belch. And of a conversation, in the dining room, about informers. 'There'll always be narks,' said the Fat Man. And the singing in his ears: 'You killed her because your body wanted it!'

'I killed her because she disgusted me. Full stop.'

'Should I kill everyone who disgusts me? Then why not do away with the Fat Man? He's vile enough . . .! You go down by the steps of no. 95. No problem crossing the roof. You turn into Riera Alta and as he goes by you drill him. He comes home every day between three and half-past. No one will see, no one will know. You come back the same way you went out. OK? Let's see who's got nerve! Why do they call people who jump down into the ring "capitalists"? Simply out of cruelty and sarcasm?' Sleep, like the waters of death.

He got hold of a snub-nosed Astra 9 and fixed the day for the following Monday. He had never fired a gun. He went to bed early the night before, set the alarm for two, in case he slept through. Before supper he had another look around the predestined spot and the hidden entrance-way. He dined calmly, went to bed fully dressed – 'Let's hope no one sees me in the street' – and slept like a log until a minute before the time he'd decided. He went out without a sound – he had oiled the lock and hinges – crossed the terrace and climbed over the flat roof, slid down the drainpipe, went down into the street, and was lying in wait ten minutes before the appointed time.

His right hand ached from holding the gun so tight. Should he slip the safety catch or leave it as it was? People passed by not more than half a metre from his hiding-place. It smelt of fried cabbage, leftovers. A cat mewed from the gutter. Rafael, in order not to think, began to count. He counted up to one hundred and fifty-eight. It was more than six months since the Matilde business. Yes, quite a bit more. True to forecast, there was no moon. You can't beat the calendar! Supposing he decides to go by on the other side? It's not his habit. He had resolved that if that should happen, he would delay the attempt until the following day. Half an hour must have passed. Only his hand existed. Steps in the distance, a car braking. He barely heard him come, saw his fat-bellied profile – like a painting by Nogués – in the dim light of the gas lamp. He counted: one, two! He leaped from his bolt-hole out into the street and fired through his pocket. The blast and the recoil left him bewildered. He tore at the trigger. No good. The Fat Man had collapsed, howling. The night watchman, in the distance, was pouring his liver into his whistle. Across the sleeping city, growing concentrically, other whistles answered. Rafael took to his heels: regained his room without difficulty. The gun had got stuck, it was a hell of a job to unload it; then he tore a strip from his jacket to remove the perforation. Eventually he heard voices, much less excited than he had expected. He was about to go to the door, already undressed, when he heard the Fat Man muttering. He pulled the door slightly open.

'What's up?'

'Nothing,' replied the blackguard. 'Occupational hazard! See you tomorrow. Sleep well!'

'A bullet in the forearm,' Espinosa told him, having found out from his wife. 'He knows who it was. Crooks, the lot of them. Let them get on with it! I expect the one who shot him was as much of a thief himself.'

'Pity they didn't get him!' Rafael said, to see what it would bring.

'Why? What's the point? One bastard more or less won't change the world.'

Serrador told González Cantos.

'No, son, no! Personal attacks are only a defensive measure. The world will be won in the streets. And symbolic acts will pass into history. No one believes in symbols any more, not even the Italians! . . . Save that for the Civil Guard.'

'But when?' said Rafael, only half joking.

'That's up to them rather than us.'

Time, of itself, does not settle doubts. 1935 ends in a fog.

Just then the Fernández brothers look him up.

'We've been down that road too.'

People are talking to them about the Falange:

'They're anti-capitalist and anti-Catalan, which can't be bad,' says Atilio. 'I tell you, black on red: without discipline we'll get nowhere. The Falange's programme is not that far from the Confederation's.'

'Yes, but on the other side!'

'No, Serrador, no! It's a case of attacking capitalism from within.'

'Doesn't it tell you something about national-syndicalism?' insists Jaime. 'Besides, they have the same flag as the CNT.'

Rafael finds all this rather cheap and mean: like selling your soul cut-price. He would like a world of heroic actions. He doesn't dare say it to anyone, but he is not far from believing that great individual deeds could change the face of the world. The same old itch to kill traitors. Drunken blather or tilting at windmills, he tells himself.

'There's no commitment. Come down to the café with us sometime.'

He went. They met towards half past two in the afternoon, in the Rhine Gold. Rafael was shocked to find himself drinking coffee in such a swanky place.

'Hey,' he asked one of the Fernández pair on the first day, 'this name "Rhine Gold", is it a hint or something?'

'Of course not, man! They haven't a cent. Not yet.'

'And as we're first in, we'll become the masters,' added the other.

That shift was served by a waiter Serrador knew from the PSUC, Joaquín Lluch: dark, emphatic, and a gossip. The fact that they met within earshot and to the knowledge of a political enemy predisposed Rafael favourably; he decided not to take it all too seriously. (At bottom, Serrador does not believe in the possibility of a serious Fascist movement in Spain, nor in the triumph of Communism. 'I believe in death and I want a just world, without rich or poor. Outside of that, what do I know? What do I want? What do I believe in? Nothing!')

The leader of that gang of eight to twelve members, depending on the day, has not an ounce of fat on him: gaunt, dry, lean flesh burned brown by the sun, stony head erect, piercing rook's eyes, alert and incredibly quick to turn and take hold, above a long thin nose which in profile acquires a Roman or Cordoban look; furrowed brow, thin spiky hair, shaven chin, grooved like the buttocks of a peach when he juts it forward and clenches his fists in some gesture of determination; then his pupils shine like polished jet, or small black olives. High shoulders, and a strong, arched chest; cheap clothes, washed threadbare; grey cloth jacket, trousers either darker or lighter showing his contempt for tailors and trivialities; long hands, long nervous fingers; a heavy smoker, he drags on cigarettes in rapid puffs from the lips rather than the throat. He walks with long strides, swinging his arms; you can tell his bony frame a mile away. Abrupt of speech, close-mouthed, used to giving and obeying orders, his military manner concealing a basic timidity and a crippling shyness about his own feelings. Only two things matter to him: courage and Castilian literature; everything else, less. Thirty-five or thereabouts; a highlander at heart, with his emotions in his two hands and the will to lock himself away, under discipline, in cold bare places. His deep love for the baroque and the sensuality of good speech is not apparent in the street: he attends to whoever accosts him and treats their smallest concern as of the greatest interest; his indulgence gets the better of him, a losing battle. His name is Luis Salomar; he was born on the border between Vizcaya and Santander, in one of those country houses long on years but short on money, with wealthy relatives in the ports – Bilbao and Santander – who migrated in search of business, leaving the family name and one brother back in the old country home. Through snow-filled winters, with time to spare and stacks of books collected through years and continents by a distant adventurer uncle, he had become a man without difficulty though without a mother, she having died far off in his childhood; caresses would always smell of servants to him. He fell in love very young with one of his aunts, pale, fragile, cheerful, thirty wee years wrapped in a blue shawl; there was no end of a rumpus when the family caught a whiff of warm flesh. Luis fled to North Africa, eighteen and broken-hearted, to join the Legion. As luggage he took a book of prose poems and the urge to die killing infidels. The whine of bullets and the slow, white, fervent, devout existence of the Moors revealed the possibility of a heroic life without immediate need for graves or vultures. After two years he received a letter from his pretty aunt, from Barcelona, where the black looks of her relatives had driven her. Salomar bought himself out after the fall of Alhucemas and went to the 'City of the Counts'. Presence made the heart less fond, but left them good friends. The suitor had returned with a book and published it, with some success, albeit confined to his northern homeland. It was obliquely commented upon in one or two cafés in Bilbao where people met who had a more moral than material relation with politics, and little doubt that they could maintain this posture indefinitely. Our man wrote well, with much rolling of drums, in the style and to the taste of the children of Don Pedro de Eguilior and Don Miguel de Unamuno. 1924 and 1925 went swirling by.

Salomar loved Barcelona with a vengeance. He paced through it with the air of a conquistador, feeling as if he was living in some immensely rich Indies where sky and earth were Spanish by force of arms and the dwarfish locals barely worthy of their fate. He attached himself to the city, loved its tonic atmosphere and whiff of battle. By right and charter he felt an abode was owing to him there. He found one and made it his own, much to his taste, in the Calle de

Fernando: an attic room with a small terrace, which he lined with bookshelves and filled with volumes bought during his daily prowls through old bookshops. He concentrated on the mystics, not for salvation but for the style – coiled, baroque, brilliant, flowery, flamboyant, intricate and difficult – and the pleasure of the words themselves; he read kilos of Golden Age preachers, wallowing enraptured in obsolete terms, antiquated styles, archaic proverbs, making a file to collect words, phrases and sayings no longer used and even forgotten: he piled up thousands which he sorted out late at night, in very neat card boxes. He spent whole periods of his life confronting Isabel of Castile, Gonzalo of Córdoba or Fray Luis of Granada: he emerged from those head-to-head jousts laden with ripe trophies from Imperial Spain. He wrote with difficulty, the constant concern for his models preventing him from fluency; he went over and over his efforts ten times and more, removing all spontaneity and sacrificing all doctrine to good expression.

Little magazines were springing up in every Spanish provincial capital at that time. The dictatorship left people with time on their hands, and idleness engendered splendid ways of saying things, helped along by Góngora's commemoration, the feast of the *Soledades*. Poetry became the be-all and end-all among the younger generation, and there had rarely been so many young and gifted poets alive at one time: Lorca in Granada, Alberti in Puerto de Santa María, Guillén in Valladolid, Salinas in Madrid, Diego in Santander and Gijón, Prados and Altolaguirre in Málaga; and their teachers, Juan Ramón Jiménez, Miguel de Unamuno and Antonio Machado. Salomar decided that Barcelona could not survive without a magazine, and founded one. He joined with bards suffering from publication sickness, clerks on heat for print, vague literature teachers, Catalans craving to be mentioned at literary soirées in Madrid: no one who came up to his ankle. With his scarce resources – he scraped along on translations – and his tenacity, the magazine got by and he had his own literary circle.

Luis Salomar lived on milk, fresh fruit, nuts and the occasional bit of salad shared with his tortoise, just as the milk was shared with his cat. Love became an adolescent memory, and as for coupling, the by-no-means-holy surroundings of his dwelling-place ensured both frequency and variety; many a strumpet would return to the scene without charge, won over by his goodwill, manliness and lack of malice. His aunt, from time to time, would come to tidy up the garret; though not his desk, always neat, with no waste paper. Barcelona, segregated by the harbour as she had been for centuries, bound and liberated his senses. He allowed himself, without remorse, and when he had friends, binges which ran from red to white and back again. He liked raw Spanish wines, and old Castilian and northern dishes: Rioja sausage cooked in wine, Galician hotpot, roast lamb, or potato omelettes two fingers thick, cold and greasy, sprinkled with oil and garlic, soaked in Rioja or Valdepeñas, with Manchego cheese, black cherries in syrup, fritters, pastries with almond custard on top, all sandwiched between the inevitable bottles of Sanlúcar or Moriles. He insulted any companion keen on foreign tipples by dubbing them pansies, blubberlings or frogs; he was always last to leave, returning to his pigeon loft very erect though completely sozzled.

For him there were only Spaniards and Arabs; then –
awaiting household orders – the Italians and the Dutch.
Opposite them, the enemy: the British. Alongside them,
those who had gone astray: the Portuguese and the Latin
Americans, who one day would have to be brought back into
the fold, willingly or by force; and in the middle, a half-loved
field of flowers and battles, France. José Antonio Primo de
Rivera's movement suited him, naturally, down to the very
ground; Primo understood that Luis Salomar was a useful
element for his spineless, brainless, foolish playboy ranks; the
highland writer, ingenuous, a bachelor, hard and obedient,
modest in spite of his masculine pride, provided a solid base.

The other participants were of the most diverse stamp,
recruited at random. Three or four fine young gentlemen of
greater or lesser rank and style, the rest mostly smartarses:
gamblers out for a lark, a card-sharp, a pickpocket they hid
from the cops for eight days by passing him from one house
to another; the occasional Catalan with a longing to be
Castilian, although these rarely put down roots, for all that
Luis used to greet such traitors to their mother-tongue with
open arms and especial warmth; all of them brown-nosers to
the Chief, weeds come to salaam the future triumvir. A couple
of Treasury employees, a journalist, a proofreader, but above
all, daddy's boys: the sons of bankers, nylon manufacturers,
makers of underwear, oilskins and rubber goods; the sons
of coal storers, fruit exporters and marquises gone up in the
world. Two doctors, an insurance salesman, two students and
a lawyer also passed through. The only workers, and that's
saying a lot because they hadn't worked for months, were
the Fernández brothers. Serrador felt lost. They had been

discussing some meeting in Valladolid, but the conversation fragmented: some talked about the cinema, some about dancing, some remained on the original subject, some veered onto books, business, cars, the magazine.

'Hallo, Rubio!'

A heavily-built young man came up to the table, pleased as punch with his own image and person, chestnut moustache, padded shoulders.

'Out there in the streets,' he ranted, 'so-called socialists or communists are on the rampage, forcing all the shopkeepers to close. I was in Casa Morell when two of the wretches came in. "Shut up shop at once," they go, quite cheerfully, as though in their own homes; and they stopped a customer coming in. He just turned straight around and went out again. If that had been me! . . . Though it's beneath a gentleman's dignity to have dealings with such scum.'

A swarthy man sitting opposite Rafael cut him short:

'I'll have you know that I am a gentleman.'

'I don't doubt it,' replies the recent arrival.

'And a socialist,' the man calmly finishes.

Complete silence fell.

'Of course, my dear fellow, of course!' said Rubio, and went and sat at the far end of the table. They changed the subject.

With the collapse of the dictatorship, conditions looked up for provincial and occasional magazines. Their begetters for the most part became candidates or took their first steps in politics: the regime might change from one day to the next, and that reinforced visions of stepping into other people's shoes. In 1930 the bourgeois world was republican. When the supposed panacea was actually proclaimed, almost by a fluke, it was as if disillusion flowed immediately from word to deed, and it turned out to be be too much of a good thing: those of good name saw it as a personal insult, and those with good credit as a menace. To be a republican once there was a Republic no longer held the same appeal. And when the Socialists tried to introduce timid reforms, those with means and the Radicals moved off their backsides and pulled away the rug. In November 1933 the Spanish right – the serious right: the Church and the feudal lords, with their generals in tow – realized that they could take to the field and win decisively, and they began to prepare their uprising of July 1936. The CEDA provided good cover: unknowingly, for the most part, and bent, it seemed, at most on restoration; it occupied itself in repairing what little damage the Republican government had supposedly done to its supporters. Lerroux was the procurer, the epitome of the pimp. Also in there, and on the up and up, was the Spanish Falange. Those in a position to do so gave it a hand: the military, for international convenience, as a direct route to Rome and Berlin, where they were welcomed with open arms; the monarchists, considering it a raucous ally which could be dismissed with a flick when the time was right; the Church, only too happy, with nothing to lose: the Falangists praised to the Heavens the imperial grandeur and external glory of the Holy, Apostolic and Roman Catholic Church. None of them paused for a moment to consider the national-syndicalist doctrine. They could not have cared less; Falange for them was a mask, an open sesame, a wheeze, a free pass.

In the days when the magazine was still exclusively literary (it died about the time of this narration), only two members of the group remained, benevolent leftists who did not take Luis Salomar's organization seriously. 'He's just playing at soldiers,' they told themselves. One, the man who had replied to Pedro Rubio Masferrer, was an Andalusian baker and poet. At his side, and the life and soul of the party, was Don Prudencio Bertomeu, a famous publisher, white-bearded and bewhiskered, a tall fine figure of a man, who wore white shirts and boots on all occasions, and was no end of a wag. It flattered him to think that everyone knew who he was, which was true of Barcelonans of more than fifty – the world, as far as he was concerned. A great friend of Ramón Casas and Santiago Rusiñol, he understood little of what went on around him; he lived in a reduced Barcelona, all whalebone corsets and classical scrolls. He caused uproar with the following:

'I get criticized,' said he, 'because I share the necessities of my sex with girls of eighteen. In-cre-di-ble, my friends, in-com-pre-hen-si-ble. Though what else can you expect of people today! But let's-just-see-now! Yes, they say, if only you had re-la-tions, re-la-tions with ladies with whose age you coincide – do you hear me, co-in-cide! . . . I'm sixty. Sixty! And it turns out that I coincide with women of forty-five. In-cre-di-ble! No one knows what law says so: but sixty male years equals forty-five of the female. Just-you-list-en-to-me-now!'

The man sat back in the dark red seat, closed his fist and banged it on the table, though with parsimony, in case of misfortunes with the glassware.

'Do some senses grow old and others not? Touch, for-ex-am-ple, is it less im-por-tant than taste? Than smell? Than sight? Do they forbid men of my age to eat sucking pig? Yes, gentlemen, suc-king-pig! No? If people were con-sis-tent, they should ob-lige us to eat grandfather pigs, grand-fa-thers! And no veal after we turn forty, and no asparagus tips. At my age only ripe or pickled ones. Farewell young pigeons and lamb! For-bid-den to see et-chings after forty-five. Historical paintings for you now. Oh, no sir, everyone would shout! Then is it fair that when I like to touch soft-firm-skin and things in the right place, just because time has gone sli-p-ping-by I must enjoy wrin-kles and flab. Ig-no-rance-of-life, my friends! Envy. One has to be con-sis-tent! Why force a man to change his opinions? I was a conservative when I was young. I still am. I like old wines; but when they're good, I prefer this year's. Young flesh, my friend, at twenty-five and at sixty!'

Rafael Serrador did not know what to do with his hands or his mind. It was the first time he had ever heard anyone talk like that. His companions, he too, scattered exclamations and oaths as they spoke, but such a lengthy exposition of so forbidden a subject sounded strange, even boastful, to him. Everyone gave noisy approval to the publisher's witty remarks.

'Right, Don Prudencio, right!'

One got up and as he left, said:

'I've got things to do.'

'What have you got to do? Write and that's it!'

'Isn't that work?'

The waiter broke in:

'You intellectuals have no idea what work is. No idea!'

Most of them protested.

'There's something in what he says,' remarked a shop assistant, not too sure of himself.

'Why?' asked Salomar, turning rapidly to Rafael, although the interrupter was further to his right. ('He lived in profile . . .', said one of the literature teachers, parodying the famous line; and in fact he always was at an angle, sideways on.) 'It's what I do . . .' There was no hint of contempt in his tone.

'No,' replied the one thus addressed, rather timidly: 'Don't get me wrong, but when you work, you leave some trace, and we don't. Do you see what I mean? I work in a shop, just like a servant works in an apartment. She sweeps the floor; I sell and arrange the goods; tomorrow she'll sweep the floor again and I'll do the same again, too. If she stopped sweeping and I stopped arranging, then you'd notice.'

Yes, thought Rafael, it's as if I gave up plating the rails or didn't polish them, and the noise of the workship started up in his head: the cables, transmissions, belts, motors, drums of polish, all in uproar, reducing all the other senses to hearing, turning him daft.

'But your work is visible and ours generally isn't,' said a Catalan teacher.

'Yes, maybe so,' went on the shop assistant, 'and that may be why workers despise people with books.'

'If only that were all there was to it!' said Joaquín Lluch. 'But every day we repeat the same gestures without knowing why we make them, for no other reason but Saturday's pay.'

'Isn't that reason enough?'

'Yes, you work today on the basis of yesterday's results. You move forward.'

'We,' said Rafael, and everyone looked at him, 'we look after the means of production, regardless of what comes out: a screw is always a screw . . .'

He stopped ('Why have I spoken?') and said nothing more. And yet he'd wanted to say something important, but the concept escaped him. 'What must they think of me?'

'That was the advantage craftsmen had,' said Pedro Rubio.

'Of course!' Salomar agreed. 'They left something behind. What there isn't any trace of is them. That's why the peasants don't want to know about socialism and other such trifles.'

'They prefer stubble to trouble,' proclaimed a beardless youth with a high-pitched voice.

'Well said, Don Carlos!' Salomar saluted.

Punning was a way of thinking for those present; with their noddles vacant, language saved them. Their enthusiasms ran from Unamuno to Muñoz Seca.

'Riff-raff see only the muscular effort in work,' insisted Pedro Rubio.

The waiter:

'We know that for you, Don Pedro, the people are riff-raff. No, I find it quite natural! We . . .' He did not dare to finish the sentence, and started again: 'This feeling about physical work doesn't come from the people, it comes from the bourgeoisie.'

'In that case,' replied Rubio, 'there must be a lot of bourgeois people among the workers.'

'I wouldn't argue with that,' said the waiter, moving off to attend to another table.

'Yes,' belched a monkey-faced lawyer, 'that's where hatred of the liberal professions comes from. They measure work by their calluses.'

'And they're right,' broke in the leftist baker.

'No, sir!' rejoined a bit-part actor from the Teatro Barcelona who was passing the time making little balls out of newspaper, as his blackened fingers revealed. 'It's the same with us. They think acting isn't working, just playing.'

'People can't conceive of work done for pleasure,' went on Federico Morales, for such was the name of the poet and bread benefiteer. 'Mankind sees work as a punishment; when they see somebody writing for pleasure, studying just for the sake of it or writing plays to amuse themselves, they conclude that person can't be working. And they're right, if they believe in original sin. That's why the unions all disapprove of amateurs.'

'Can't abide them!' said the actor. 'But that's a different matter.'

Morales shot him a teasing look.

The lawyer:

'The only liberal profession most people can agree on is engineering.'

Luis Salomar:

'A canal, a bridge, a road can be touched. Human beings want to see things. Whereas hearing, air . . .' He paused. 'That's why the greatest enemies of schooling are the people. If they'd ever wanted to study, no one would have stopped them. A furrow can be seen, but a word: pure wind. That's why they hate teachers. I don't think it's a bad thing: there are too many. You should learn what you need for what you're going to be.'

'The people,' intervened Jaime Fernández, 'feel the same contempt for politicians.'

'Yes,' replied Salomar, 'when they're not in power. That's why the opposition must be suppressed.'

'The root of all evil,' Rubio butted in.

'Don't talk rubbish,' Luis insisted. 'Power is the basis of everything; it suppresses contempt. People think ill of politicians because of their instability. It's the only advantage of the monarchy, and the explanation for puppet regimes.'

Rubio took the stand:

'There is no other force but force,' and he stuck out his chest. 'The respect men have for intelligence is nauseating. Some people are shocked that the plebs know who Zamora, Samitier or Paulino Uzcudun are, yet haven't heard of Luis Vives or Menéndez y Pelayo. Is Luis Vives's intelligence more to intelligence than Paulino's muscles are to muscles? Did Menéndez y Pelayo make, create, manufacture his own intelligence or, like Paulino and his muscles, does he owe it to God? Well, then, isn't the one as admirable as the other? At least Uzcudún trains and looks after what the Creator has given him; whereas as far as Don Marcelino is concerned, I believe his brains were first-class from the start. I have biceps, therefore I admire those with more of them than me. If I have nothing inside my skull, how can you expect me to admire an egghead? What's happened is that intelligent men have been shysters. They fooled the powerful with tricks and arse-licking, and for far too long now they've been running the show. People were taken by surprise and there's the result. But when did you ever see a country ruled by intelligence rather than force? Because force of habit – but force nonetheless – makes all of us want to masquerade as frightfully-intelligent-people. I can respect a man if he's stronger than me or shoots his gun more quickly, but because he knows more Latin? Come off it, man! The weak have always been a damned nuisance and they're still a damned nuisance to us. Let them return to the maternal cloister! I don't despair of throwing Christians to the lions.'

'And this long speech,' chimed in Federico Morales, 'have you produced it from your sternum or with your forceps?'

People started to get up, because of the time. Rafael set off up the Rambla de Cataluña. Salomar accompanied him.

'Are those the people who are going to save Spain?'

'They're good lads,' said the writer. 'I'm not interested in men but in ideas.'

'And in the name of those ideas you'll lead them to their deaths?'

'It shouldn't come to that! But what would be left of them if they died in their beds?'

'Their lives.'

'Life has no importance for me.'

'I don't care about my own, but I care a lot about other people's. To die for them would be a fine thing; for an idea, grotesque.'

'What matters is history. Roads, monuments, books, all that can be won with armies. And armies are not the personal characters or the lives of their soldiers, nor their ethics. Armies are made of courage, weapons, tactics. Men aren't much use in the face of a machine-gun firing off seven hundred rounds a minute. For one hundred and fifty years, people, the masses, have despised politicians; but what should be despised are certain human emotions, so as to convert men back into what they always were: God's foot-soldiers in the hands of the chosen leader. The French Revolution was an absurdity. Our children will blush to recall it. To think that people want to govern the world through sentimentality! . . .'

He stopped and fixed Rafael with his small, dark, likeable eyes:'Against equality we shall establish hierarchy; against liberty, discipline. Nobody ever had any illusions about fraternity, other than the brotherhood of arms. The time has come to sweep away all this dead wood piled up since the birth of mad Jean-Jacques of Geneva. Compassion is a Judaic invention. And I don't wish to speak ill of either Jews or Arabs: there are too many of us.'

'And the poor?'

'For us there are neither poor nor rich. There is an Empire and each man's obligations towards it.'

'An empire!'

'Don't think we're so childish as to see ourselves playing with Cuba or Flanders. It's the idea of the Empire that matters. People worry about tomorrow as if today's harvest weren't a product of yesterday. Let each Spaniard think about what has been, and pay for the sacrifices that a past of that calibre costs, with arrogance, with pride, with potency. Well, see you tomorrow, Serrador!' he said, turned quickly and went.

That evening, Rafael went to the bar on the Parallel. The Chauffeur, the Metalworker and González Cantos were there.

'The Falangists? Bah, not worth bothering about! Nor fascism either,' said González. 'It's all part of communist tactics. It suits them, with their Popular Front; but we're not falling for it.'

'I talk to you about fascists and you start ranting about the communists,' said Rafael.

'Frankly, as far as I'm concerned . . .'

'You don't know what you're talking about.'

The big man looked Rafael up and down:

'Listen, go wipe the snot off your face and come back when I'm not around.' He could hardly get over it. 'No, but did you hear the little brat! Who does he think he is?'

Rafael was at a loss.

'I told you to clear off. No mother's son who hasn't learned to shave tells me I don't know what I'm doing. Understand?'

'Forget it, man,' the Chauffeur intervened.

'Forget it, be fucked! He's out the door right now, with his snotty nose and his communists!'

'Right you are,' said Rafael. 'Cheers!'

And he went.

He talked to Espinosa.

'I told you,' said the latter, 'you were on the wrong track. The fascists consist of those who really are, those who are without knowing it, and those who are without saying it. You'll always go along with the dissidents. You want to solve problems on a personal basis, and it can't be done. The worst of it is you're aware that's not the right path, but you persist, knowing you've no way out. I'm not trying to lure you over to us. You'd be thrown out after two days. You're too fond of doing as you please, without any spirit of sacrifice. You've lived by yourself for too long. Solitude has to be paid for.'

He gave him some leaflets.

'If you ever come to communism, it'll have to be your own choice . . . You'd never forgive me for having enrolled you.'

'You're right,' replied Serrador.

'We're always right,' smiled Espinosa, 'and that's something else that bothers you, like so many others. What you want is to be wrong, and save yourself in spite of everything. And, by saving yourself, save all the rest.'

They closed the workshop fifteen days after the foregoing and Rafael found himself out on the street. For about a month he looked all over for work, with only the pittance from the union to get by on. In the end he just wandered around the harbour; enjoyed the rain; started to masturbate again. At night he would go into any cheap *café cantante*. In one such, three months after their first conversation, he met Luis Salomar and some of his friends.

He couldn't say why, but Serrador likes these places. He finds them relaxing, with their tiny stage, their dancing girls, singers and sex, yellow half-light, warmth, background music, sweaty armpits and tobacco. The workers come for a good time, straight from the job, with the grime still on them. A theatre lobby is filled with freshly-scrubbed men and women of means; these music-halls are visited casually, people come and go without rhyme or reason, hang around five minutes looking for their friends, sniff the atmosphere and when it doesn't fit the mood they wander out again and try next door. There are shopkeepers who come every day to take coffee and quietly read the *Noticiero Universal*, glasses and buttocks firmly planted, every so often glancing sideways at the show; a few soldiers; rather more sailors and marines; pimps lurking by the stage, keeping an eye on their property; dockers, men out of work; the honourable couples of the quarter; girls on the job and their sponsors flashing quick smirks of superiority at the flock of artistes waiting in the boxes, unengaged. At the back, separated by a curtain, dark screen, partition or glass door, silent men play *julepe* or *burro* with worn chips and greasy cards; as they're all card-sharps, the game is honest. In the bar, at the back, to right or left, the waiters collect the orders, tinkling spoons the only sound. All these people come down to two groups: locals and non-locals. The former are in the majority, plus the casual visitors, those who've just been whoring or are about to.

The pornography on stage is simple, and of two kinds: the first consists of displaying what you've got – it's all a poor girl owns, and belongs about as much to her as to the first young blade with a fancy for love – and usually appears in the first part of the show; the second is a matter of mischievous insinuation, speaking or moving with innuendo, to humorous or embarrassing effect. If an artiste has both talents she's gold-dust, her name attains incandescence above doorways and half a metre on posters. How far they can go depends on politics, the governor and his police force. The Republic is prudish and it's been necessary to resort to subterfuges in order to keep going; under the administration of Anguera de Sojo, the wretched girls invented bloomers with artificial fluff, which got around the law while still permitting some excitement; they were known as 'Anguera de Sojo knickers'. Government intemperance banned them in their turn; ingenuity is rarely rewarded by the state. The show begins at half past nine, and lasts till half past twelve. At that time the super-tango begins, reserved for the artistes and the young swells. The stalls are hastily removed, whilst waiters and caretaker sweep the floor of peanut shells and newspapers dropped by the crowd; butts are collected to make roll-ups; blobs of spittle are covered with sawdust. The flower-girl fixes her make-up, the orchestra moves from one side of the room to the other. In the poorer dives this is a sad and lonely time of day; the waiters stand chatting around a table waiting for the curfew to fall on some well-heeled soak; the tango dancers and showgirls spend their time in the rest room, some kick off their shoes and doze on a divan; another lolls back in the bar. In some obscure box voices can be heard: 'These stockings cost me four pesetas in Casa Vehils!'

One, two, three couples dance; then sit whispering around a table, trying to figure how they can do the *régisseur* out of an hour. A young man, randy or exhausted, tries to persuade the artistic director to let a showgirl out before five in the morning; he can usually win half an hour with her, as long as no precedents are set.

Towards half past ten the undercover police come round, bells ring and all the artistes put their bloomers on. The audience, who are in on the secret, shriek, shout, protest; the showgirls retire without saying goodbye.

'Go away! Get them off!'

Those who arrive at this time stand by the door for a moment.

'They had them off yesterday, I swear!' says a young lad.

'Let's come back tomorrow, might have better luck,' says the other. They leave. The man on the door watches them go with a knowing look.

At Juanito el Dorado's, the stage is in the centre of the room; elsewhere it's at the rear. Old backdrops hang down: a garden or just a smooth tarlatan, black, grey, green or blood-red. A blackboard at the right of the actor swivels over; the compère chalks up the title of the sketch about to be performed, and presses the red button which signals the pianist to strike up the tune. The songs have titles like 'Fragrance of Spain', 'Twin Carnations', 'Córdoba Born', 'Flower of Madrid'. The dance numbers prefer straightforward geography: 'Granada', 'Holy Mount', 'Lisbon Fado'. A German girl dances a waltz on tiptoes; the audience is sensitive, and applauds her dislocation. One daring girl performs the 'Fire Dance'. The quintet always includes, without fail, a bald man; the pianist wipes the sweat and dandruff from his lapels with a half-white, half-dirty silk handkerchief. The stars have their own 'set', bright red or damask, with their name inscribed on the front, shiny with silver paint.

> Oh, what a grind,
> To think a poor girl's driven
> To waggle her behind,
> Just to make a living!

The audience is abstemious, it orders lemonade and coffee. Up in the boxes the young toffs quaff Málaga wine and Codorniú champagne: either because there's a crowd of them and it works out cheaper to share a round, or because their pick-up is a hard nut to crack. The procuresses bustle to and fro between the lavatory and the boxes:

'She'll be here in a minute, she's with a friend.'

Then she runs to the other end of the club shrieking at the top of her voice:

'Don't nod off, Paquita, lover-boy's arrived!'

And then, in an aside:

'Lord save us from uncorking, Peque nearly got off with him instead!'

The man in charge of the lights is a very important person. The artistes have to pay him, and he charges according to how many colours are required. One night when this official kept missing the artistes with his spotlight – which can happen due to inexperience, inebriation or failure to pay – and sent the light in exactly the wrong direction, Rubio, who could be amusing when drunk, shouted:

'With all this wandering between right and left, you'll end up a sceptic, firefly! A sceptic, my friend!'

'Like your mother!' replied the electrician, blind drunk. They pulled them apart, and there was no more to it.

Somehow, out of all that – from the footlights and the arc lights, the tawdry costumes, the spangles, the glow of the sets, the mystery of the performance; the clicking of the castanets, the elegant swaying of the dancers, the stately uplift of their knees and the delicate tip of their pointed toes fleetingly piercing the air; from the whirling of frills and flounces, the flashy trimmings, the dust from stamping heels, the liveliness of a pasodoble and deep rending of a fading voice, the latest hit in fashion out in street and square, the peal of a fandango, the melody of a *seguidilla*, the beat of a bolero; from the world-weary singers and the bitter lyrics with their saucy, suggestive edges worn away by the indifference of the spectators or the impotence of the voice, from the *apache* singers in black skirts, or country maids with bonnets and lace pinafores; from the fringed shawls and spangled dress-coats – somehow there floated up, by some magic in the air, a haze which lent brilliance to the grimy and decrepit, joyousness to the sad at heart, plenitude to the ragged, firmness to the flabby, and made the down-at-heel desirable once more. A pathetically over-painted old woman breaks into a *guajira*, cherry-cheeked, green eye sockets, white double chin: the spoons fall quiet. A 'knock it off!' is drowned by those in the know: 'Quiet!'

Two girls come out and shake everything they've got in time to a *son*, tulle handkerchieves aloft. 'Up your mother! your aunt! your grandma!' They wheel and gyrate, moving their buttocks, starlike, in orbital cycles. Time takes you down to the dregs (the older they come, the drunker they fall): a fat old bag rubs her crotch against the stage jamb, up and down, wobbling her sagging behind.

'Attagirl, saucy!'

It's the dancers who perform the miracle: nimble feet, twirling arms, spinning bodies; toes, soles and heels, thumping away. At it, to it and away! The spectators shout them on through a gipsy dance, a *jota* – go to it, darling! – a fandango.

'I saw the Argentine's debut here . . .'

The audience forgets the face and figure, and sees a wafting breeze of words, a line that snakes with panache, arms raised gracefully aloft, legs gliding to the rhythm of blood, flouncing hands that round off a song with elegance and wit.

Rafael sees the foolish expression on every face, all carried away, spirit suspended; alert of eye, willing of ear, all else forgotten; outside of time and space, other than the five or six metres of the stage set. The light shines on them from the side and front footlights, some with open mouths like fish about to bite, some as if peeping from under cover; all suffused by a certain beatific purity and tranquility, faces distended, rather like those of dead men, but with the warmth that enlivens everything.

The curtain opens on the last act. Out comes the top chanteuse in her gold lamé costume crowned with ostrich feathers:

The day that I leave
This saloon full of leeches
You men will not need to
Bust out of your breeches!

The band plays the march which signals the end of the cabaret.

'The satisfied public goes back where it came from,' says one of Luis Salomar's companions.

'The parade of the billy-goats,' comments a passer-by.

There is a moon outside.

'Let's go for a stroll.'

Going for a stroll consists of crawling from tavern to tavern with the aim of ending up somewhere between two and three in the morning, around a lamp, bottles of Priorato to hand and fish soup, omelette, olives, cheese or fried eggs laid out in front, drunk as newts but highly solemn, discussing the future of Spain, punctuated by the occasional wild hurrah! from Salomar, whose eyes are brimming with life.

'Where will you find lamb to equal Spanish lamb, or a poet like Fray Luis, even if he was a bit of a Jew?'

'Granted, but we still always do everything at the last moment, and carelessly. The incredible thing is that sometimes it turns out well. Improvization is a Spanish weapon.'

'You do not look ahead. Or vorrk in stages. Small stages.'

'Nor do we need to.'

With Luis Salomar and Rafael Serrador are a Swiss and a young Catalan, the latter a teacher of archaeology or some such: an idle lump with affected manners, an aristocrat come very far down in the world, related to families of mercantile renown, whom he doesn't drag in unless he really has to; Vienna and London always on the tip of his tongue. He has a certain poofy air, without being one, and is determined to prove this on all occasions to any and every painted lady, which doesn't protect him, in the 'taxi-girl' establishments to which he is addicted, from exchanges like the following:

'I tell you he is!'

'Please yourself, love, but I tell you he isn't.'

'How much do you bet!'

He claims to be an authority on wines and meats, but is no more than an amateur, as in everything. His name is Bosch, De Bosch; he considers the particle very important: Jorge de Bosch. He is what might be called 'distinguished', as aunts say of their nieces once they reach a certain age; sports fine trousers with a fine stripe in them, is well-read and even better connected with the Barcelona gentry; very fond of a quiet binge and quite capable, for a trifle, of betraying a friend. He was a priceless man for the Falange. He made it his business to find out what was going on in the Lliga and among the Carlists and gave the information – free of charge, it must be said – to Salomar, who had a weakness for heraldry and prepositions.

The Swiss is called Walter something or other, a man of some hundred kilos and limited, but cool and lucid, intelligence; angular and dark. He was an insurance company representative and despised his profession; frequented the cafés of Montparnasse when he passed through Paris; read the latest books in the language of wherever he happened to be, and was more than a match for any of Salomar's young swanks in the matter of reading. Tied to appointments and commitments, he would get up from the table at the time arranged, no vintage of manzanilla could stop him – sober or not, because he drank as much as anyone.

'Here in Spain,' he said, 'you call disorganitzation freedom. And the funny thing is, it's true. In Germany no von vould drream of connecting the two things. Here, frreedom consists of peeing ver you feel like, especially if it's prohibited. Anyone who did that in Englant would be attacking the frreedom of the English. That's enough to upset any von.'

'The English are a load of pricks, or rather cunts.'

'Bravo, Don Jorgito!' exclaimed Salomar, by way of welcome to the professor.

'To an Englishman,' went on the Swiss, 'frreedom is the vay vot exists is organized. To you it's a myt.'

'I bet English workers live better than Spanish ones,' said Rafael, already drunk.

'For you people lots of things are just verds. Bla-bla. But that doesn't mean they're unimporrtant. You vould all die for tem.'

'Word or death!' said Bosch, pointing with the stem of his pipe.

'And we choose death. Hurrah!' cried Salomar.

'You're capable of fighting over mere verds. Spanish honour is full of that . . . what do you call it . . .?'

'Wind!' said Luis.

'It's no yoke,' reproved the Swiss. 'A German vould not understand.'

'We are a nation of orators,' chipped in Rafael.

'And Italy is a nation of opera singers. You,' said Bosch to Salomar, 'and he' – meaning Rafael – 'and I, would die so that a washbasin be not called a sink, or bowl.'

'Arrant nonsense,' ruled Salomar.

'Life's something different, I don't know, just seems to me,' Rafael cut in.

'Quiet, crapface!' retorted Bosch, due to a stiff swig of brandy he had just swilled down. 'Don't you believe it!'

A whore, friend of Salomar's solitude, came in.

'Come over here, strumpet,' went on the young gentleman. 'Come here, flower of my ejaculations. I haven't a sou: I've just given Luis every last peseta I had, a not insignificant sum. Shhh! don't tell anyone, fine and discharge!'

'Watch your tongue, scoundrel!' warned Luis Salomar, suddenly serious.

'What does it matter! We're all friends here. As two and two make four' – he paused, thought better of it, and changed the subject. 'Don't you agree, pretty one, "that love should sell his glories dear, is true and fair exchange": is it not so, little whorelet? "If I would have good government, it will cost me goodly lashes."'

'Olé!' applauded Salomar. 'Cervantes said so and that's good enough for us. They want us to leave. So let's go to the Caracoles, since by now the shop assistants and outsiders will have gone home. No, no, come with us! That rogue has some black olives fresh from seasoning, and until you've tasted them you haven't lived!'

They went out into the street. Salomar paired off with Walter.

'The truth is that we Spaniards are ultimately incapable of objectivity. We always see things from the inside outwards, on the slant, in black and white. You won't understand, it's a figure of speech. It's the same with people. What the hell! You others have no blood in your veins and you let yourselves be talked round; this, that, the other, what will people say, fairness, you scratch my back, and all that ... Long live subjectivity! El Greco couldn't have been anything but a Spaniard. Picasso, too. God made the world and the Spaniards deformed it. Here we paint with the end of our pen ... cils! And anyone who doesn't like it can get stuffed. Then they slander us by calling us individualists. What we are is men, and all the rest puppets on a string who tremble in the slightest breeze! Left, right, left, at the orders of My Lady Majority of the Delicate Parts! We are as we are and not as others want us to be. Hurrah! That's why we call barbers and guitarists "Maestro", because they have a definite effect upon us; but as for teachers, some hopes! Eh, professor, if they called you Maestro, what would you say to that?'

The professor, slouching back on one of the Rambla benches, shouted:

'Who cares!'

'Take no notice,' said Salomar. 'He's a good chap, but a Catalan.'

'What is poppet?' asked the Swiss, very drunk and working out his phrases from a distance.

'A puppet?' replied Salomar. 'A dummy. Don't you know what a dummy is? A marionette.' He bounces up and down. 'Don't you know what a marionette is?'

It was late. Bosch went off with the whore, the Swiss to his hotel, and Rafael and Salomar along the Ramblas, at first light.

'What do you intellectuals know about us workers?' Rafael, the worse for drink, was unburdening himself. 'If any of your people ever came out of our midst, then they've forgotten, turned traitor, or rather coward; to be a traitor you need a certain amount of courage. You look after us, but from a distance. A platonic affair. Do you think,' he asked confidentially, 'that taking charity is tolerable? If for no other reason, we've got to put an end to this world. You protect us through logic and justice, but not for us, our humanity or our blood: to defend ideas. Capitalists are idealistic: they give goodness away with money. Yes, man! In the banks, for every thousand pesetas they get a gold star for good behaviour, for every hundred thousand, a rank; millionaires are captains-general and good as gold.'

The bitter wine rose up his gorge.

'I don't know if you can understand me. You don't care about our true situation, our squalor, our hunger. You appreciate it in the abstract, through spectacles and gloves. The people sense that: that's why they resort to violence. Then you act all surprised and offended: you love us so much! Really: all you give us is the vomits! If there were only some human warmth in you! But you said it the other day: what you care about is ideas. To hell with ideas! Man and his filth . . . when that awakens human brotherhood in you and not just a feeling you can savour in your clean, well-fed solitude, then we'll talk.'

'You include even us?' asked Luis.

'Great writers, and our defenders, but living with lounges and bathrooms. And dressed by the finest tailors.'

'That's unfair.'

'I know and I don't care. Because it's true. You just have to scribble two lines and everyone takes notice. What if this, and what if that . . . You get up at twelve, and you think that if you write that you get up at twelve, people will be agog. And then you remember the poor little workers, and hail fellow well met!'

'That's a low, crude way to talk . . .'

'Yes, sure!' (Rafael thinks of Matilde.) 'Balls! We don't understand one another . . .'

'But we'll come to understand one another, which is what matters.'

'What matters to you is the relationship, the externals. I want to be understood.'

'You're sozzled, Serrador.'

'Yes, yes . . .'

They had reached Plaza de Cataluña, with the day. Serrador sat down on a bench.

'Long live Vidal y Planas! What do you know about anything? We understand what's going on better than all those bloody fools of yours.'

The sparrows were flushing the last of the night away from the dark corners.

'You are better than that,' Luis said after a silence. 'I don't know why you're not yourself. Aren't you working tomorrow, or rather today?'

'Not today, not tomorrow, nor ever. Be seeing you!'

And they parted.

'What have I got to do with all these people. I don't care about any of the things they care about. I'd like a straightforward world, where we could move about freely; they want to give orders, or, even worse, control the relations between men. I want to be like everyone else and everyone else to be like me; they look for distinctions, because that's all that matters to them. They dwell on differences, I on similarities. They want to spy from sentry boxes and note eccentricities, I want to live out in the open, where nothing is hidden. They look for hiding-places. I look for the light; for them light is an oil lamp, for me it's the sun. They think that Diogenes business is brilliant; I think it's rubbish. Not the idea, but the clowning about, given that we have daylight all around us . . . I consider them people apart; they despise me whilst believing they esteem me, making it show. For them ideas are a shawl, something that doesn't quite make a cape, they move it up and down, they don't know how to face the bull: for that you need parts they haven't got. They strut about with tassels up their arses and wool over their eyes. The meeting in the café is their good deed for the day: a lifebuoy . . . Revolutionaries my arse! So why do I go? Do I feel flattered? Do I expect to get something out of it? What can they teach me that I can't learn somewhere else? Imperial Spain! Does it entertain me? Maybe. Intrigue me? No. I'm not bothered whether I go there or anywhere else. Solution?'

The red glow of dawn rose to his throat along the tram rails, down the electricity and telephone wires, the radio aerials, the closed windows and roof tiles, strangling him where he stood.

'They're as hypocritical as me. As who? That *me* just slipped out. I'm alone, alone, completely alone.'

He shouted it, by now along the Parallel. There was no one else around. He drew his pistol and, aiming at the sky, fired until it was empty.

THREE

Prat de Llobregat

A few days later, Jaime Fernández sent a message asking Serrador if he was in work. When he replied that he wasn't, they suggested he take up painting Falangist slogans on the walls at night; he could make twenty pesetas; there was no danger, he could do it between two and five in the morning. Rafael accepted: 'What the hell!' He spent the daylight hours asleep; since the factory closed, he had slept a lot. At ten p.m. he would meet Salomar in the Golden Lion, a German-style coffee house on the Ramblas, near Plaza del Teatro; the family scions did not attend these evening meetings. The Swiss, Bosch and an uncle of his, an old man who liked to amuse himself among young people, were often there, along with the odd teacher from the Institute. Now and then an old friend of Salomar's would turn up, a socialist named José Lledó. State advocate, of marriageable age and bon viveur, with curtailed ambitions, he possessed a large library of books and an affection for poetry, the origin of his friendship with Luis. Everything about his face was big: chin, mouth and temple, in a field of wrinkles. To crown his mournfulness, this domehead was losing his few hairs and growing a sad bald patch which further extended his interminable forehead; the coffee-house lights glinted on naked scalp. It was the only topic which could make him lose his composure.

José Lledó used to tell Salomar that the day they, the fascists, triumphed, he, Salomar, would be hung.

'You don't realize that your fascism comes from your love of Castilian. That on the one hand; on the other, if you are ever in power, your organization will be so unlike your dreams that you will be the first to rise against it. Your force is fictitious and factitious. Fascism in Italy and Germany is based on a tangible force, capable of putting a solid number of deputies in Parliament, and even a majority. Here you haven't managed to get one out of six hundred elected. Like it or not, in those countries fascism has been a popular movement.'

'Wait till we take to the streets,' said Luis.

'What for? One of two things: either you'll go it alone and be crushed by the Civil Guard, or you'll go in with the military, who will gobble you up as soon as they get you round the corner. You're just poor little guinea pigs, believe me!'

'That's what you'd like to think!'

Here Bosch's uncle – nice fellow but a bit dim, eyes asquint – intervened.

'Wouldn't it be nice if no one went looking for trouble!'

'Fascism in Spain,' continued Lledó, 'is an invention of the young toffs. There are hardly any of you decent types. . .! It's easy for a clever man, more so if he's intelligent, to make it with your backers. He just needs to appeal to their vanity, with noisy dedications and the like, and clamber up on their shoulders. You are an open field for all the scoundrels: all they have to do is demean themselves a bit to get in. The pure souls like you can be counted on one hand. There are no obstacles for the social climber, which is not meant to be a joke, though it's not such a bad idea; incense can provide a smokescreen for every sort of dirty trick, and the rich, so long as they don't have to see anything and can hear themselves praised to the heavens, will pay whatever price is asked of them. What do these people think of themselves? They're all obsessed with the world's opinion, but have to bring it down to their own level of dishonour. So as not to despise themselves they despise everyone else; I don't envy them their wee small hours, but perhaps I flatter myself too much. For them greatness is mere show, appearance, parades, uniforms, pure form.'

'Soon you'll be blaming it all on Góngora again!' said Bosch.

'Leaving aside the exaggeration, there's some truth in that, my young friend. Not Góngora, but the taste for him . . . That's why Hitler loathes rationalist architecture and Picasso. It's all self-hatred and its corollary, the longing for death: result, war tomorrow. All futile tomfoolery, lack of vision and understanding, perfumed with acts of worship by night and day. As long as the Duchess of X invites me to sup, and then feeds me for the rest of my days . . . You know some of them, don't you? I'd rather starve, which is what decent folk do.'

'And the people,' said Rafael.

'You,' Lledó continued, 'take life as a whole. Within species, a species is only a species; language is a great thing, it reveals ghosts. Like something owed to you, like a drunk's breakfast God puts before your eyes each morning: workers, peasants, swallows, dwarfs, swordfish . . . And so on, in general – with generals – by generalities or genres. A genre's a genre.'

'Have you finished?'

'But a man? A man? Just one? One tiny, miserable, human being? That doesn't exist and never has existed for you! No pity, no charity, except towards another generality: the poor; but like that, *en masse*, as a whole. And you fly on overhead, so as not to get upset: there are so many of them!'

'What about you?'

'I do more or less the same, but I know I'm contemptible. You are proud of your shit, you glory in it. What's worse, you want to fight thinking about the past; something fixed and solid, with limits and a frame, like some historical painting. A true religious print. I once told you you were dead. I repeat it. For the best of you, Spain is a museum and a library. For you: because for those who are pushing you, the petty intellectuals, it has another name, and they know where they're going. You don't want to face the fact that we live off our means. Ends don't exist, there are no other ends but our means: the ideal is a horizon: try to catch it, booby! You'll never get anywhere; that's why you'll die of shame, those of you that have any, at the means to be used. And your Spain, up in the clouds.'

'Dear oh dear, my little lawyer, my little lawyer, we're going to have to hang you!'

'Do you think I don't know? Despite my fear, my incompetence and my cowardice...' He returned to his subject: 'All the hack writers who have joined you do so with the notion that *It honours me to be misunderstood by the ignorant...*'

Salomar went on with the recital: '... *for such is the distinction of learned men: to speak so that all seems Greek to the people; one does not cast precious stones before swine.*'

'The worst of it is,' Lledó continued, 'that because they only speak double-Dutch they've thought themselves Góngoras,

Mussolinis or Hitlers. Juan Antonio' – that was what he called José Antonio Primo de Rivera – 'is nothing more than the son of a dictator from a good family. You've shat on yourselves, my dear friends!'

'You're disgusting!' shouted Luis Salomar.

February 1936, and Barcelona blazed with discussions: the elections had just given victory and power to the Popular Front. Companys and associates had been released from prison that morning.

'Ten years ago,' says the squint-eyed uncle, 'young men – I know this from my own sons – talked of nothing but football. To hear them talk about bullfighting you'd have to go back to Joselito's time. Such a shame.'

'There's no denying Spain has changed!' agrees Salomar. 'If Rubén Darío disembarked today, one can't imagine him writing *Pray for us, For we have neither sap nor bud, No soul, no life, no light*, etcetera . . . The young have returned to politics, that's their strength.'

'The nobs have,' counters Rafael. 'The workers are where they were before.'

'And the libertines,' assures Jorge de Bosch.

'So,' says the Catalan professor, self-important, emphatic, leaning his bosomy chest into the table, 'you don't believe there can be great poets so long as politics absorb the interest of the country?'

'No, man, no! Poets are above circumstance, they can adapt to anything, and, if they're any good, sing a good song; it makes no difference whether they glorify a leader or a rotting salad. In Spain, though, we've found something worth dying for, and that's a great thing for our generation.'

'You're a barbarian!' says the socialist.

'Neither that, nor the contrary.'

The old man joins in again:

'One can always place oneself above party politics.'

'Then the party is you,' says Bosch. 'Anyone who wants to balance up good and evil ends up in between, lukewarm, wishy-washy, half-baked, a mongrel with no hope of descendants, a mule.'

'Suits the she-ass, nephew!'

'There is no great writer without imprisonment and exile,' Salomar goes on, 'or ministerial seat. I say writer, not poet. Poets are creatures who can chirp as well in winter pastures as on dunghills.'

'What about Lope de Vega?' adds the podgy professor.

'Wasn't Lope a poet?' Salomar asks in surprise.

'. . . and arse-licking a political tactic?' chips in Lledó. 'And I don't mean to rehash what's already been said, but never believe Cambó's boys aren't playing politics. Remember dedications past and present. They just lack Lope's genius, today.'

'A hack novelist writes hack novels,' says Salomar triumphantly. 'Sometimes I suspect that Blasco Ibáñez is not as bad a writer as I tend to imagine . . . You Catalans think you can settle problems by inventing prizes and handing out flowers. Fat lot of good that does! You'd do better to put them all in prison. Leave the poets out of it.'

The Catalan teacher, something of a poseur with his baritone voice, bombastic buttocks and foolish sagacity, can't decide which card to play: whether to defend his fellow Catalans, or go over shamefully to the other side. What he would like is a chair in Madrid.

'Look, Luis,' he says finally, 'I think you should sit down and write a book about the mystics, and stop fooling around.'

'The foolishness is yours, professor,' says Salomar, stung, 'and as for writing, those are my onions, as the Frenchies say. Writing, for me, is a battle against death. And I'm just as happy fighting one way as another.'

'I could understand your position if you were on the other side of the barricade,' comments Lledó. 'But your political attitude, your pessimism . . .'

'The one doesn't affect the other. There are no tracks in this field. I shall save myself by fighting all out, or by force of words. It's all the same! A man who's not interested in politics is not a man; be he ever so wise, he's still a bug that gnaws at its own guts; but as for taking the air, or appreciating colours, or the scents of fields and streets . . . At most he'll want to save humanity by fiddling about with microbes, and that doesn't interest me or anybody else, as far as I know.'

He paused, they drank up their coffee.

'Faced with life,' he went on, 'there are only two positions: to give orders or to obey them. Must we make up a third: ignorance? Drivel, that's for poofs. Purgatory's a betrayal. All this may be skeletal and elemental, but Spain is a land of skeletons and there's nothing we'd rather kill ourselves for than sophistries. And as we eat badly, what's more, life doesn't matter a damn to us.'

'You mean,' interrupted Rafael, 'the workers eat badly.'

'The workers eat badly and the rest don't know how to eat,' replied Lledó. 'Catholics and anarchists have always cared more about the next life than this one. And there are more than a few of them! Here we live or die for tomorrow! And now you Falangists want to resurrect yesterday. The poor old Spaniard will end up crucified. It's just as well you won't succeed, my illustrious friend.'

'I'll hang you yet,' smiled Salomar.

'Where?'

'From a tree on the Rambla.'

'Can I choose which one?'

'Why not! The very branch!'

And they walked on to choose their trees. One each, in case the other should win.

'What I can't stand about the people is their contempt for spiritual things,' said the Catalan professor, in front of a poster.

'To despise something you need to know it. Were you born knowing who El Greco was?' asked Lledó, with no attempt at a pleasant tone. And without waiting for a reply, he joined Serrador and walked off.

'Salvation lies not in ourselves,' said the lawyer, 'contrary to what is preached by so many of those who prop up the world. It's not in others either. It's in the relation between the two. People apply to their being the laws of their existence. That's why Christianity has sunk so low: they've swallowed but they haven't digested it. Being good has passed from good deeds to repentance: we get by through the Magdalene's juices. Words, my young friend! They're the Renaissance's great dirty trick. And if repentance is not public, what is it? That's why the Russians . . .'

'What about the Russians?'

'There are still true Christians there, my illustrious friend. Once the whole world turned Catholic, there was no way to be one. It's the curse of the majority. The day every man's a communist, you wait and see what's left of Marx. This is a country of penitents where nobody does penance.'

'So you think that when the whole world admires the Catalan primitives I went to see last Sunday on your recommendation – and couldn't make head nor tail of, by the way – there won't be anything to them any more?'

'For me, perhaps not, and I'm forcing myself to answer you. But it's possible.'

'You're a cynic.'

'And in the bad sense of the word, my young friend. But going back to what we were saying: what's wrong is that man has come to think that the spirit is enough to save him, whereas what he needs is to act, to perform good works. But in our time nobody does anything except for their own profit. If anyone, whoever he is, works for the general good, he's looked on as a Quixote and a fool, and they won't let him be – they would all have done things better. Would have, because when it comes to actually doing them . . .!'

Lledó was obviously alluding to some personal adventure. What? No one knew much about the details of his life.

'The most highly regarded man,' he went on, 'is the one who does nothing. Yet to me there is nothing more moving than to see a man risk his life for his fellows, without thought of gain. Seriously!'

'Do you believe that someone who risks his life, knowing why, is not enriched by it?'

'Not always. The one's got nothing to do with the other. Not even in a strictly spiritual sense. Death has nothing to do with the spirit. Nothing, my dear fellow, nothing! Nor with life. Death is a thing apart. Worth taking into account. But on one side, in a niche, for special occasions.'

'And what do you do, then?'

'Me? Nothing. That's the problem! I don't think paying my party subscription is going to get me to heaven. And the worst of it is, I never will do anything. I've had things too easy. No one's going to put me in prison. Besides, I'm lazy and I have a low opinion of myself. If the opportunity came, I'd let it escape.'

They parted on very friendly terms. Then, once he was alone, Rafael went over his prearranged itinerary, which he picked up each day at seven in the evening at a draper's store in Calle Balmes. One evening he said to the counter assistant:

'I want to speak to Don Luis Salomar.'

She looked surprised.

'Wait here,' she said.

She came back shortly:

'Go on through.'

The shop was very small; the back room, slightly larger, overlooked a garden which had another exit. Luis came out to meet him.

'What's up?' he asked. They were more distant than in the past.

'I looked for you in the café.'

'Yes, I couldn't go today. What is it?'

'I'm being followed at night.'

'I know, they're our people. Don't worry. Anything else?'

'Nothing.'

'See you tonight, then.'

As he went out, he crossed with the Fernández brothers.

Three nights later, when he was daubing a fence along the Diagonal, close to Pedralbes, he was startled by an exchange of shots. People were firing from both directions, catching him in the middle. He was wounded in the arm. It didn't hurt until afterward, and then not much. When their chambers were empty the gunmen disappeared, leaving him alone. When he got back to his room he found Rubio going through his few things.

'They got me out of bed. In case there was anything that could incriminate us. What happened?'

Rafael told his story:

'It'll be the Generalitat police. They're changing them. We're going to have to keep our eyes peeled.'

'But you're hurt! You should have thrown yourself to the ground.'

'Nothing serious,' said Rafael, who had tied up his arm.

'All the same, come with me. The idiots protecting you thought the others had done you in.'

They went to the house of a doctor Rafael had seen at the meetings in the Rhine Gold. He treated him and said that within a week, only the scar would remain. The following day, Luis Salomar gave Serrador five hundred pesetas.

'Rest up for the moment,' he told him.

'This España is screwing things up,' snorted Rubio.

España was the interior minister in the Generalitat's new government.

'Do me the favour of shutting your trap!' snarled Salomar.

Other Falangist leaders were going to the café now: a bespectacled lawyer named Bassas, and a Murcian whose name Rafael did not know. With time and familiarity Serrador was gradually coming around to the theories of his fellow-participants; he noticed it himself, with a mixture of reluctance and indifference.

'Look,' Lledó said, one night in the Golden Lion, 'the bourgeoisie has become incapable of talking about anything but their physical necessities and associated pleasures: food, women and locomotion.'

'What else is there to talk about?' asked Rubio, who happened to be there.

'Politics and art, my fiery friend. I'm not saying the bourgeoisie doesn't talk about politics or art, but that they do so only on the basis of their own needs.'

'You'll be telling me next that the working classes talk about politics and art purely for pleasure.'

'We were referring to intellectuals,' replied Salomar.

'And what's an intellectual?'

'A man who has a moral relation to politics. Or for whom politics is a moral question, if you prefer.'

'Ah! And what's politics, mister more-or-less-socialist lawyer? Because I don't suppose you're referring to whether Martínez Birria is a minister, or retired . . .'

'Politics is the history of power and its spirit.'

'Balls to the Marxist! And art, oh great definer?'

'The reward, the payment from God, my young friend. Most vexatious for that eminent old gent, but there's nothing for it but to fork out! To me, subjectively, it's the form of truth: when all's said and done, the power of power . . .' He paused. 'Or if you like, the power of reproduction. Excuse the lecture.'

'Do you think Velázquez saw himself in *The Lances*?'

'How can you doubt it, old chap! Test it out: take any painter a picture that's not his and tell him it is . . . We say of a canvas:

it's a Rubens, not painted by Rubens. And don't cry sophistry! Artists are the only people who can see themselves without the aid of a mirror. The artist is a man who can recognize himself in the inanimate world. That's why I believe in God. Now he really was an intellectual! Someone must have said that before me, I dare say. And the world's in his own image and likeness, what's more.'

'So you believe that an intellectual is a man who wants to leave his mark on the world?'

'Stop there, my young Catalan professor, I did not say that! Two inaccuracies in your supposed definition. It's not enought to want it, you have to have the power. That's one! And it's not a question of leaving your mark, anyone can do that; but of continuing to be yourself after death. Trace or face, toes or nose, that is the question. Immortality, old friend, was invented by Cain, the first academic. An intellectual, my young Catalan professor, is a man who imposes his style on the world. Whatever it is.'

'Yes,' said Rubio, 'what's important is that when Leonardo shits, everyone should be able to tell the Mona by the smell he leaves 'er.'

The conversation went on in this style, and from styles to songs, from songs to singers and thence, through natural weakness, to red wine.

'Art,' said Lledó to Serrador, in the early hours, 'art, my dear fellow, is the desire to see oneself, to see oneself coming, a maze, a labyrinth of mirrors. To see and be seen. The worst thing you can say to an artist is: I don't remember your name. That's the question, to give birth to something that won't move, to give birth to death. Movement belongs only to God.

From time to time humanity forgets its own condition, or remembers it, if you like, and plays at being God, and there's an epidemic of dictators. Little gods and big pricks, that's your intellectuals, my dear chap! "Shove over and make room for me, I'm better-looking." Rabble, my young friend, rabble, and God's their photographer! Beginning to get the picture now? At the end of every course, God, who is a high-school teacher, takes each generation's photograph.'

Serrador didn't understand a word. All that verbosity wounded him.

Days later Rafael arrived at the Rhine Gold earlier than usual. He chatted to Joaquín Lluch.

'What are you doing with those people?' the waiter asked him.

'What difference does it make? Aren't you in bed with all those republicans of every colour? Do you believe more in Casares Quiroga or Prieto than in Primo de Rivera?'

'You only notice what's in front of your nose!'

'Stop worrying, you'll see. Life's today, not tomorrow. Your leaders are too cautious; they just split hairs, endlessly; and so finely, they pretend that fanatics and Catholics are just the same. That doesn't wash with the workers. You think you're the bees' knees, but you'll never make the revolution that way. The CNT could do it; you'd like them to, to take advantage of them, but they won't let you. You're too much in hock to the bourgeoisie. You communists . . .'

'I'm not a communist!'

'I know, you're in PSUC. Do you think the proletariat are stupid? Most of your slogans suggest you do. Well, don't think it'll do you any good. You may convince those who flatter themselves they're clever; but those who are serious . . .'

'Do you suppose we don't know that the bourgeois state only looks after the bourgeoisie? Do you suppose we don't know that the most democratic people, and the most republican, are the first to fire on strikers if they so much as begin to cast off their slave condition? Do you suppose we take seriously all that stuff about the equality of citizens before the law? In everything that counts, the bourgeoisie defends only the bourgeoisie.'

'Then what's the Popular Front about, and all that other tomfoolery of talking the language of our enemies? Do you really imagine you can deceive them?'

'As if we were that strong! Come off it, man!'

'You lot are just a bunch of jokers. We have to unite to defend the democracies. But nobody is mortgaging tomorrow for it. And everyone who goes against that unity is a traitor, making way, intentionally or not, for the common enemy. What's the matter with your arm?'

'Nothing. Did it at work; roller got stuck.'

The others started to arrive, Morales first, radiant ever since the elections. Unusually, Jorge de Bosch and his uncle also came that lunch-time. Salomar turned up with Bassas and a policeman from the Generalitat: a poor louse who pimped and narked for sheer pleasure and no profit, wallowing in his own baseness; tongue looser than a parrot's and face uglier than a dog's, with a dirty collar, black tie, and ankle straps always dangling down over dirty boots. Ramón Navarro by name.

'The fact is,' he told Serrador one day, 'I've never taken anything seriously. Nothing seems worth bothering about.

That's why I'm poor in every way. Does my life matter to anyone? Nothing's important, and we'll all be dead in the long run. Neither poverty, and I'm surrounded by it, nor misfortune really get under my skin. I like lots of things: football, bullfights, women, music. I look, I see things, they're a laugh for a moment and then – to hell with 'em! I'm sentimental, though, burst into tears over any soppy song. Music's what I like best, you know what I mean? Music is like hearing the dead speak. It seeps through the walls, it says what you want it to. Because I'm envious, that's what I am. I say that, and people laugh and don't believe it. They should have my body and a mirror. And I've felt that way since the first time I went to a prostitute. If she laughed then, I've laughed plenty since!'

It was true: they feared him in the brothels.

'They're replacing all the officers in Security,' he told Salomar.

'All of them?' said Bassas.

'All of ours.'

'How many?'

'About sixty. Besides, España has brought in those from the UMR.'

'We were better off with Casellas.'

'Yes,' said a new arrival, 'or with Dencàs.'

'What do you know about the Civil Guard?'

'It seems they're not changing any of their officers for the moment,' replied Navarro. 'They've named Lieutenant-Colonel Hernando head of the Assault Guards.'

Bosch's uncle chimed in:

'Gentlemen, why can't you leave us in peace? So they've beaten you in the elections, so what, you'll win others!'

'And in the meantime, what of Spain?' said Salomar.

'Do you think yourselves indispensable to its history? Wouldn't it be Spain without you?'

'What – make the revolution when we're all gaga?' roared Rubio.

'Here in Spain,' replied the cross-eyed moneybags, 'there's never been a revolution and there never will be. What there have been, and will be again, are counter-revolutions.'

'We're a race of counters, contradicters and contrarians, doing and saying the opposite of the next man,' said Bosch.

'The Republic came out of the dictatorship,' the old man persisted.

'Long live intelligence!' someone grunted.

'We live off the stupidity of others –' and the elder raised his voice, to show that the interjection had not passed unnoticed. 'Here there has never been an organized revolutionary movement; we have a certain talent for conspiracy, but our plans consist purely and simply of destroying what our predecessors did. And the people like changes, novelties and crises. If not, why do we have so many? We're all reactionaries here. Left against right, and vice versa.'

'And the day the dance really begins,' said Rafael, 'and the people hold the score in their hands, do you think we'll go on playing?'

'Of course. Spain breathes through her open flanks. And no one can cure her. If the workers held power – absurd thought! – the same conflicts would appear among them as among us. That's what we are: a country of contrabandists and contra-bandits.'

'Counterplots, countersigns and counterfeits!' chips in Salomar, greatly amused.

'Even deformity and vice are a national theme, from Velázquez to Goya. Blockheads, dunderheads and death's-heads, gaping out of their ruffs and stiff collars.' The despised Don Ramón had surprised them all with his sally.

'Well said, Don Ramón, well said!' nodded the Swiss. 'I say the same as you. When they could have done something, with the Rrepublic, their saint was sent to heaven – that's how you say, isn't it – and they forrgot what they been meaning to do. They just changed all the names. And waited for the manna. With beaks open wide.'

'And look what fell in!' exclaims Salomar.

'A rrevolution can only be made by completely changing the burreaucracy. But totally; othervisse the burreaucracy ends up eating the rrevolutionaries. This isn't only my idea,' he said modestly. 'The office staff have not changed, nor has Spain, so I am happy.'

'Ah!' replied Don Ramón, encouraged by his success. 'Don't worry, it'll go on a bit longer yet. Those who have other hopes may as well die now. The world is like unto itself, there are no new germs. Chess is more varied. That's why the liberals' – to him all left-wing parties are 'liberal' – 'are poor fools we let into power every now and then, so they won't get bored and can work themselves into the ground. The world is full of suckers, simpletons, cynics and atheists, and they must be given what they deserve. That's politics: the art of fools for smart guys.'

And Don Ramón, man of means, slowly lights a Havana cigar.

'Do you think,' Serrador asks Walter in an aside, 'that revolution is a question of bureaucracy?'

'The leaders decide it, the people make it, the arrmy secures it, the burreaucracy consolidates it.'

'We don't agree, Don Ramón,' Morales was saying to Bosch's uncle. 'I may be what you call a fool, simpleton, sentimentalist or whatever; but I'm with the weak, the most and the least.'

'Excuse me?'

'The most numerous, and the least fortunate. That's why I'm on the left, and not ashamed to say so. Just for that reason. I can't accept that any decent person' – there was a brief stir – 'can be in agreement with the present organization of society. I find it monstrous that anyone should think things are all right as they are, when some have nothing to eat and others are stuffing themselves. Mind you, I believe everything can be sorted out without any need for violence or revolutions.'

'In the end,' quipped Bassas, 'you're for a dictatorship of the lame against those of us who leg it correctly.'

'Why not? Go on, split your sides.'

Rafael remembers a phrase from someone – González Cantos? – in the Victoria: 'Politics is a toff's game: the only serious thing is to smash their faces in.'

The baker left. 'All these idiots who preach eternal peace are our best allies,' commented Bassas as he watched him go. 'We must always agree with them, even if we do them in later: bunch of masons and Jews! But they disarm the masses and put them to sleep. The great gelders of our time. I take my hat off to them and sweep their path.'

In those first days of July there were great upheavals. Eugenio Sánchez, a writer of some renown, came from Madrid to have talks with Salomar, Bassas and the man from Murcia, whose name Serrador still did not know. Sánchez's Galician head had been turned by Italian history and landscapes, and the contorted tripe of undigested German theories; no one could follow the delicate thread of his arguments as he wove them into whatever shape suited his purpose.

The top men stopped appearing at the café for two or three days. Late one night Salomar and Sánchez bumped into Lledó, Bosch and Serrador. Lledó had been a friend of the recently disembarked writer when the latter, not three years before, had been a Socialist candidate; with several mistresses, a leading role among the talking sheep at the 'Granja el Henar' café, and the wife and children left to rough it who knows where.

Now here he was with his fluted voice, deep and yet mellifluous, so soft-spoken that you never knew where you were, having to make up half of what he said. A voice like Eugenio d'Ors, who was in a sense his mother – his father, unknown – and a way of talking which made titled ladies 'fall for him madly', a bug he'd got from Don José Ortega y Gasset, to the amused derision of former comrades.

'You've gained chains, Sir Sánchez! I say this because of that bauble, my long-forgotten friend,' sniped the socialist, on account of a wristwatch the other was wearing.

The writer made a vague gesture and pronounced a few unintelligible words.

'We were discussing the Crusades,' Lledó went on, keen to make his presence felt, since he knew it was intolerable to Eugenio Sánchez. 'Cross-referring, you might say. What do you think of the Crusades?'

The man of the moment shrugged his shoulders and began to speak to his intestines: no one could make out a word.

'No!' Lledó interrupted, 'you are right! You like the word: crusade. It sounds good. And you are all crusaders. Cross-bred!'

'Don't be funny,' Salomar rebuked him.

'I'm extremely serious! You want to burst upon Spain like colonizers, but make the world believe you were responding to a broadly-based popular movement, just as people remember the real crusades to this day. In reality it was a colonizing expedition by the Pope and the Capetians. A colonial expedition: what think you of that, my muffled friend?'

The new arrival began to mumble again.

'You take this for a land of infidels ruling the Holy Places, of which there are plenty, from Covadonga to Santiago by way of the Virgin of Pilar. You want to treat the Spaniards as Indians and half-breeds, and think you're doing us no end of a favour. The crusaders took advantage of Moslem anarchy at the start of the twelfth century. But then the Mamelukes –'

'Centuries have passed,' says Salomar.

'Not that many! And anyway, do centuries count for you? The point is that you want to treat Spain as a conquered country, basing your claim on tradition and history; without giving a damn about the Spaniards and their troubles. And that's what you see, Luis, in Fascism: that old yearning to be a conquistador, with the Spaniards playing the Indians, in the worst sense of the word. Conqueror of yourself: gnawing at your own entrails on the one hand and at ours on the other, like vermin. Empire, what empire? Are you going to sit down and dream that the Balearics are Sicily? The Canaries, Florida? Your whole programme is literature, armchair chatter!'

'You're off your head!' said Luis.

Sánchez started to talk to his beard again.

'There are a lot more of us than you imagine,' insinuated Luis, like a child with a new toy.

'Do you think I don't know? There are many more of you than *you* imagine: all those who don't believe in the creative power of the people.'

'You, for example.'

'Quiet, villain!'

Sánchez mumbled a farewell.

'He's very talented,' said Bosch, when he'd gone.

'Handles his affairs well, too!' remarked Lledó. 'Cheerio!'

The next day Salomar said to Rafael:

'Come at eight.'

'Where?'

'Same as last time.'

When Serrador had gone, Rubio said, referring to him:

'Spain is a land of social climbers.'

'Do you think every farmhand or peon from Medina Sidonia wants to be a gentleman?' asked the beanpole Bosch.

'If he dared to think it, yes. In Spain there are those who don't know what they are, and those who don't know what they want; the rest are scoundrels, and then there's us. Don't forget that in 1912 we still had sixty per cent illiteracy; today, how much? Fifty? Just as well they don't exist.'

'And you're capable of killing anyone who reminds you of them,' rounded off the waiter, who was listening leaning against the counter, georama of shining chrome.

'Vot I don't understand,' said the Swiss, 'is how you are going to rreconcile Fascism and the Churrch. Fascism is at base anti-Christian. And your rrevolution, if it happens, it will be for the good of prriests.'

'Get away, man!' said Bassas.

'Time vill tell!' concluded Walter. 'And now I go. Prrrick fuck cunt!' his usual parting line, to the delight of his companions.

That night, at the draper's, Luis asked Serrador to sound out his anarchist friends for their attitude in the event of a 'national' movement.

Rafael went to the Victoria next morning; they greeted him as though he'd not been away for more than a day.

'González Cantos was sorry for what he said to you,' said the Chauffeur. 'Come back, he'll be glad.'

Rafael followed him out and put the question to him.

'I can't say,' the anarchist replied. 'It depends on the committees. But I don't think there's any doubt.'

'Weapons?'

'No. But it doesn't matter. The situation is completely different from the 6th of October. This time the government will help us . . . There's a good chance of success. I believe that counter-attack is more effective. The others will be the rebels, the government the victim; between the two, we can make ourselves the masters.'

'What about the transport strike? And the construction workers in Madrid?'

'That's got nothing to do with it.'

Rafael told Salomar he believed the CNT would take to the streets.

'Without arms?'

'They're confident the government will supply them.'

'Bah! We must repeat that we have no quarrel with them. Quite the contrary! With those meddlesome socialists, yes. They're on strike right now. You must insist.'

'They won't understand.'

'All the same, we'll print some leaflets. I'll give you twenty-five men, you see to it they're handed out.'

Two days later Salomar asked Rafael:

'Are you any good with a gun?'

'I don't know.'

'Tomorrow, half past four, Plaza de España. Wait for me by the fountain.'

'We'll see each other in the café.'

'No. Four a.m.'

Rafael had to wait no more than five minutes; Salomar arrived in a car and made him sit in the front. The car took the road to El Prat. Once there they turned right and a kilometre further on, passed through the gate of a farm. In addition to Salomar there were four young men Serrador did not know. Not a word was spoken. Once past the gate they saw about fifty men scattered about a garden and an orchard, most of them young, their shining faces and breeches bespeaking good family backgrounds, all with blue shirts and the yoke and arrows of the Falange, in red, above the left nipple. They lined up in pairs as soon as they spotted Salomar. The roll was called in the sun, between a ploughshare and a pond. The farm was surrounded by high, freshly whitewashed walls. At one corner, standing on a ladder, a sentinel spied out the surrounding area.

In front of the carefully tended orchard, carnation beds with neat little fences, pink coping everywhere; gleaming yellow corncobs and crimson strings of dried peppers hanging down from the roof; tangled bell-shaped vetch flowers following wire netting along the sun-blistered walls; a path runs from the farmhouse to the outer gate, lined with white oleander interspersed with amaranths, geraniums, lilies and *amormíos*, and, at their feet, bordering the gravel, dignified pansies hold high their purple heads. To the right, some almond trees, pomegranate and quince shrubs, half a dozen hazels; further off a cabbage patch, light green, blue and topaz in the early-morning light, with a sheen of iridescent dew; followed by an artichoke and melon bed closed off by crossed canes where peas are seeding. Aloes, prickly pears and *murcianas* grow at the foot of a wall; behind the house, a yard with rabbit hutches against the wall, and a huge grey dovecot high above; at its feet, a wheelbarrow; between its wheels, two geese and their brood.

The dondiegos begin to close their purple flowers; above the pine trees, filters for dust-storms, the sun marks out its territory and casts long light shadows on the still earth as it emerges from the sea.

In front of the little phalanx, stiffly at attention with right arms raised to the sky, struts a cock, erect of comb, martial of spur, whilst his hens brood and cluck not far away.

Against the yard wall, three white and roughly human-shaped targets are propped. Salomar goes into the house and comes out with three pistols in his hand: a Star 6.35, an FN9 revolver and a Mauser of the same calibre. They start shooting in pairs, one taking note of the shots. When it's his turn Rafael fires the whole chamber without hitting the target. The animals yelp, howl, grunt, squawk or bark, according to their abilities. Dogs answer in the distance. A white cat, undaunted, tail aloft, passes between the marksmen and the cut-outs.

The exercise over, everyone tucks in to breakfast. Salomar assembles them afterward and delivers a lecture on the history of Spain. He began three months ago with the Catholic Kings, and he's still on Charles V.

'After Philip II,' he says, 'there was no more history!'

'But I thought –' ventures a beardless youth.

'You don't think, you believe!' shrieks Salomar, beside himself with fury. 'We are bringing back the motto of the University of Cervera: *Preserve us from the woeful curse of thinking*. We believe and you obey!'

The telephone rings: Ramón Navarro warns that the police are looking for him. They have arrested Bassas!

Luis Salomar dismisses his flock and sets the next meeting for two days' time.

In the car on the way back, he tells Rafael to wait at the same time and in the same place.

'Get them to drop you where you like now.' Salomar gets out before they reach the city gates.

Rafael found himself alone that afternoon in the Rhine Gold.

'Looks as though they're on to them,' said Joaquín. 'There's talk of a military uprising. If they want trouble, they'll get it! They'll be stopped dead in their tracks.'

That night, Salomar, wearing a huge pair of dark glasses and a hat, walked down the Ramblas with Lledó. He looked like a villain out of Quevedo; all he lacked was the stick and the dog.

'I think we've come to the point of no return, old pal,' reflected the socialist. 'On the one side those with wants, on the other those who want for nothing. Those who have are asking themselves, pretending to be surprised, what is it they want? As if they didn't know . . .! The mere status of proletarian is ennobling: bondsmen, the Bible calls them, and that's much better. They are obliged to ask themselves: what do we want to be? And from that moment they are already better than they were before. Your people, on the contrary, want to debase themselves – pay the lowest contribution possible. They know what they are and what they have. What you have is what you're worth. And they have no illusions. A man is as good as his illusions. You can do your worst now. You're well and truly done for, old chap.'

'Enough of your stories! What matters is to stay awake and get cracking,' said Luis. 'Dreams are an affliction of the constipated.' And he pulled the brim of his hat down as far as it would go.

'Suppose you could have three wishes . . .'

'Me? Not much! I should like to see all the Catalans hang while I stroll among the gallows, amidst the smell of rotting flesh; with the birds of the Ramblas up above; and our squadron out on the sea.'

'To die like Garcilaso,' said his companion, 'having reduced the Quixote to a pile of scrap paper.'

They walked on in silence.

'What about you?' asks Salomar.

'Other than waking up tomorrow to find myself President of the Council, nothing!

Bientôt nous plongerons dans les froides ténèbres;

163

Adieu, vive clarté de nos étés trop courts!'

'You can take a running jump with your frogtalk! Recite in Spanish, like a man!'

'Very well, mister general, sir:
How vain the prizes
for which we vie and run,
for in this treacherous world
e'en 'fore we die we lose each one.'

'*Olé!*' said Salomar. 'Let's drink a bottle of amontillado in a drinking den Bosch has discovered down some alley in Escudillers.'

With the wine between them, Salomar warns Lledó, in an off-handed way: 'Watch out for yourself!'

'You think my time's running out?'

'Yes. We're face to face at last, at the end of the road.'

In the Interior Minister's office are assembled the heads of the Civil Guard: General Aranguren, Lieutenant-Colonel Escobar, and Brotons. The minister is a tall man, ruddy, with a thin and elongated nose; he looks younger than his fifty-five years.

'Gentlemen, a military uprising against the Republic is being planned. You don't have to answer this question. I am a man of few words. Can the government count on the Civil Guard?'

'If the movement is aimed against the legitimate government, without the slightest doubt. As always,' says the general.

'And you, gentlemen?'

'At your orders!'

'Word of honour?'

'Word of honour!'

'Now I shall put you in touch with the Superintendent of Public Order, Lieutenant-Colonel Escofet, and the Chief of Police, Lieutenant-Colonel Vicente Guarner. You will work out a plan for suppressing the expected movement. I have a list of the officers involved: it will be communicated to you later.'

'Those involved must not have command,' says Aranguren. 'Because I suppose you won't arrest them . . .'

'Obviously, not without proof!'

The soldiers depart and the minister's private secretary comes in.

'Did you know Escobar's a Catholic, and his sister a nun? So we're gambling with Barcelona: heads or tails, church or state.'

'And?'

'On the edge!'

In the woodworkers' union, a few CNT representatives are gathered.

'How many guns?' asks Ascaso.

'None. The stuff from Pueblo Nuevo: a machine gun, you know the one, three automatics, thirty Winchesters,' states García Oliver, low and hard.

'We need to talk to Companys,' says Durruti.

'It's Barcelona we need to deal with!'

'He'll send us to España.'

'We'll talk to España, then.'

'There's a case of revolvers in Hospitalet,' someone says.

'How many?'

'Twelve.'

'Get hold of the plans of the armouries; when the moment comes we'll go and fetch them in the early hours. The fascists will begin their movement between between four and five a.m.' (García Oliver lowers his voice, smiles, and ends the phrase after a brief pause, as always.)

'Then what?'

'We'll see!'

'Who's taking charge of the operation?' asks Ascaso.

'In the capital, García Oliver. Nobody sleeps as of tonight.'

'What do we know about Zaragoza?'

'Nothing.'

'And Valencia?'

'Ready.'

Shooting practice was over. Rafael knew several of those present that morning: Rubio, the Fernández brothers, Ramón Navarro. Salomar assembled them on the ground floor of the farmhouse. He had them all line up.

'Blue Shirts!' he harangued them. 'The games are at an end! The moment of truth has arrived!' ('In for the kill,' thinks Rafael.) 'Let us take our Spanish traditions into our hands. You have them between your fingers, within reach of your triggers. The freedom and decency of Spain are in our charge. You will all shortly answer for a free, united Spain, answer as one: "*Presente!*" The liberty of all is to be turned into the liberty of the Falange. All for Juan Antonio! The time for talking is past: now for discipline! Disagreements are at an end: now for discipline! Contrary efforts, at an end: now for discipline! Freedom, at an end: now for discipline! The Falange is entering into its glory: let us honour its dead! Tonight each of you will receive your battle orders. Spain for ever!'

'Evidently,' thought Rafael, 'he is no orator.'

They waited to be dismissed, but Salomar addressed them again.

'Comrades, there is a Judas among us. If I've spoken in his presence, it's to convince him that he won't be leaving here today. I know who he is. If he comes forward I'll allow him to end his own life. If not, I shall have him shot like a dog. I give him fifteen seconds.'

Rafael Serrador felt he'd turned to stone. It could not be him, and yet he realized that deep down at his root there was a shadow of a doubt, his lack of faith. No one looked at anyone else, for fear of giving rise to suspicion. Who among them felt sure of never having said a careless word? The men Rafael did not know were no more than twenty years old. One of them spoke up:

'I told my father last night that we would soon be . . . I'm ready. And my father won't talk.'

Salomar cut him short: 'Not you. Him.' And he pointed at Ramón Navarro.

They all felt as if the roof had been raised, as if the air had suddenly rushed in; they felt lighter.

'It had to be a policeman! Stool pigeon! Traitors die twice over.'

'A corpse, whatever you say, is still a corpse,' said the runt, in a voice rather higher than his natural pitch.

'But you'll have to think of two places and two ways at the same time. It's hard to die in peace like that.'

'I want to talk to you alone,' he indicated to Salomar.

'What for? To tout your trash again? No. Besides, I'm just carrying out orders. Thanks to you one of our triumvirs is now in prison, and us only at liberty by a miracle. How pleased with yourself you must have felt when you got here! And when you were listening to me. You didn't know it was your death sentence. A state of war is declared. Guzmán and Robles, tie his hands and take him out into the yard. Gregorio, Ruiz Aldaneta, Batlló and Matas, take picks and shovels from the shed on the right as you go out; dig a trench between the dovecot and the wattle fence. He's nice and short.'

'How deep?'

'Sixty, eighty centimetres. If we had more time ...' he shrugged. 'But it will teach you a thing or two. And now draw lots, the six eldest, to see who shall have the honour of sending him off to hell.'

None of the boys had moved a muscle.

Cowering in a corner of the yard, Ramón Navarro flattened himself against the right angle of the whitewashed walls. The shadows speared his face and right shoulder. Opposite, a few barrels; beneath their wheels, small trickles of wine running towards a pile of manure. The air vibrating with summer and heat. His guards have gone, but a man is coming towards him. They close the wooden gate. The hinges squeak. It's possible he was not afraid, that he didn't care about dying, but his body tried to curl itself into the wall. He was sweating inside, his skin dry, gleaming, brilliant. The eighteenth of July, almost midday, everything blue. A fly buzzes at his face. He shakes it off without even realizing, by moving his head. The fly has become two flies. Flies gather round those who are about to die. The man coming towards him finds that shudder distasteful; he looks like a horse, he needs a nosebag and straw.

'He's going to kill me. Oh God, how absurd!' He couldn't think of anything else. The sun, the dungheap, the flies. The only things that came to him were words, quite empty now. 'Oh God, how absurd!' Opposite, in the shadow, the chicken coop with three grey hens. A cock approached, in the sun, pecking at dreams, then lifting its crest with such self-satisfaction that it seemed to wish to hide its shameful truck with seeds and worms and to dominate the world with its red and green feathered sheen, its cold, impersonal little eyes.

'Why didn't I try to make a run for it?' Iron bars across the gate. Outside, the vines are peeping in with their blue flowers and there are sunflowers in seed, black, ready to burst. The sun casts so much light that Ramón Navarro has to squint.

'To die like a rabbit, a rabbit.' And all of a sudden he saw an enormous rabbit winking its eye at him. 'And I'm wetting myself.' The cat in the granary. He feels as if his whole body is smarting.

When the assassin got within four paces of the runt he fired at his stomach. The wretch folded his arms, holding in his abdomen. How had he got them untied? He bent double, which allowed the executioner to put a bullet in his head without leaning over: he just had to stretch out his arm; the wall was spattered with blood and brains. An ass brayed in the distance.

'He won't be the only one!' said Luis Salomar as the allotted killer fixed him with his gaze as with a burning nail. 'There's not much to killing a man, since the invention of gunpowder!'

'I couldn't have done it with a knife. As it is . . . I feel I've taken poison!'

'A drink will soon fix that!'

In the distance Montjuich loomed out of the mist, like a huge shield.

'Why did you talk in front of Navarro?' Rafael asked Salomar. 'And what if . . .?'

'So he'd repent the better, and gain entry more easily to the heaven in which he never believed.'

At three o'clock in the afternoon Don Juan Manuel Porredón announces himself to His Excellency Don Jesús de Buendía y O'Connor, ex-minister to the monarchy, an imbecile, and en route through Barcelona.

Don Juan Manuel is a banker, Don Jesús was born a chairman of directors.

'My dear Juan Manuel . . .!'

'My dear Don Jesús . . .!'

'It seems to be in the bag.'

'All over, Don Jesús, bar the shouting! And about time!'

'How are things here?'

'It's possible they'll be able to resist, but it's a matter of hours. At worst, another 6th of October. Goded will arrive at eleven, once he's sorted things out in Palma. The plan is simply splendid, it can't fail. The only problem was Madrid. And in Madrid we're not making any move just now. In the other capitals they are unarmed. As for the political parties and the unions, pah! . . .'

'What about the Civil Guard, and the Assault Guard?'

'As to the first, I presume you're joking. As to the Assault troops, what can they do against the army in the streets, once war is declared?'

'And Zaragoza?'

'Don't worry. Cabanellas in Zaragoza and Queipo in Seville are the surest of all. You can't beat ingratitude! The problem is Aranda in Oviedo, but there he's very isolated. Besides, his friend Lerroux is not hostile to us.'

'So?'

'Nothing, everything will turn out swimmingly. Sanjurjo will arrive in Burgos, Franco is already in Tetuán. The planes have arrived as promised. The only disaster is that one or two have had to land in Algeria.'

'Do we know how France has reacted?'

'Quiñones has very good connections there. Besides, as it's a Popular Front government, they'll be very careful not to get involved with us, *les réactionnaires*. They'll treat us far more kindly than your friend Léon Daudet would have done!'

'To sum up, then . . .'

'Franco will join Queipo's uprising in the second region. Goded will take charge here. In Valencia García Monje is at a loss, but the regiments are out on the streets.'

'Which is what matters. Go on.'

'Furthermore, Mola, from Pamplona, can reach anywhere he's needed, though he won't be. Galicia is ours. Just a matter of issuing a proclamation. What can Casares's ridiculous government do? Can you tell me? Surrounded, fenced in, with the enemy at his front door, he'll have to surrender.'

'I'm expecting great things of that silent threat in Madrid. It's a novelty.'

'Sanjurjo will tie up the threads. It's a matter of days. Our friends might be a bit more prudent, though; in Amsterdam, Almadén mercury shares have gone through the roof.'

'And here? What will Llano de la Encomienda do?'

'Weep! Legorburu is more than adequate until Goded arrives. You know him, the general in charge of the artillery. And with Fernández Ampón. But above all we have Moxó, the colonel at the Military Academy, and Adalberto Sanfeliz.'

'The Italian mercury stocks haven't made a move.'

'Whether Italy joins the council or not, once union has been achieved they'll rise like foam.'

Lieutenant-Colonel Guarner enters the office of the Minister of the Interior. He takes a book from his briefcase.

'It belongs to an officer under my command. He left it in the guards corps. Inside I have found this sealed letter with the Captaincy-General's emblem. I didn't want to open it without your permission.'

'Open it.'

Tearing of paper. Guarner reads it and passes it in silence to España. It's an order to declare a state of war.

'Undated,' comments the minister. 'With the General Staff's seal.'

'And signed by Colonel Moxó,' notes Aranguren, who is present.

España calls the captain-general by telephone.

'Listen, general, despite your denials, it is so. Lieutenant-Colonel Guarner is coming over with the document.'

Guarner is just leaving when Brotons, Escobar and Escofet arrive.

'Gentlemen,' says España, 'Commander Sandino, in charge of the airfield at El Prat, has offered me his unconditional support. I am sure that if all orders have been carried out, the movement is certain to fail in Barcelona.'

On a map are marked the police posts, the barracks under watch.

'I have increased the number of men in the Diagonal,' says Escofet. 'There is no post with less than two hundred.'

'I don't believe in miracles!' says the minister.

'I do!' replies Escobar.

'Well, let the miracle be done and let the devil do it!' sneers Brotons.

Guarner returns:

'The seal is false; the signatures authentic.'

'They've even made the seals!' says Aranguren. 'They've got money this time!'

'Yes, it's looking serious.'

'What about Madrid?' asks Escofet.

'Who?' counters España. 'Moles? Esplá? Casares? Pozas? They all exude confidence and call me an alarmist!'

'Alarmed and disarmed is what they'll be,' mutters Brotons into his beard.

At three a boy brought Rafael Serrador an order typed on yellowed paper. 'Headquarters, three o'clock.'

That afternoon he called at the draper's, where they gave him the password: *'End of the road.'*

PART THREE

'And thus it was the earth did start to roar'
—Juan Ruiz

ONE

Late Night, Early Morning

It was time to take up a position.

'Yes, our era is a war of positions. And you have adopted the easiest, the most comfortable, the most dishonourable,' Lledó told Serrador.

'Why, O prince of morality?'

They were walking in the direction of the University. The newspaper vendors were exhausting their evening supplies.

'No, no *Noticieros* left, nor *Noches*. *La Rambla*! *La Rambla*! 18th of July 1936!'

'You think you're the whole world. I can't understand it in a worker, my fellow-bondsman.'

Lledó's voice was hoarser than usual; he walked with customary ungainliness, unconsciously pushing up the bridge of his spectacles with the forefinger of his right hand when they slipped down over his nose, a gesture Rafael would sometimes mimic to comic effect.

'You judge politics as though it were a machine designed to make you happy. Like glove to hand. To sort out your personal conflicts.'

'Isn't it the same for you? How can you look after everyone else if you can't cope with your own problems?'

'That's no argument. I wasn't born a proletarian, my friend, and that's what hurts. Do you believe people are going to die for your conscience? To save Rafael López Serrador?'

'I don't believe anything.'

'It's not that you don't believe anything: you don't believe *in* anything, which isn't the same. You underestimate the world. That's your strength but also your downfall: just so you won't be despised, most of all by yourself.'

Lledó stopped:

'Listen, haven't you ever loved, really loved, a woman?'

'Do you buy all that nonsense as well? What does that matter to the rest of the world?'

'To the world, not a toss, but to you, yes. And as for you, you are the world . . . For you, my young friend, nothing has a price, or rather, the reverse, you put a price on everything. That's called contempt. I don't know if you've ever come across anything noble. If you have, you've missed it. That's why you don't believe either in the people or in yourself, since you don't believe in man; and you take refuge in vain ideas. In the name of that emptiness you want to subjugate Spain. Don't your very entrails protest . . .! Those of us who have no price, who won't sell ourselves, though we may be worth nothing – which would be a reason for selling oneself – despise you!'

'Well, this is turning into quite a night! And, in all honesty, my fallacious sermonizer, what do *you* believe in?'

'In my own conscience. In my virtue as a man. You know what I really believe in? It's going to sound old-fashioned and strange on my lips: I believe in honour, honour for all!'

Lledó stopped on the corner of the Parliament building. The lights disappeared as they grew smaller and closer together in the distance: the night was heavy and uneasy; radio stations blared from every open window, snaring the passers-by and their newspapers. All ears were cocked, hunting by sound. 'Melilla, Prieto, Pasionaria . . .'

'Honour for many, respect for all. Do you like it? I offer it as a definition of socialism. The anarchists are content with just half: respect for all. You, I'll grant you this much – I'm too honourable for my own good! – you will fight for the sense of honour as fame and glory, show and window-dressing, for the sake of appearances and the good opinion of others. For you honour is not a moral quality, something that brings self-respect; it's your reputation, an external sign, a palpable reality, something you can touch and value, something which is even a matter of words, titles, money, debts. Honour for some and blindness for all. I also offer you a definition of your concerns: not "from" but "to"; not "from the inside" but "towards the outside". You're not interested in the human being; what counts is his shell; not the person but the garment, the aspect. I won't deny it's very Spanish. Here nobody is surprised at paying for appearances with their life. Theatre. You love to show off: in Christianity, surplices, chasubles, damascenes. I know it's magnificent to die for a word . . . Heroic, but not honourable. You make the same confusion between worth and wealth.'

'Anything else?'

'Yes. As always, we are the idealists; it will cost us our lives, but we never learn; we, honoured to be honourable – and dishonoured by you . . . Until the day arrives . . .'

'I ought to mention that I have nothing to do until nine, and then, food.'

'You like to live off lies. You fall for everything phoney and artificial. You flail at the air. You can't see men, so you replace them with peons: serfs, foot-soldiers. For your leaders, there are land-owners and *lieu-tenants*, and that's all: a man is just a peon. Toilers, tillers, labourers, wage-earners: all peons. Viewed with terrible contempt. All that matters is winning the game. They pay them six *reales* per day of life. They say they pay them, though what they do is to buy them. Do you know what a farmhand is worth: all of him, his hair, his talk, his sperm, his nails, his strength? An average of eight to ten thousand pesetas. Slavery's abolished, my cocksure young friend, but harvest watchmen and shepherds are still bought and sold! Do you know what a worker is worth? It shouldn't be difficult for you to calculate. And it's no good them not wanting to do it. Rebel, and you die. It's against that death that your comrades are fighting, while you stab them in the back, my dear little wrecker. But that's because you're worthless: you give yourself away. It's not that you really despise anyone else, you despise yourself. To hell with the blood of the turners, polishers, workers with wood and metal! . . . You are gentlemen! Gentlemen, those who are about to die salute you! But this time the ring is bigger and there are no barriers between us, nor upper levels to save you. You consider us animals; we'll become wild beasts. You've taunted us: bulls we'll become, killer bulls. Prepare your swords! There will be bulls in the field this Christmas!'

'Finished now? Good night.'

Serrador turned and went. All to play for, thought Lledó. Busloads of young men dressed in white drove noisily by. 'The People's Olympics tomorrow. Everyone to run the half-marathon. All records to be broken.'

Rafael slumped on his bed for a moment, before going down to the dining room. At the top of his chest, the base of his throat, escaping through the handle of his sternum, he felt and heard the beating of his heart and the pumping of his blood, worlds orbiting through his emptiness.

The only speaker at dinner, in the Pearl of the New World, was the Fat Man.

'Now we'll show them a thing or two! Because Casares will last a minute and no more. Holy Father. You can't tell me Franco has rebelled in Africa without agreeing it with all the others. Now we'll see where our fine friend Azaña ends up.' The fatface guzzled away with evident satisfaction. 'They thought the world was theirs. No respect, no order, nothing. I'm not including you, Don Rafael, Mr Espinosa, but you know what I mean! One strike after another. We'd had seven years of dictatorship like seven suns. Not a squeak out of God, and bully for business! You there, what do you want? Work, sir, work! As for your eight hours, and your forty-four, and when I have forty-four I want forty! What do they expect? Me to work for them? Whatever they're given, they're never satisfied. People get tired, and with good reason. I strike at you, and strike you again. No, we've got nothing against the workers! But now we'll see what's what! Every now and then it's good for the scum to see who's in charge. As for their autonomy, and their City Council, and their Generalitat, now they know where they can stuff it . . . Pardon me, ladies. Besides, a good thrashing never hurt anyone. I'm not talking about the workers. We know they're decent people. It's the leaders who have to be taught a lesson. They live by making trouble and lining their own pockets. They levy the unions and then, "Let's live it up and undermine society!" I've been a republican all my life, but not for a republic like this, where the Socialists are in charge . . . A republic like that, I'll make anyone a present of it! You can't beat tradition, gentlemen! An old man is telling you. Who was the real republican here, in Spain? Don Alejandro, nobody else! Now we'll get our own back! I know you're decent people. That's why I'm talking to you with my heart on my sleeve. Hey, Desi!' he shouts at his saint-swallowing wife, out in the kitchen. 'Have you bought bread for tomorrow and the next day? Because this will last at least two or three days. Buy ten pounds of *bacalao*. You have to be prepared. We've got rice. I was in the club this afternoon. Someone tuned in to Radio Tetuán. The broadcasts finish with 'Long live the Republic!', and they play Riego's anthem. Desi, coffee for everyone, it's on me.' And he brings out the brandy and glasses.

Everyone excused themselves. Rafael had no desire to stay with his intended victim; but just to be different, he accepted.

'Now it's our turn!' repeated the glutton, patting the great pot of his belly.

'Do you think so?' said Rafael, for something to say.

'Who else's?'

'The Army. The Falange, the King, I don't know!'

'Come off it, man! No, man, no! What decent people want is work, and' – turning roguishly to confidences – 'Don Alex for President of the Republic and Gil Robles for President of the Council. They both pee through the same hole!'

'Whatever you say,' said Rafael, who was not in the mood for an argument. 'I'm going for a walk.'

He bumped into Espinosa, who was going upstairs. The smell of stale oil and leftovers caught in the throat. Espinosa turned, two stairs further up.

'Are you a Falangist?'

'No.'

'But you're with them?'

'It was you pointed me in their direction.'

'Things are different now. It's not a question of theories any more. They'll take to the streets tonight, tomorrow or the next day.'

'Oh?'

'Don't tell me you didn't know!'

'I didn't say anything.'

'I take you for a decent lad. Why lie? Do you realize what you're about to do?'

'Bah! You or the other gang . . .!'

'The only difference being, we're complete opposites.'

'For me, opposites . . .'

'Enough. If I see you in the street, I'm daft enough to aim in another direction.'

Espinosa went on up. Rafael hesitated on the landing. 'Good luck!' he shouted.

'I don't need it, I have something better,' the communist replied, invisible.

Rafael went down to the front door; the night seemed so unbearable that he went back up to his garret. 'We're taking to the streets. For order, discipline and all the rest of it. And I . . . Lledó is right. What matters to me is my own freedom; as for the rest, who cares. Beware of Fat Men! In syndicalist terms, it suits us. You bet it suits us! The fact is, everyone has their head full of empty words. We shall see . . . So, for the sake of honour, my dear friend? What a mouthful that was!'

Walter is deep in conversation, immersed to his armpits in a goatskin armchair; a middle-aged Catalan is in front of him. A foundry owner.

'Look,' says the host, 'my two sons are in the Falange. I have never interfered in their affairs. But whether they like it or not, I'm taking them to France tomorrow! Look: where people make their mistake is in believing that tomorrow the world will inevitably go fascist or communist. So naturally they become anti-fascists or anti-communists. They think capitalism is done for, that they need to resort to subterfuges to survive . . . It's ridiculous! All it shows is the power of propaganda. I'm not saying that capital – France, Britain, America – will not ally itself at some point with one of those two forms of low-life; but only to gobble up their ally after defeating their enemy.'

'You don't think you will have to commit yourself?'

'Not on your life . . .! That's why I'm off to Toulouse, to wait for my compatriots to sort themselves out. All I support is peace, industry and commerce.'

'You think the militarry will have a quick and easy victory?'

'They hold all the trump cards. Barrera and Sanjurjo can rely on the support of Germany and Italy. Look, Italy and Germany are extremely interested in us, whereas France and England couldn't care less. Full bellies are blind.'

'To me the vorrld is under the sign of A. Africa for Italy, Asia for Japan, America for Germany. Italy is interested in

Spain as an African power, and Germany as an American one. Stepping stone or gangplank.'

'Look, politics is a matter of gangplanks. And now if it's all right with you, let's talk about serious matters. You're staying on, aren't you?'

'Ya, to see vot happens.'

Relishing the semi-wakefulness, taking it easy, his head among the tassels of the bedspread, his crown against the headboard, Rafael makes a tremendous effort to lift his left wrist to his field of vision: two o'clock. 'Half an hour to go, half an hour laid out like a rug before me, to do what I like on, a carpet of flowers.'

Indolence, sluggish current, slow march, tunnel, night: to just float on the water sustaining myself as I am now, belly to the sky. Weary slide. Still two o'clock. His arm falls, swinging, as though he were dead.

'Soldiers of the Republic!' says the colonel of the regiment billeted in San Andrés. 'Soldiers of the Republic! A communist plot against our Republican institutions has been uncovered. But we have been able to unravel the threads of this skein so treacherously woven in Moscow against our Spanish liberties. Moving with exemplary speed to punish those responsible, the government of the Republic has declared a state of war. There is now no other authority but military authority. Before order is even disturbed, it will be restored by the glorious Spanish army, which, once again, will know how to sacrifice itself for the Fatherland. Soldiers of the Republic! Now you must march out into the streets to show that our arms defend all law-abiding citizens! Our shining tradition will not be broken, etcetera, etcetera' – the colonel coughs, composes his sky-blue sash in front of the full-length mirror; looks at himself behind, and in profile. 'A bit podgy, colonel, sir, a bit podgy!' he says, satisfied with the general effect. He calls his orderly: 'Ask the gentlemen to come in.'

In the square on the Vía Layetana, where a little to the rear the General Commisariat of Public Order raises its three modest storeys, eight vehicles stand with their engines running; guards swarm everywhere; every so often, cars race down the broad avenue at full speed.

'Yes, the Commissar General on the line. Right, keep watching and keep us informed.'

Another telephone. 'Is that you, España? I'm informed that plainclothes men are moving into the San Adrián barracks. The Icaria as well? Right, I'll get back to you.'

He hangs up the receiver, listens to the sounds from the street. Cars go by with their accelerators hard down: it sounds like an underlining, the closing of an account, the end of a chapter or the beginning of another: out of the silence and into it once more; that rising hum and distant death on the downward slope seem to him like whip-lashes on the shoulders of the night. 'New life, death; tomorrow – already here – really will be another day.'

In a run-down café in the upper part of the city, Luis Salomar paces up and down as far as its dimensions allow; with his arms crossed, in front of Rubio, who sits with his elbows on the table staring at a bottle of brandy. Salomar is thinking that within an hour, the three hundred men under his command will be at their posts.

'Do you think any of them will be missing?'

Rubio shrugs his outsize, well-tailored shoulders, and knocks back another amber slug. Luis keeps coming and going, arms crossed, hands resting on his biceps, fingers reaching to his shoulders.

'What are you thinking, captain?' blurts the other, from his cups.

Salomar stops dead, turns quickly towards his questioner. Looks at him with his little eyes of living jet.

'About the arrival of Don Quixote in Barcelona,' he replies, 'galleys on the sea, streamers and pennants. Bugles and hornpipes. The sound of artillery "piercing the wind". The knights sallying forth from the city . . .'

The Fat Man is reclining on a rep-covered sofa. He reaches out, a last-gasp effort, towards the table, where the stub of a cigar has just gone out. The old reprobate manages to reach it and sucks noisily as he relights. The bangled hand of the number two procuress appears through the blue velvet curtains.

'Had a good rest?'

'Where's Pepita?'

'In the dining room, with some fellers. All the others are busy.'

'Tell her to come up.'

'Right away, Don Joaquín.

Madam herself arrives, displacing air, bouncing flab.

'What do you want?'

'Fifteen thousand.'

'That all?'

'A thousand packets, plus commission.'

'So there's trouble coming, big-time!'

'What's it to you? Will it stop people smoking and enjoying themselves? Revolutions are for fools; me, I'm a town councillor. Cough up and fetch me a coffee!'

The barbarian adjourns his buttocks to the softest part of the seat.

Espinosa walks towards the party headquarters. 'Against a Fascist enemy, the government considers itself just another belligerent . . .' Well, now we'll see, Mr Casares! In the doorway to Central Office he runs into Joaquín Lluch.

'It seems Azaña tried one of his tricks this morning. Martínez Barrio, etcetera. But it misfired . . .'

'The newspapers say –'

'Pah! . . . All our people in Melilla have been arrested.'

'How did we find out?'

'I don't know.'

'And here?'

'Today or tomorrow.'

'What about Madrid?'

'Nothing yet. They're talking about Seville, Pamplona . . .'

'Where are you off to?'

'Corner of Diagonal and Balmes.'
'Good luck!'

Colonel Moxó is in his office in the Captaincy. Lieutenant-Colonel Sanfeliz is listening to him.

'At half past four the squads will leave to proclaim the state of war. As soon as that's done we can proceed in accordance with the law.'

'Any news, colonel?'

'By telegraph. They're still in control of the telephones. Excellent news. To the best of my knowledge, war will have been declared in Pamplona, Zaragoza, Huesca, Logroño, Burgos, Valladolid, Zamora, Salamanca, Orense, Lugo and La Coruña.'

The colonel counts on his fingers and consults his papers.

'Seville?' prompts his inferior.

'Seville, Granada, Córdoba.'

'Not bad!'

'Not bad.'

'At what time will the general touch down?'

'Between ten and eleven.'

'What if the squads are fired on?'

'Then the columns set to go out at seven will go out straight away.'

Atilio and Jaime Fernández are talking, leaning against a wall in the courtyard of the Atarazanas barracks. They are wearing blue shirts, pistols dangling over their buttocks.

'Quite a tour we'll be making of the town the day after tomorrow!'

'Can you see the faces on some of those sons-of-bitches when they see us coming!'

They feel as if the Canfranc is within reach of their hands. They fall silent.

'Smoke?'

The telephone rings and resounds in every newspaper office.

'The government is in control of the situation. Nothing to report.'

'No news. The government . . .'

'I know nothing. Good night!'

'I've already told you. I know nothing!'

'The government is in control of the situation.'

'Didn't you know that we newspaper people never know anything?'

'But is there any news?'

The doctor looks at him from behind his spectacles. He doesn't know whether his stomach hurts or not. There are moments when he thinks so, but as soon as he tries to tell, it stops hurting. And vice versa. He feels himself gasping. Why is he gasping? He doesn't want to gasp in the doctor's face, but he can't contain himself. What have they put on his chest? All the children were around just now. 'Who has gone to the station?' He tries to ask but can't. 'Don't forget, be careful when you go up into second. Blasted clutch!' It's not that he can't speak; he knows perfectly well what he's trying to say, but they can't understand him. As if they'd all gone deaf. Perhaps Rafael might understand. 'Who's gone to the station?' His wife approaches. He makes a sign. He talks, and she doesn't understand his gasp. So many days without shaving! 'Who's taken the coach to the station?' His belly hurts, oh God! his belly hurts. And his chest, what a weight! 'Who's gone to the station? What will happen if I die? The railcar leaves at six. I can't get air, I can't! What time is it? It will have left Segorbe by now.'

Lledó walks alone, hands clasped at his back. What is it about the air that makes the trees sound different? What sound of footsteps in the wind? He hears the earth as if he had his ear to it. There are more people sleeping on benches than usual, that's all. 'Nothing in the streets; nothing along the pavements; and in the sky left clear by the branches, nothing: the constellations. The bourgeoisie puts everyone's blood to sleep. Cats, snakes, cows and pigeons all asleep. Bedbugs are another matter. The vegetables are asleep. The drowsy wind drags itself along through the hollows, the squares, the broad streets; without the strength to force alleyways, it wanders through waste grounds, open spaces. Around the outskirts of the city men keep watch in all the barracks. All around us the lights of the guards' detachments: Hospitalet, Pedralbes, San Andrés, and closer. How time falls and passes! Giral, head of government, what a joke! What's funny about it? What will I do tomorrow? Stay home. Young Francisca won't let me go out, nor will her good mother. As long as the wireless is working! Am I a coward? Yes, I am. I know where the truth lies, and I don't much fancy dying for it. That speech I made to Serrador should have been directed at myself. Two maids and a bathroom prevent me from being a person I can respect. I disgust myself, but not too much. If there were other reasons . . . And I shall accept posts, and everyone will say that that's the way to serve the Republic, and I'll end up believing it. But as for risking my neck tomorrow . . .! I'm a passionate spectator, but a spectator. Watching the bulls from behind the fence. What courage! And just there, hard, heavy, behind the ear, that buzzing: how is it in the Republic's interest for me to be shot? I shan't serve it better, etcetera. Bourgeois swine, to bed with you! And sweet dreams. Do I disgust myself? Do I not disgust myself? I disgust myself. Half past two. Trouble in the Eighth. No one could convince young Francisca of either my honour or my cowardice.'

González Cantos and the Chauffeur are in the front seat of a truck in Calle Roger de Flor.

'Is the transport workers strike still on?'

'Yes.'

'How did you get hold of the truck?'

'It's the Union's.'

'Is the construction workers' strike in Madrid still on?'

'Yes. They haven't released the prisoners. Antona, López, Mera and Marín are still in jail.'

'I told people it wasn't the moment to be obstinate. Where are we going?'

'Over to Pueblo Nuevo for supplies.'

'Are they on the move?'

'We've just had a phone call saying there are plainclothes men going into the barracks, one and two at a time.'

In a squalid room in the Nouvel Hotel Barcelona, in Calle de la Unión, Jorge de Bosch has a harlot trapped in a corner. The washbasin is fixed on the wall with shiny screws, the enamel bidet is peeling. Towels hang from the chromium rail; a bit of worn linoleum curls on the floor. The bed, pulled back, is untouched. A screen is placed by the window. A harsh light falls from a bulb barely covered by a tulip shade which ends up as a rose. A rickety wardrobe with scratched mirror stands alongside the two characters. On the marbled top of the bedside table sits the flabby lout's wristwatch. On a seat and on the tired arms of a bright green armchair, with dark flowers blurred by time and worn by fondlings, clothes lie where they fell. Toff and tart are as naked as their respective mothers bore them. The trollop's thighs thin as they fall, stomach slack, udders war-weary; scarlet toenails match scarlet fingernails on hands folded across those sagging breasts; a faceful of pockmarks, beautiful blue eyes, blonde mop, bony shoulders. The good-for-nothing looks her straight in the eye. He knows her weakness: the slut is revolted by anything sticky, slimy, sluglike. The roué knows it and his eyes blaze. With her helplessly ensconced, the idle lecher rasps out words of love, searches for lip and lobe, as she vainly tries to defend herself against the disgusting stream by covering her ears.

'Snot!' says the cowardly blackguard. 'Slime, gob, spittle, saliva, sputum.' His honeyed, amorous voice begins to crack.

'I'll fill your mouth with live snails, with phlegm, slobber, spume! You'll be completely covered in viscous humours, slug-slime, spit, splatters, white, green, yellow; stickiness, pus, sperm . . . !'

The little sickling bites her knuckles. The man spreadeagles her against the wall. The consumptive sinks her nails in his shoulders, retches and vomits down the proffered back, as the professor sets about his business.

Minister of the Interior to general in command of the Fourth Region:

'I hear that in San Andrés the colonel has assembled his troops and addressed them.'

'Impossible! But just in case, and for your peace of mind, I'll send a general there at once.'

Serrador looks again at his watch. Half past two, almost twenty-five to three. He gets up, goes to the wash-stand, fills the bowl with water, wets his face. He goes down to the street through the darkened house.

A body turns over in the narrow bed.

'Promise me you'll stay home tomorrow!'

'Let me sleep! I'll do what I have to do. Women!'

A baby wakes and starts to cry.

'General Llano de la Encomienda? España here again. They tell me that men in plain clothes are entering the Pedralbes barracks after giving the password.'

'I'll send another general right away. But I can assure you my subordinates will see to it that nothing happens in Barcelona.'

The gate to the Icaria barracks is locked. From time to time a bare head pokes out through the shutter. A hundred metres on, the local nightwatchman and a policeman are openly on patrol.

'Look,' says the nightwatchman, 'you can stuff this game, standing here fishing with a long line, or go straight to the bloody devil! What do you think I am! I may have been born in Alcantarilla, but not yesterday and I'm Barceloneta-bred.'

'Yes, but fishing without a rod has its . . .!' the eye of the Generalitat calmly starts to say.

They have been approaching the gateway to the building. It opens and five men in shirt-sleeves burst out and grab the disquisitioners by force; they hustle them into the entrance-way and without a by-your-leave begin to give them a proper thrashing. The policeman reaches for his gun. A buckle crashes down on the back of his hand. The representatives of the civil authority howl, to no avail; their captors beat them with their own lightsticks to humiliate them more, prick their arses with the sharp end of the shaft. Then they shove them, black and blue, covered in muck, ribs well battered, back out into the solitary street.

'Our best wishes to your masters, young explorers! There's plenty more where that came from, coppers!'

The blows hurt more than the insults.

In the night there was no one. The darkness had always reminded him of a blanket, something with which to envelop and protect himself; now he realized he'd been deceived; the night was on nobody's side. Not that it was hostile, just outside of him, indifferent, dead. Noises reached him not through his ears but through his throat, as if he were hearing himself. His footsteps sounded longer, resounding in his memory, in the emptiness. The cracks of light below the doors to some of the bars, open-mouthed at ground-level, only emphasized the darkness. He had never looked so tall on pavements and walls.

'It's not the night, it's me.' He felt the handle of the revolver against his thigh. Everyone was in a hurry. The streetlights hissed. No whores or pimps on the Calle del Conde del Asalto; nobody beneath the archways to the Fifth District. Distant solitude. In the sky, sure signs of milky dawn. Cocks crowing, and as he approached the Ramblas the birds all warbling like a brook. Rafael had a glass of wine in The Giralda, still open. No trams broke the silence of the Rambla Central; people sleeping flat out on the yellow iron benches. No one in Plaza del Rey, the lamps beneath the arches multiplying shadows. A man disappears in the distance. In the Calle de Escudillers there is still noise coming from the Ideal Room and The Penguin. Sitting out on the kerbside, a girl in evening dress and a young upper-class swell. A tango is playing. From an open window, the strumming of a guitar;

further up, along the channel of the narrow street, he seems to divine the first battles between the day and the morning stars: the hour denies it. A group comes down the Calle de Aviñó. Serrador quickens his step. It's not yet three when he gives the password at the back gate of the Captaincy. They take him to Salomar, in an Isabelline room, white and gold with couches and armchairs covered in yellow, and matching curtains. An enormous painting with an elaborately carved frame: a windmill and a long column of troops marching through a dark landscape. There is no carpet: the black and white paving-tiles cast a chill upon the whole. Salomar, in the centre, chats to five young men Rafael remembers from El Prat, among them a trouble-maker who has some grudge against him. They salute one another, Roman-style. Luis Salomar hands him an embroidered badge, with the yoke and arrows; Rafael fixes it to his chest. It weighs heavily on him.

'General Llano de la Encomienda here. Is that you, Minister? You see? Four in the morning, and nothing has happened. Just as I said. I'm going to bed. Good night!'

Montjuich against the sky, and Tibidabo still lying back in the shadows; half past four rings out, late, on the tower of the monastery at Pedralbes. Cactuses, marsh-mallows and willowherbs confused in the blur of morning. Down below the barracks gate opens, squeaking; a large squad marches out, in good order; it sets off down the wide, open avenue. The police, the ministry, the Civil Guard commanders hear at once. Orders are transmitted. The police reserves form up at strategic points.

'What have you said to them?'

'Putting down a communist movement, to some; putting down a fascist one, to others.'

'The general?'

'Resting in his rooms.'

'Get him an escort. Send in the Falange delegate.'

Salomar enters Colonel Moxó's office. They go over to the window. At eye level are the tops of the palm trees of the Paseo de Colón; behind the warehouses, a strip of sea, early morning topaz. In the solitude, a dog sniffs at the dockyard railings.

'Now our men are converging from all the peripheral zones,' says the colonel, 'towards the centre of the city. They can't hold out. Cornered. These new barracks are all perfectly located. Strategy, *señor delegado*! There's nothing anyone can do against good organization: from Sans, Hospitalet, Barceloneta, Gracia, San Andrés, they're heading towards us. We are in the centre of that open fan, we are the screw on the ribs, the handle. The general will feel a complete idiot. Not that that takes much.'

There is a map of Barcelona on the table. Moxó points out to Salomar the route of the insurgent regiments.

'The confluence.'

Salomar approves; looks out at the slow dawn. The chief picks up the receiver.

'Get me San Andrés.'

'The telephone's not answering. It's not ringing,' replies the guard. 'You can only speak with the direct line to the Interior Ministry.'

The colonel looks at the time. A clock of gilded brass tells it, from the mantelpiece. Cupids wearing crowns tick in rhythm: five past five.

An orderly comes in with a letter. He opens it, calls his adjutant: 'The Bordeta troops have reached Plaza de España. Tell them to leave a squad on the Parallel, on the corner with the Rondas, to ensure the link-up. Yes, twenty or thirty men will be plenty. No other news? All right.'

The day rises up out of the sea.

The Paseo del Diagonal cuts across the Plaza de los Hermanos Badía, with grass verges and a few small trees; it then continues, without houses to frame it, and takes on the name Pedralbes. Four kilometres to the sea, and the city in between. The troops from the Pedralbes barracks march from there to the centre, with a band of trumpeters in front. At each street entrance civil guards stand at the ready, rifles cocked; a bearded captain is in charge. Four hundred men is more than enough for the new arrivals. At the third volley, not even their tails remain. The first was into the air; by the second, there was no one to aim at.

Up in the northeast of the city, close to the sea, stands the Icaria barracks. Close on a hundred men emerge, under Captain López Varela. They head for the North Station. Three hundred assault troopers wait for them to reach the Plaza Palacio. They allow them to march right into the lion's mouth. Five minutes later López Varela, wild-eyed and wounded, enters the Interior Ministry building as a prisoner.

'In God's name, don't kill me!'

'We don't kill anyone here!'

And he goes to the hospital. Eighty men volunteer to serve the government. Six or seven have managed to flee back to barracks. The others disappear, leaving their jackets as security.

In Plaza de la Universidad, the very heart of Barcelona, at the foot of the ornate monument to Doctor Robert, some CNT affiliates are making plans. A squad of soldiers from Bordeta arrives along Calle de Cortes. The anarchists fall back, firing their pistols, towards Calle de Balmes, looking for doorways. One of the corners of the square sees the first worker fall. Five forty-seven by the University clock. Now all the cocks are crowing. There are no more shadows. The sun, above the city, gleams on the windows of the open-air fairground on the top of Tibidabo mountain.

TWO

Morning and Noon

On the corner of the Parallel, facing the harbour, facing Montjuich, lies the Santa Madrona barracks. The colonel assembles his troops.

'Soldiers of the Republic, the time has come . . .!'

Three shots ring out and the officer crumples to the floor.

'Long live the Republic, soldiers, long live the Republic!'

The other officers flee. The troops give chase. Three traitors hole up in the flag room. They fire through mouldings and panelling. Several soldiers fetch a beam and all together they smash in the door. A wounded officer lies slumped on a bench, the rest stampede through the offices. They find themselves corralled. The paymaster's office windows are opened, to pass through pistols. Everything crashes down in a heap, papers, ink, typewriters, blotters, penholders, ledgers and pouncet-boxes. Rifle fire. Someone has had time to flee the officers' sleeping quarters by the rear doors, breaking through the partition walls; two trickles of blood run down towards the floor. The plaster dries and darkens it. Sergeant Valeriano Gordo has taken control of the mess huts. The soldiers shout their enthusiasm as they charge about the yard. Sergeant-Major Manzana cries freedom. The soldiers scatter throughout the Fifth District. Manzana sends word to the

Confederation: 'In conclusion, two machine guns in working order.'

The guns, behind mattresses, point down the Parallel.

'We ought to send someone, a man who's not on file, to Atarazanas and Plaza España,' Moxó says to Salomar. 'To find out what's going on. Damned nuisance about the phones. Until they reach Plaza de Cataluña . . .'

Salomar goes out to the waiting-room and calls Serrador.

Up in the brick-built hotels of Plaza de España, the hundreds of young men in town to compete in the People's Olympics, due to begin at eleven a.m., appear at the windows. They see soldiers at ease in the middle of the square. Three light aircraft in the sky. A French sprinter (100 metres in 11 seconds), who speaks a bit of Spanish, goes down for information.

'They're probably covering the race,' suggests a Swede. 'I heard the President is coming to the opening ceremony.'

The Frenchman buttonholes the first rebel he meets. They get on famously.

'Uprising in Barcelona!' The conscript looks up at the planes and points them out to the athlete. 'Fascists.'

'Fascists. What about you?'

'Anti, anti-fascist,' replies the soldier, convinced he has come out to fight a reactionary uprising.

They are ordered to line up. A small lieutenant with an irregular moustache approaches.

'Who's this?' he asks of the foreigner. 'One of us or a red?'

'*Moi?* Sprinter!'

And he raises his fist.

There is no way of getting through to El Prat.

España looks at the same ocean that two hundred metres below him Colonel Moxó sees and doesn't see. The planes go by: piloted by Ponce de León and Meana, Villaceballos and Giménez, Bayo and Herguido.

'All sheets and canvas out onto the roof!' shouts the Minister of the Interior. They spread the cloths over the brick terrace and paint on them, as large as possible: SAN ANDRÉS. The planes fly down to within thirty metres.

'They must have read it easily … To think there are no other planes in Barcelona …!'

'They're carrying hand bombs and some twenty-pounders.'

'The San Andrés troops left at six. It's six-fifteen. They'll catch 'em right out in the open.'

España slaps General Aranguren on the back. He realizes, and grins.

The President of the Generalitat is in the office of the Director-General of Public Order. There has been no news for a quarter of an hour. In the distance, lost in the anxiety, a few shots. The Vía Layetana, deserted. The wail of a siren, a ship leaving or arriving unawares.

After a 'Forward!', an orderly salutes.

'Mr García Oliver and Mr Durruti to see his Excellency the President.'

'Send them in!'

'What's going on?' asks Durruti, quizzical and forceful.

'Waiting,' replies Escofet. 'The detachments came out and were routed. Too easy. We're still waiting for the main bulk of the soldiers.'

'Santa Madrona is ours,' says García Oliver, forceful and intense.

'Some have reached the University via Cortes. That's the only place they've broken through so far,' adds Companys.

'They control the Parallel, but the Air Force has dispersed the San Andrés column,' Escofet informs.

'What about the Ramblas?' asks García Oliver.

'Clear.'

'Then nothing is lost.'

'Who controls the Telephone Exchange?' asks Durruti.

'We do, but I'm not sure what's happening. We can't get through.'

'Until after,' finishes Durruti, putting a certain stress on 'after'.

Down below, in a car, sits Ascaso.

'Get everyone you can together in the Plaza de la Constitución, within a quarter of an hour,' says García Oliver. 'Send someone back to Pueblo Nuevo to tell González Cantos that with the comrades, plus those from the docks, he's to see what he can do with Icaria. Let's go!'

They climb aboard the car, which drives on. García Oliver keeps talking as they turn into the Layetana and Jaime I.

'As always, they've conceived it as a purely military operation, without considering the revolutionary topography of Barcelona. And that will be their undoing. Every revolutionary movement in Barcelona has begun and developed in the Fifth District. As long as we hold that, nothing is lost. They are acting on the orders they receive from the Captaincy. If we cut that off from the barracks and the detachments, the day is ours; we can then attack their strongholds, without communications or leadership. And isolate them.'

'Telephones?' inquires Ascaso.

'Smashed. It's obvious: they're converging on the harbour, the Captaincy, Atarazanas, etcetera. They can't slip through and link up on the left-hand side: they'd have to pass right in front of the Interior Ministry. That's not on. It seems they haven't even tried through the middle. To them the Ramblas are taboo.'

'Traditionalist fools. They want to surround the city centre.'

'It's clear as day. So the only line of communication left to them is the Parallel. Let's get going!'

In the Plaza de la Constitución there are three hundred men; they unload the machine gun, the three sub-machine guns, the thirty Winchesters. García Oliver calls the leaders together:

'Divide into three: one group to go to the Schilling armoury, another to Laplana, and the rest with me to Beristain. Meet up again at the corner of the Ramblas.'

Locks burst, doors bulge; the three hundred emerge once more, the lucky ones with shotguns, some with collector's pieces, most with pistols of variable calibre and no ammunition, others just with cartridge belts. García Oliver assembles them at the entrance to the Ramblas.

'One hundred of you stay here with Durruti, a hundred with Ascaso, the rest with me. You, Durruti, divide up your

men: fifty down towards Atarazanas to stop them coming
up this way; I don't think they'll try; fifty towards Plaza de
Cataluña, to stop them coming down. You, Ascaso, along
Conde del Asalto, towards the Parallel, to come out by the
power station; the rest, follow me.'

'Keep to the walls, and watch out for the roofs!'

García Oliver goes up as far as the Llano de la Boquería.
The clock on the corner of San Pablo has been hit: half past
eight for ever. Someone is firing out of a window, some from
roof terraces; the anarchists riposte, somewhat haphazardly,
from the street. The attackers smash shopfronts, the attacked
shatter apartment windows. First blood comes not from lead
but from glass.

Durruti and his men have reached the Plaza del Teatro; they
go round keeping tight in to the Principal Palace's walls.
Rebels in the Hotel Falcón opposite are free to take pot-shots
at them.

'Get back!' bellows the leader.

The men crowd into the entrance of the local cinema;
others from across the Rambla have already taken refuge in
doorways; they are carrying three wounded companions. On
the pavement, in front of those who brought him down, lies
a body.

'Stay where you are!' roars Durruti. And he goes, alone,
for the fallen comrade. He hears shots. Seven, five, six. 'How
bullets sing! That's a carbine.' A ricochet hits him. 'They can't
reach me with a pistol at that range. One man is not much
of a target. We'd have to go like a Sunday-school outing for

them to knock us over!' He returns without the fallen man – a bullet in the brain. He knows what he wanted to find out. He calls to the men across the way. He sends ten of them to Plaza del Rey via Escudillers:

'Soon as you're in Plaza del Teatro, keep to the wall of the hotel and go on in. They can't see you or get at you. There aren't more than six or seven of them.' (At least fifteen, he thinks.) 'They're in the rooms on the top floor, to the left, and on the roof. As soon as you reach the staircase, fire up the well; then we'll come across the square. It should all be over in five minutes.'

And it is. And those without pistols now have them. Durruti stations his men to the left and right of the entrance to the Ramblas, ten in Casa Juan, five on the balconies of an adjoining brothel, five more in another, one floor higher; ten more posted up on the roofs; the rest he keeps with him, in the street. Those in the buildings pile up cushions against the windows. The whores are screaming, huddled together inside. The men don't even see them. Death is too close, and victory within reach.

'Today is the day after tomorrow,' thinks a resident of the Parallel. Shots are heard towards Atarazanas. 'Ascaso's people.' All those men jostling together there are fighters from other times: men who run and hide after emptying the chamber. Months, years waiting for this moment to fire, properly esconced in a corner. Firing as they please. Not only in their own right; for others, too. Giving their hand a treat; fighting openly. They shoot for the joy of shooting, as if the lead they are sending carried, aflame, the furious right to live of Barcelona's enslaved humanity. They feel at one: the wounded and the dead don't count; because they are not themselves, but their union, their relation, their desire, palpable in their hands, in their chins; above all in their eyes, in their glistening skin, weary after three or four sleepless nights. The bullets stand in for sleep, the explosions for night and silence. Each has his life in his hands, looks at it, notes it, knows what he is living for. They are, they exist; they are not X or Y; they are all one; linked, united in this glorious sunny morning by the shots that now echo all around.

'This is the life!' one of them says to Durruti.

And another: 'Heaven!'

Rafael Serrador, from a doorway, notes this overflowing. 'It's not learning that's drummed in the hard way...' No one took any notice of him, no one looked at him, though they knew him, though someone might have clapped his shoulder as if to say, 'Good, you're here: here we are!'

No one down the middle of the Rambla, no one on the pavements down the side, no one in the paved gutters. Only bullets come and go. Rafael Serrador, arms folded, sees men's faces and their tongues of fire. 'What's drummed in the hard way is life.' He is overawed, imagining the entire city violating the skies, frightful phallus, savage fist on high and blood in the air.

A head looks out over a balcony and shouts:

'How's that for a labour tribunal!'

Serrador remembered something González Cantos had said:

'There is no other justice but ours, only cowards need arbitration boards, tribunals, all that palaver! And then those same people talk of dying for one's country? What's it to be?'

'Are you asleep?' someone asks as he goes past. Men were arriving from all over the disembowelled city. Rafael Serrador envies those who are shooting. He remembers the Castellón train, Domingo Ortega's low pass. He feels in the air – in life? – something he'd never suspected it had: meaning. 'To live without meaning. Blind, deaf, dumb. These people have a reason for living. They are fighting with good reason, they have a reason to be. For the first time I see people living in movement: dying on the horns of the bull. Hurling themselves between the horns. This thing that was mine alone, feeling, is now an external thing which links one to another, each with all. He remembers a phrase of Lledó's, which he'd forgotten: 'When a man thinks by allowing himself to be led entirely by his feelings, his intuition or his fantasy, he is alone, completely alone.' These men were guided by their reason. To be alone is to be by oneself. To be in agreement with oneself is to be alone. Solitary inhabitant of my own desert. He remembers the hall in the Captaincy, and how each man there seemed locked within himself. Serrador realizes that he is not in agreement with himself. And that it's not these men who interest him, nor himself, but the relationships of men among themselves: fraternity.

All this he thinks without thinking it: like air, like the sea breeze reaching his hidden post from across Atarazanas: with a flutter of finches, fresh clean air, the colour of salt, the feel of water: parted by bullets that fly whistling by.

For the first time Rafael López Serrador sees himself from the outside. And he feels like a man. 'Up until now I've been like the arch of a theatre. The greatness of the bull comes from its incommunication, its animality. What an animal, what a stupid brute I've been! And how the world gleams! To think with reason and not with feelings. What a stupendous animal I've been! It's not a question of agreeing with people, but of wanting something. I've never wanted anything, just let myself be carried along. My loneliness was my own feelings. I've lived inside myself, thinking that the world was a tangle of alien fences. And these men are here, together, moved by one single feeling, feeling themselves to be men. And for that reason, not caring about death. Then reality exists; I can touch it: I am touching it.' And slowly, carefully, Serrador stretches out his hand and caresses the stonework around the dark doorway to the brothel. The Chauffeur comes careering past. Shirt-front undone, black shadow over his vest, stained with sweat, a pistol stuck in a jockstrap instead of a holster, matted hair, with four days' stubble, a gashed arm, half a cigar in his mouth and that absent look, the look they all have, in his eyes. Serrador blocks his path to shake his hand, damp, sticky and cold with sweat.

'All right, all right!' says the lame meteorite. 'The time has come, but let's not get carried away . . . Now you'll see what's what!'

('These men have faith in one another. Is that fraternity? It doesn't matter to them whether I exist or not, whether you exist or not; what matters is what unites them, what separates us, if you like: a certain human air, confidence in death and disregard for pity. What will remain when the enthusiasm wanes? Memory. In effect, with this memory and that hope, perhaps one can live.')

Bullets whine.

'Get back or you'll be hit by a rebound!' they shout from the other side of the street. ('I've discovered a life.' And he looks at the palm of his hand.)

'Yes, mate,' shouts a man as he leaps outside, hard on his heels. 'If it comes with a beard, it's San Antón, and if without it's the Immaculate Conception!'

García Oliver and his men have reached the end of the Calle de San Pablo without problems. They know every corner, every shop. Two hundred metres away in front of them, the Parallel; on the pavement outside the Moulin Rouge, a platoon of twenty soldiers with their officers. García Oliver sends fifteen men via the Teatro Olimpia to cut off a possible retreat by the squad towards the bulk of their column; he sends a similar number to the left under cover of the Teatro Español, to prevent their march to the harbour.

'When we start up the machine gun, fire away for all you're worth.'

He goes into the Bar Chicago, opposite, and on its upper floor sets up the machine gun. The shock produces a natural reaction in the soldiers: they scarper back into the little theatre at their rear. The rebels imagine, as they are caught in a crossfire, that the attackers are many more than they are: they surrender after half an hour, waving a dancer's costume which they must have taken at random from some dressing-room. The soldiers come down with their fists in the air. Three without jackets: the officers. Gordo and Manzana, victors at Santa Madrona, arrive at that moment with the two machine guns captured there. García Oliver dispatches one to Durruti; with the other two and his swollen ranks he advances up the Rondas, step by step, towards the University.

Captaincy, Military Governorship, Atarazanas, Customs House – the head of the rebellion – all cut off from their forces.

'We've taken Barcelona with a hundred men and a machine gun.'

'Flattened them.'

And indeed, tracing a straight line from Montjuich to Badalona, everything is in the hands of the government.

'Right, let's take it one step at a time,' says the thin, hard, but really quite small, man of the FAI.

Down along the Paseo de Gracia march the rebel troops.

Durruti is in España's office.

'I've got thousands of men and no weapons! I want you to give them to me.'

The Interior Minister replies deliberately and emphatically:

'I don't need you.'

'You put too much trust in the armed forces.'

'That's up to me. I can put the rebellion down entirely on my own.'

'Listen, if they make it to Atarazanas . . .'

'Don't worry about it.'

Durruti heads back towards the Ramblas.

'What's up?'

The guard is panting, sweat runs down his forehead.

'I don't know how they got through, but they're in Plaza de Cataluña. They've taken the Colón and the Telephone Exchange.'

'The telephones?'

'Yes. The lieutenant in charge of our force has gone over to them. Those in Plaza de la Universidad have gone into the Patria Restaurant and adjoining houses.'

'Right.'

'At your orders!'

Companys is sitting in a corner.

'If they manage to make contact with the Captaincy,' says Escofet, 'it's going to be tough.'

'Yes,' says the President, 'very tough.'

It is a quarter to eleven.

Durruti gathers together two hundred men.

'They won't give us the weapons. We're going to where they are: the Artillery Depot.'

Using the only telephone still functioning in Barcelona, General Llano de la Encomienda calls the Interior Minister.

'I'm being fired on, minister!'

'Come over here, then, general.'

'Can't. I'm trapped in my quarters. Give the appropriate orders for them to stop shooting.'

'I'm very sorry, general.'

España turns to Lieutenant-Colonel Escobar:

'They've reached Plaza de Cataluña, they're occupying the Hotel Colón and the Telephone Exchange. Get them out of there!'

Up the Vía Layetana march the Civil Guard, in two columns of five hundred men, keeping close to the walls; up the middle of the street strides Lieutenant-Colonel Escobar, he whose sister is a nun.

From the balcony of the Public Order offices, Luis Companys watches them arrive: light almond uniforms, black boots, shiny black three-cornered hats, rifles at the ready, fingers on the trigger. Gunfire all around the city and Spain's finest moving up from the harbour towards the rebels along the solitary fearful street. On whose side are these hard men? There is no telephone. España has been informed that two hundred metres further up, in Plaza de Cataluña, are the rebels, controlling most of the Telephone Exchange, masters of the Hotel Colón, and – Paseo de Gracia?

The troops move slowly forward, with their lieutenant-colonel in the middle. The fate of Catalonia ... Their commander has now caught sight of the President of the Generalitat, springs to attention and salutes, and the Spanish Civil Guard marches on.

Companys looks at Escofet and says nothing.

Outside the barracks, fifty thousand men hungry for rifles. From roof to street, from street to roof, a trelliswork of shots fired just for the sake of it. A column of smoke starts to rise above the city.

'It must be along the Diagonal,' says one small boy to another.

'Yes, let's go.'

And they set off, running towards the fire.

The pigeons fly high above Plaza de Cataluña. In the sandpit in the centre, two dead horses and another kicking the air ... Should anyone be counting, there are twenty dead bodies distributed pretty much everywhere, watched over by the bullets. When the Civil Guard arrives, only the most determined continue to fire. Five minutes to take the Colón. Not even that for the Telephone Exchange. Out from the hotel, looking small in his shirt-sleeves, on the arm of a youth, comes a bald figure with a short beard, fist on high: Don Jacinto Benavente, Nobel Prize for Literature.

Lledó, up in his gallery, sits chatting to a friend and neighbour, an art teacher at the Instituto Balmes.

'Don't give it too much thought. Half these people running about with guns don't know what they're fighting for. I, who do know, am staying indoors. If that's not what you call cowardly ... And yet I don't mind dying.'

'Yes, you do.'

'Possibly. If you prefer, I *believe* that I don't mind dying. But these people scorn death. The difference is fundamental. I won't answer for tomorrow, but today, in the intoxication of revolution, they are heroes. I was reading Vauvenargues last night –'

'You were reading Vauvenargues last night?'

'Yes, my dear chap, and I offer that as further proof of pusillanimity.'

'And what did our friend Vauvenargues, whom I do not have the pleasure of knowing, although I've heard the name, say?'

'"Ce n'est pas à porter la faim et la misère chez les étrangers qu'un héros attach la gloire, mais à les souffrir pour l'état; ce n'est pas à donner la mort mais à la braver." These people you can hear are mostly just fighting for the sake of it. Because their bodies and their blood demand it. They hunger for glory. The janitor just told me that this morning some group or other broke through a barricade defended by I don't know how many men, a large number anyway, on the Parallel. And that the attackers were no more than a hundred. We Spaniards have never known how to be many. And Barcelona is not the Amazon. It's how good people are that counts, not how many.'

'Yes, and the part is equal to the whole.'

'I'm delighted to hear that from a professor of art. Anyway, when there are a lot of us no one can abide us. We always tend towards fractions.'

'And factions.'

'Pleasure lies in the fragments, the sections. Everything Spanish is out of proportion, like its writers. We always end up in sections. Yes, in sections and selections. Cut to pieces.'

They move towards the balcony doors. Smoke rises slowly.

'They want to live the revolution and die. The communists are probably right. But I, my dear draughtsman, and don't you forget it, I, a coward incapable of shaking off the debris that envelops me . . .'

The men accompanying García Oliver on the Ronda de San Antonio have grown in numbers; some wearing army helmets at an angle, or on the back of their heads; others, new belts. They are all smiling without knowing it. They push on.

On reaching the Calle de Muntaner, they fall like flies; flow back like spilled water towards the doorways. The city clocks, one after another, strike twelve.

A servant in a doorway, saucepan of milk in her hand, asks: 'But what's going on?'

THREE

Afternoon and Evening

The telephone rings in the office of the Interior Ministry.

'I should like to speak to General Aranguren.'

The receiver is handed to the commander of the Civil Guard.

'Colonel Moxó here, on behalf of General Goded, to see if we can resolve this.'

'The minister is here, you can speak to him.'

The telephone at the other end hangs up without further ado.

For two hours the insurrectionaries hold out in the Patria restaurant. After this time, the troops surrender. Some officers continue shooting from the private rooms. Only snipers remain in the centre of Barcelona.

On Avenida Icaria the dockworkers and the volunteers from Pueblo Nuevo, under González Cantos, open fire on the barracks. Those in charge meet in the hallway of a jute factory to deliberate.

'We need to go in through the harbour. It's pointless to try anywhere else. And in front of the harbour they have two well-defended machine guns. They can't come out, but we can't get in. And there are guns and cannon inside. The cannon are useless to them. What can they fire them at? But for us, they're the key. No building can withstand them. For them, to bomb the city would be as daft as firing into the sea. We've got to go in and get them. But how?'

'We have twenty dead and more than fifty wounded.'

The avenue is wide, and the machine guns rake it right across.

'And they're good shots.'

'Yes, officers and gentlemen of the Falange.'

'We need to make a barricade and keep pushing it forward, to gain ground.'

'The trouble is, there are no houses overlooking it.'

'Right, then, if you've no better ideas! We could build them, dammit!'

Cecilio Puche, a dockyard foreman, utters an oath and explains:

'In the docks they've just unloaded bales of paper for *La Veu de Catalunya*. How about that for a trench for four pairs of monkeys!' (The *Veu* is the newspaper of the Lliga.) He belts out the appropriate orders.

'Fetch the barrows as well!' Puche exults.

In the centre of the avenue a dead body lies sprawled; a little to the right, a horse in the same condition; between the two, a Mauser. Those without weapons look at it from doorways and corners, but no one dares: two hundred metres away are the fascist machine guns, which haven't jammed. At the entrance to the street, the workers place themselves a hair's-breadth away from the path of the bullets. The corners of the buildings are just bare brick and stone; bits of plaster and splinters from the edges cover the ground. New arrivals join the back of the column, equipped with the spoils from other barracks.

'Don't push!'

The feet of the attackers mark the trajectory of the projectiles.

Rafael Serrador watches all this with his hands in his pockets. No one says a word. Someone pushes out a cap on the end of a stick. Ten centimetres from the corner, a volley of bullets whistles by. It's as if the streets were made for battle, and men for fighting. From time to time a boy decides to chance his arm and empty his gun at random. An old man rests his double-barrelled shotgun against the wall; he sits on the floor, back to the wall, brings out a lunchbox and opens it; out comes a fine-looking tortilla and a big lump of bread, wrapped in newspaper.

'Let's have a bit!' someone pipes up.

'Don't be stupid, soon we'll all be dining at the Ritz,' says another.

A young man Rafael knows from the Victoria goes and sits down next to the old boy. He answers to the name of Tramp. Tall, good-looking, olive skin, long hair, sunken cheeks and rough bristles, very white teeth between fine pale lips, wearing a crumpled but well-cut suit, fraying at the cuffs and turn-ups. He sees Serrador and greets him as usual with a cold:

'Hi!'

'What are you doing here?'

'What's it look like? Watching.'

From Santa Rita prison, Madrid, as he himself says, he likes his words dry and clipped.

'Look, chum' – he used to dispense his opinions in taverns and on benches, with a patronizing air – 'everybody's always someone else's bourgeois. Well, not me. I don't want to be anyone's bourgeois. Every man-jack lives off someone else's sweat. Not me. And to go that road, there are no two ways about it, only one: to do nothing. But nothing, do you hear? Nothing. Neither work nor think. Just live, what's called living, and that's it: take the sun; eat if anyone'll give you anything, and sleep. Full stop! No one can take the sun and your sleep away from you. Now, as to eating . . .' He stared at his neighbour's tortilla.

As a child he'd been sent to a college out by the Escorial, because his family was quite well off; right from the start he refused to study. 'They taught me to read behind my back, because if I'd cottoned on . . .! The trouble is, you can't unlearn it. I go mad when I read a sign and don't realize I'm doing it.'

He ran away at the age of ten with a schoolfriend slightly older than himself; chance put them on the train to La Coruña. Halfway there they were discovered, under a seat, by an Englishwoman nervous about bandits, and the inspector handed them over to the Civil Guard. These worthies, faithful to tradition, administered a thorough thrashing, despite the shrieks of our hero at the top of his voice:

'My uncle is a captain! My uncle is Captain Fuentes!'

They took them to the officer in question, just in case; he was stationed in Madrid. The boy complained of the beating: the evil uncle congratulated his subordinates and returned the stowaways to their respective homes. Our lad's mother was a frivolous woman, free with her favours, fond of flirting and courtships: involved at that time with a nosey good-for-nothing irritated by the boy's impudent gaze. One afternoon when the child caught some particularly moist glances, he went for a frog, imprisoned for this very purpose, and carefully introduced it into the ample maternal bed. They held their peace, but sent him back to school. There the boys were watched over at night by an effeminate-looking monk, who soon showed certain preferences for our friend. He, knowing a thing or two by now, allowed his chin to be chucked, and became the preacher's pet; until one day the holy brother tried to get repayment for his good deeds with something more than squeezes. That famous evening the lad stuck a fork in the monk's left nipple. The pederast said nothing, but our young fellow could not bear his sad, gormless gaze of gentle reproach, and three days after that almost homicidal act he set off to the station once more. His first adventure had taught him to mistrust the upper classes, so this time he chose a third-class seat to hide beneath. He reached Gijón. He discovered the sea, the port, a craving for food. He was shocked to see women smoking pipes and that world of damp rubber: mists, drizzle, wet winds, fog. He roamed the docks, befriended a cabin boy: the thing was to embark, never mind where to. To survive he wound sails, pulled in nets, helped to carry the sardine catch to the sheds. The civil guards caught him sitting on the jetty. Stubborn as a mule, he came out with the same old tale: 'My uncle is a captain', this time to better effect. The pair thought it might well be true, and as he was a missing person they contented themselves with handcuffing him. They went from the North Station to see the famous uncle, and found him, but he, weary of his nephew, denied him. At which point they turned nasty:

'Let him have it, so he remembers who his uncle is!' And let him have it they did. 'I've been thrashed plenty in this life, but never again like that . . . I still have the weals!'

They sent him to Santa Rita:

'The happiest years of my life. I lazed about no end, spent most of the time in a cell, for doing absolutely *nothing*. Then my mother bought me a perfumery to keep me occupied. After four days I'd given away all the stock. It was in Argüelles; I expect they still remember. There were some fantastic fights, husbands suspecting affairs . . .

'I'm a gentleman through and through; that's right, my boy, nothing less than a gent. As posh as they come. So what if I'm a tramp as well? Do I bother anyone? Have I done anything wrong? So what if I don't work? Proud of it! I eat a little less than other people, no complaints. I can't see how anyone can live by exploiting their fellows, nor how those who are exploited can bear to live. It's a lack of human dignity. Let them do as I do: take it easy! I neither give orders nor take them: I support myself.'

'But what about the rest of the world,' his audience objects.

'The world? That it's about to go under, you mean? Well, bon voyage!'

The tramp gazed at the tortilla and its fortunate possessor.

'I haven't eaten for two days, comrade . . .'

The old man looked at him.

'Have you earned it?'

'What do you mean? I never earn anything. Some hopes!'

'But have you sung for your supper?'

'Why should I?'

'Screw me, you seem 'alf-daft!'

The old man's name is Fermín. He is unshaven, with hollow weatherbeaten cheeks, wearing a thick cloth cap despite the intense heat, pink vest, corduroy trousers, sandals; a gipsy from Pueblo Seco, on the slopes of Montjuich.

'Just one lump, man!'

The Romany with the tortilla looks at him with twinkling eyes:

'Fetch!' he says with his mouth full and pointing to the corpse, the horse and the rifle.

There is now a swarm of flies around the dead man's head, and a black stain is spreading through the dust, beneath the face turned to the ground.

'Fetch us that broom, and we'll have us a party!'

Everyone has turned to listen. The Tramp rubs his chin.

'Deal or not?' taunts the gipsy.

'No time like the present!'

Our man gets up, stops a moment at the corner, takes a look and takes the leap. They fire on him, the daredevil falls behind the horse as cover. Has he been hit?

'No,' the old man assures them, 'don't wet yourselves.'

Now he gets up from behind the horse and reaches for the Mauser, crouches, picks it up and dashes back the ten metres separating him from the alleyway, without anyone firing until it's too late. He wipes his knees earnestly.

'They must have thought you'd come out of the mangy nag's entrails!'

He gives the old braggart the gun, and starts to eat with great restraint.

'You can keep the stick,' Fermín says, meaning the rifle.

'Me? Come off it, what do you take me for?'

Rafael can't keep still, takes a walk round the block. The bales of paper start to arrive from the docks, carried on carts. First they pile them up in the alleyway. All the dockers are as one in the sweat that darkens their vests and glistens on their bare chests.

'Why was I going to fight these men, when they're the ones who want something? They don't want the rich in charge, even if the world collapses. Isn't that enough? They think they'll achieve it tomorrow. That was yesterday, and today is tomorrow. The Salomars love yesterday, death and cenotaphs. When you're alone, you like death, you cling to memory. You can't help it. But whatever these people are doing, they're doing it to live, and that's what saves them. It's not things in themselves that matter, but why they're done. Espinosa would say that what's important is to do the things that need doing and . . . what am I trying to convince myself of?'

'Hey, you, flyblow, lend us a hand!'

They mean him; with the bales. First they line them all up along the wall of the jute factory, which is at right angles to the avenue. Then they start to push them out into the centre of the street dominated by the rebels who, when they see all that bulk appear, without realizing what it is, shower it with bullets. No projectile can pierce a roll of newsprint. It wasn't all plain sailing; sometimes the bales turned off course and then had to be righted at the risk of offering a target. It took an hour to set them up in place across the avenue. There was room for thirty bobbins: two men slightly wounded. The ardour of the workers, boosted by the arrival of a company of assault guards, was prodigious.

'New arms, new life!' crowed González Cantos.

And the sun, high above them, melting everything.

'Three men per roll,' decreed González Cantos. 'Two armed men behind each, from among those with rifles. Hi there!' he said to Rafael when he noticed him. He hadn't seen him since he'd thrown him out of the bar with a flea in his ear. 'Start pushing there. And you, and you.'

It's a case of shoring it up, taking the strain, pushing in a straight line without straying, under pain of getting shot. ('What does that roll of paper weigh?') Strung out across the street they look like a giant steamroller. From the North Station, locomotive whistles: the general strike was not declared at the same time throughout Catalonia, and some trains are still coming in. The passengers mill about on the platform and around the ticket office. Windows shatter.

'This is the tops!' Heads bowed, arms outstretched, hands at full spread, all their strength concentrated upon their palms.

'This ain't lending a hand, it's giving both of them!' says a wit.

Shoulders are the thing, and placing your feet squarely. Serrador feels like an Atlas. 'Thinking is a grey and gloomy business, still and melancholy, a memory. Family memories. Push, load, pull, carry, move, force: that's living. Thinking is defending yourself against life and death. There's no better way to forget than by doing things, creating movement, pushing.' If the one to the right can't push as hard as the one to the left, the one in the middle can make up. The impact of the bullets ripping into the paper is not noticed; a slight breeze, perhaps, as a machine-gun volley drills right across it; when the holes come round to your hand, a metre further on, they're still hot.

The rebels have no upper floor or roof terrace from which to halt the advance of this fantastic rolling dam. The walls which surround the barracks, too high, prevent it. The façade, riddled with holes, has been stripped bare. Rafael Serrador thinks of the fascists in front of him, seeing that great mass rolling forward like fate. They persist in firing. Serrador does not stop to think that he could be there opposite, that he should be there opposite; there's no room in his head. Someone is wounded in the hand, another in the foot and ankle; one man in the middle of the road is hit in the head, and twists in the air: the bale had rolled down into a depression, an unpredictable pothole, and as he tried to stop it the man had raised his head above the barricade. Amen. The avenue now slopes upwards slightly, one team can't cope and falls behind. One of the reels, suddenly, turns sideways, because the left-hand pusher strained too soon. Only eighty metres from the insurrectionaries, the brave man is left exposed. They spray bullets at him: but he stands firm, shielding his comrades with his body, giving them time to take cover. They abandon that improvized tank of wood and paper, lying on its side like the entrance to some dread cavern. Behind the barrier formed by the rest, more than a thousand men crawl along the road, protected by the extraordinary offensive parapet. In front go those who don't have weapons but can smell them in the barracks. From up above, God must be watching them, wriggling in the sunshine like lizards. If it weren't for the thunder of gunpowder, you would hear the sound of all those human bodies scraping against the stone.

'Now they're for it!'

Suddenly, at first no one knows from where, a radio speaker launches its blaring scratched voice: a waltz, then, only three seconds later, a *sardana*.

González Cantos roars, bellows, completely beside himself:

'Turn it off, for fuck's sake, turn it off!'

The music stops.

Some hand grenades have appeared. They must have been brought just now, because it's the last attackers who have them. They pass them to those ahead, without stopping from crawling.

'Pass it on, they're from Atarazanas!'

The grenades move forward like a tide, with the rumour about where they've come from. (False news: Atarazanas will not fall until next day.) When the grenades reach the front, the bobbins are only thirty metres from the fascist barricades.

'Stop! Stop!'

And they leap over the rampart. The boy who has gone ahead of Serrador curves backwards, grenade in his right hand, left elbow in the air; a girdle of blood stitched across him drains him of strength, he throws the pine cone in the air but his dead arm cannot propel it: the artefact explodes against the outer wall of the rebel stronghold. But twenty men have surged forwards, sucked in by the proximity of the enemy and impelled by their new weapon; they leave the paper wheels behind, run frenziedly to the attack, exchanging death for time. A hundred more follow. González Cantos is in a frenzy of his own:

'Wait, for fuck's sake. Wait, you stupid bastards! We hadn't lost a single man!'

But now the machine guns belong to the people. As the barracks door is broken down, the astounded officers surrender in the courtyard. The men fight to get close to and touch a battery of seven-and-a-halfs.

'This time we're going to win,' says González Cantos to Serrador. 'This is the one.'

He can hardly believe it himself, and to the surprise of those who know him begins to dance about like a savage, thumping his chest. Those who are not yelling embrace one another in tears:

'We've got cannons! We've got cannons!'

The assault troops attempt, politely, to move the people away from the artillery. An old man with long hair kisses the mouth of a cannon. No one pays any attention to the dead. A whole forest of rifles grows, the sharp teeth of the magazines in those starving hands.

Lieutenant Giménez Labrador, commander of the Assault Guard, inspects the cannon: only one is in a fit state to fire. Soldiers and workers push it outside. They fight over it. Every so often the carriage ploughs the ground, and brakes the march. The ammunition is carried by hand; one man holding a shell as if it were a baby, another with one under each arm, like elephant tusks.

'Durruti has taken the Artillery Stores!'

'That's where the grenades were from.'

Afternoon begins to mature into evening.

García Oliver walks down the Ramblas.

'It was a military coup, not a revolution. They've no-one with them! Clear as day! No-one! Fascism in Spain hasn't got a hope in hell!'

Captaincy, Military Governorship, Customs, Casa de Italia, Atarazanas: the decapitated head of the rebellion continues to hold out.

'Are they firing down Calle Ancha? No? Right: you, Ortega,

go and see Guarner; yes, the lieutenant-colonel. Don't make that face. Ask him for a tank of petrol. Got it? A tank with a hosepipe and everything. And fetch it round by Aviñó at the back of the Captaincy. And you' – he says to another – 'go for some bottles of flammables.'

'Give 'em a nice shower,' gloats somebody.

The cannon has reached Plaza Palacio. They go right round Siete Puertas and aim it at the Captaincy.

At four o'clock in the afternoon, General Goded calls the Interior Minister.

'Listen,' comes the reply, 'either fight or surrender!'

'All right, it's hopeless. But send the Civil Guard for me.'

Commander Pérez Farrás, at the head of the Civil Guard, goes to fetch General Goded. They escort him to the Generalitat. All it had taken was two shells and a few splinters dislodged from the façade. García Oliver arrives with the petrol, but with no tank, just drums, and late. The local residents, appearing at doorways and on balconies, share it out among themselves. People pour into the Captaincy building. Rafael Serrador sees Luis Salomar, watches him emerging from the crowd, against the current, naked from the waist up, gesticulating with the rest. He watches him slip away unnoticed.

Shivers of triumph run through the city, cars and trucks full of workers, men and women, soldiers with their fists in the air, cheering. There are no trams – the electricity's down – and no petrol, the bars are closed, dead horses litter the Plaza de Cataluña. But the air has turned to rejoicing. Ambulances come and go, the only bells in the city. Churches begin to burn.

'What do you expect!' someone says. 'They're easier to see than the banks, and they burn better!'

Not one shop looted, not one hold-up, not one food store attacked, not one outrage in all the delirious city.

Near the harbour, in the vicinity of the buildings still holding out, a few bars and cafés have opened and people are quaffing whatever they can lay their hands on.

A ragged peasant searches stubbornly for 'the people in charge'. He finds his way eventually to Durruti.

'What do you want?'

'A chit so they'll give me a cow back in the village.'

He gives him one.

Some little distance away, in what until yesterday was a dance-hall for nobs, a crowd of people drink sherry and champagne. The wireless is on. For a quarter of an hour Goded's surrender speech has been repeated. Now it is being chorused.

'They might just as well have put on Companys' speech from 1934,' someone says. 'Seems like those who lose and don't know how to die, don't have a lot of imagination either.'

'You can't die on two different roads,' someone replies.

'There's a name for one who plays and loses, and then doesn't pay up, as you well know.'

'You're a bourgeois and a counter-revolutionary. Drink?'

España rants away on the telephone, now reconnected.

'Guarner's to take charge of all the barracks! Guarner's to take charge of all the barracks!'

'What for? Those that have been captured are in the hands of the people. The rest . . .'

'Assemble the troops.'

'What troops?'

'The Civil Guard, the Assault Guard . . .'

'No one can find them. They've merged with the people. The formations have broken up. They've given their jacket to one, their helmet to another. Who can say where the tricorns have gone? Once they'd split into groups of two or three hundred, they became dispersed. By the time they started to wake up, there were only the people.'

'Who's going to keep order?'

'There are thirty thousand rifles in the streets.'

'Who's in charge of them?'

'They are, the people! On top of that, Guarner has another six or seven thousand.'

'*Presidente*, we have defeated the rebellion. And we don't know what still may happen. As the person responsible for public order, as the minister of the interior, I resign.'

'Have you no confidence in the people?'

'That's not the issue, *señor presidente*. I repeat my resignation.'

'And I do not accept it.'

'The big question now is Zaragoza,' says Durruti.

'Mallorca,' is the response from the Generalitat.

'We shall see.'

In the Calle del Este, night creeps from the cobbles towards the roofs. Rafael Serrador approaches a group hotly engaged in argument.

'I say no! It's a disgrace!'

'What's going on?'

'They've caught someone from Atarazanas.'

'A Falangist.'

'Why haven't they drilled him?'

'This feller wants him to talk first. Says he must know where their files are.'

'What do I care!' snaps a giant with a torn shirt and grimy arms. 'I don't give a damn if he knows where the crown jewels are! Have a bit of respect, you bastards! Is that what the revolution's for? To make prisoners sing, just like the police do? Who do you take us for? We respect the rights of individuals. What did he say? That he doesn't know anything? Then either he doesn't know or he doesn't want to tell us! He's within his rights. Everyone's free to do what they want.'

The prisoner is a pathetic, down-at-heel squirt, with dark rings of terror round his eyes.

'Human dignity – d'ya hear? – dignity! We're fighting against the police, against beatings, against papers, against contracts, against bribery. And you want to pump someone, make a prisoner sing? He's doomed? Then let him die! But decently, without squawking.'

He takes a pistol, a massive Colt, and blows the wretch's brains out.

'There, now he can see how libertarian we are!'

The night fell; the shooting rose.

CULMINATION

ONE

Night

There are no electric lights in Barcelona. Nor a moon. Only gunfire and blazing churches. Crowds in the streets move from one fire to another. The firemen tried to go out, but the people cut the hoses. The churches burn, but not the Cathedral, nor the monastery of Pedralbes. Gothic buildings are not to be burned: this is the only order the people take note of. Barcelona in darkness but with enough churches to be able to walk round the city, with the spectacle of its dead horses and flashes of gunfire from the fascists safely installed behind their balconies and murdering with impunity. A million inhabitants whose only light is a few gigantic torches. All the churches look like the Sagrada Familia now, and Barcelona smells of bonfires. Long branches, thick tongues of sparks against the blue, black night; and the smoke against the stars. People move quietly from one place to another, with their tragic sense of life in their pockets, hoping for a miracle; realizing that a new world is being born, one which may die in its infancy, as so often before in this very same bed; but they can all smell new birth; and, suspecting it, no one says anything; all that's to be heard is the crackling of fire. Fire rising to the skies and the black city with its wounded in the doorways and killers on the roofs. You can see the belly of the smoke in the light of the flames, but not its shoulders or its crest.

Rafael Serrador, leaning against a lamp-post, watches the Church of El Carmen blaze. He can't work out, in this new life of his, why they are destroying and burning, why they don't keep it for themselves. The flames pain him. By now he has asked twenty men why they are setting fire to things, and they have all shrugged their shoulders. And yet something drives them on.

He sees an old man in a doorway whom he thinks he recognizes, watching the statues being carried out and fed to a great ceremonial pyre; he follows him with his eye, doesn't lose sight of him, and approaches.

'Why are they burning all this?'

The old man peers at him and says confidentially:

'Shhh! You must always begin with the choir. Always.'

'Why?'

'It's the nub!' And, staring him in the face: 'If not, they could come back and sit there again.'

The man leads Serrador up the Ramblas:

'Come on.' He takes him up to the roof of the *Las Noticias* building.

From there they can make out ten or twelve fires.

'See, boy? Every so often you need to shake out the bugs and disinfect the environment. I was a pupil at Ferrer's school, you know? Now there was a man! They knew what they were doing when they executed him. This will be as much of a shindig as that was. Do you think they're burning things just for the sake of it? Oh no! You kill what you hate. You burn to purify and save life; to frighten off evil spirits, and restore the earth. In this world there are only two pure and beautiful

238

things: fire and nudity. Art? Tricks and stories. I should know! I make sixteenth-century virgins. The bourgeoisie and the communists think we burn to destroy, and rob to make ourselves rich. When a child is naughty here, they say to him: you're worse than Ravachol. Swine! That Ravachol business is because of those trams in Valencia that were always coming off the rails, and killed a few people. It has nothing to do with this. We burn to save life and make a clean sweep; and when we've robbed it's been in order to live. I know I don't know who you are, but I don't care either.'

The old man was completely overcome, and staring over the city, he began to whimper and snivel: 'Ferrer was a saint! Ferrer was a saint!' Suddenly he turned sharply back to Serrador and snapped:

'Because if we don't burn them they'll come back!'

'Who will?'

'Priests and devils.'

Rafael went back down to the port. He went as far as the Buena Sombra club, now converted into the headquarters for the siege of Atarazanas. There was an unholy racket going on. He sat in a corner, beside a second-hand bookseller and a man who sold Protestant bibles.

'Look here,' said the older man, 'it couldn't be simpler. Over here are them as don't believe in God, and over there are them as do. End of story. No need to say more. When the priests are all gone there'll be no more rich folks.'

'Listen, Ambrosio,' said Serrador, 'I'm not sure you haven't got it the wrong way round.'

'Who asked you, brat! On this side, nothingness, on that side, God. Tremendous!' (This was his pet word.) 'Tremendous! Of course, the joke is that for those of us who've sniffed out the truth, it's a case of nothing fighting nothing, but that's only for a select few.'

'Right,' said the bible salesman, 'they've been trying to smash our heads in for centuries in the name of God.'

'And they're not done yet, not by a long chalk!'

'I think,' said Serrador, 'that they believe in what they own, and that you're the one who believes in God.'

'Tremendous, young squirt, tremendous! As if you could teach me anything. We believe in mankind.'

'It's the same thing,' said Rafael, indulgently.

'How can it be the same? They believe in God because they're afraid of man, and God is a good standby.'

Rafael asks the Protestant propagandist:

'How come you sell bibles, being an atheist?'

'If I believed in God, I'd have to give them away! Not even He can put one over on me,' he replies with a wink, showing gums with no more teeth than one incisor, half yellow and half grey.

'I wrote a book,' rejoins the bookseller, 'in which I demonstrate that all calamities derive from the belief in God. More than two hundred quotations, and a prologue by Count Tolstoy.'

'Did he send it to you?'

'I took a cutting!'

The club can hardly cope with the darkness, despite the two or three dozen candles dotted around tables, counter and stage. The passage to the cellar was clear, and the bass drum sat on the floor with a candle on top.

Around a table several men from the FAI are arguing.

'The city's ours from top to bottom.'

'And the Esquerra?'

'Where would the Esquerra be without us? We saw that two years ago.'

'And the UGT?'

'That's another matter. But don't let's get off the point, they're nothing here, nothing! Here we're in charge. And in Zaragoza, and in Seville. And in Valencia, with a bit of luck. As for Madrid and Bilbao, we'll have to wait and see.'

'Do you think we can take power directly?'

'That's a matter for the Committee. Probably not. It's not 'our' revolution: it belongs to the right. They asked for it and they got it! But for that very reason we have to keep up our republican appearances. The hour has come to safeguard liberal democratic essences. "*Allons, enfants de la Patri-i-e . . .*"

'Stop horsing around!'

'Yes, mate, long live the Constitution!'

'What's the latest from Zaragoza?'

'Nothing. I always said that the general secretary of the Federation . . .'

'Apparently they're starting to shoot people there.'

'Say what you like, if it hadn't been for the Civil Guard and the Assault Guard, there's no knowing where we'd be right now.'

'Or where they'd be without us . . .'

'That's another matter. But let's see what the Confederation will do in Zaragoza and Seville.'

'It will depend to some extent on the governors.'

'Hush, man!' said a Valencian in the darkness. 'We've all fought for the revolution, and outside there are still barracks to be taken.'

'True enough. Today the civil guards were with us, but tomorrow? They need to be disbanded, right away.'

In another club, that of the PSUC, Vidiella and Comorera were similarly inclined.

'We've got to set up worker-peasant committees.'

Companys, after consulting with all parties, sets up the Central Committee for Militias.

'This is the downfall of Republican legality!' shouts an important official of the Lliga in the glorious patio of the Generalitat. 'It's creating revolutionary power by decree!'

'And just who asked for that, monkey-face?' sneers a passing orderly.

The reddish columns of billowing smoke continue to rise up to the dark sky, spattered with brilliant embers.

Rafael Serrador wanders the streets, bumping into people and feeling the links that unite him with other men, as though caught in a net of which he is one of the meshes, one of the threads of the night. A man strides stark naked through Plaza del Pino, shouting: 'Long live Herr Kneipp! Long live Herr Kneipp!'

A world overflowing, beside itself, without direction. Leaning against a drainpipe, Rafael Serrador thinks about water, wild water, savagely charging, swift, insistent, irresistible: like a fire bull, a rainbow of fire, above the triumphant city.

TWO

Death

For those who may have taken an interest, if I may presume so much, in the characters both large and small of this true-to-life and scarcely amusing gallery, I give below, to save pages, the list of their fates as I have been informed of them up to this day, August 17th, 1939.

RAFAEL LÓPEZ SERRADOR: dead, eight days after the last chapter, in the Barcelona Hospital, of typhoid.

DURRUTI: killed on the Huesca front, 8 July 1937.

ASCASO: killed outside Atarazanas, 20 July 1936.

THE ENGINEER: killed as a result of injuries sustained at Pinto. I don't know the date.

THE CHAUFFEUR: killed on the Talavera front, 4 October 1936.

JAIME FERNÁNDEZ: executed at Montjuich, 23 February 1937.

JOAQUÍN LLUCH: killed on the Ebro front, 20 November 1938.

AGUSTÍN ESPINOSA: killed on the Teruel front, 25 December 1937.

PEDRO RUBIO: killed in the Atarazanas barracks, 20 July 1936.

GENERAL ARANGUREN: executed by Franco on his entry into Barcelona.

LIEUTENANT-COLONEL ESCOBAR: executed by Franco on his entry into Barcelona.

COLONEL BROTONS: executed by Franco on his entry into Barcelona.

THE TEACHER who looked like Don Quixote: executed by Franco on his entry into Barcelona.

CECILIO PUCHE, foreman at the docks; the MOTHER and WIFE of MARIANO, the messenger in Don Enrique Barberá Comas's warehouse; DON PHOOEY and DESIDERIA, the Fat Man's wife: died as a result of different bombardments in Barcelona.

MANOLO, the civil guard: died on the Teruel front, 16 October 1937; SEVERIANO is safe, in Zaragoza.

In the camps at St. Cyprien and Argelès are THE OTHER ENGINEER; DON FÉLIX, of the white beard; MARIANO, the messenger; THE YOUNG MAN who liked to say 'If tomorrow was the day before yesterday'; THE PROTESTANT BIBLE SALESMAN; JOSÉ REVERTER, the Dencàs supporter; THE ITALIAN, after serving in the International Brigades.

In the Barcelona Prison are FEDERICO MORALES, the baker, and FERNÁNDEZ the Galician.

In France, in exile, are ESPAÑA, GARCÍA OLIVER, COMPANYS.

In Mexico, JOSÉ LLEDÓ.

LUIS SALOMAR, sentenced to death by a Republican tribunal, had his sentence commuted. He is now back in Barcelona, with JORGE DE BOSCH, who was director of a Republican museum during the war.

THE HERMIT was executed by mistake.

ATILIO FERNÁNDEZ disappeared.

EUGENIO SÁNCHEZ took refuge in the Chilean Embassy in Madrid; now in Italy.

THE TRAMP is still in Barcelona, as are DON ENRIQUE BARBERÁ COMAS, Bosch's uncle DON PRUDENCIO

BERTOMEU, and DON JUAN MANUEL PORREDÓN; DON JESÚS DE BUENDÍA Y O'CONNOR died in Switzerland, naturally.

THE JEWELLER'S WIFE died in Castellón, years ago, of cancer of the womb; THE JEWELLER joined in holy matrimony with MARIETA. She is the only one who sometimes on a Saturday evening, when the breeze comes up from the sea, remembers Rafael López Serrador: 'I wonder what's become of him?'

A dog barks, far away.

Paris, May–August 1939

APPENDIX I

Spanish Organizations and Institutions

The political groups and organizations mentioned below were influential during the period leading up to the Civil War.

Acción Católica (Catholic Action): militant worldwide organization founded by Pope Pius XI in 1922.

Alianza Obrera (Workers' Alliance): anti-fascist organization founded by Spanish socialist parties and unions, March 1933.

Assault Guards (Guardias de Asalto): blue-uniformed police force during Second Republic; urban counterpart of Civil Guard.

Carlism: traditionalist monarchical movement opposing main line of Spain's Bourbon monarchy and exalting separate line originating with Carlos V (1788–1855).

CEDA (Spanish Confederation of the Autonomous Right): founded by José María Gil Robles in February 1933 to combat left republicanism.

Church: the Spanish Catholic Church had been especially reactionary and supported not only the monarchy during this period but the Falange.

Civil Guard (Guardia Civil): Spain's paramilitary rural police force, founded 1844, reactionary in origin and practices for most of its history; members known for their tricorn hats and for patrolling in pairs.

CNT (National Confederation of Labour): Spanish confederation of anarcho-syndicalist unions founded 1910 based on union Solidaridad Obrera (its newspaper, *Solidaridad Obrera*, the *Soli*, was first published in 1907); closely allied with FAI.

Communist Party of Spain (PCE): founded 1921; grew to prominence through electoral victory of Popular Front in 1936.

Cuba: a key point of reference. Loss of Cuba in 1898 was the symbolic end of the Spanish empire in the western hemisphere; this made Morocco and colonies in North Africa generally the scene of a last-ditch defence of Spain's historical greatness in the 1920s and 1930s.

Dictatorship: initiated 1923 by General Primo de Rivera, ended by triumph of Second Republic in 1931 (First Republic was 1873–1874).

Diputación (*Diputació* in Catalan): town council of Barcelona, founded 1836.

Esperanto: the international language, invented in the 1870s, which became a symbol of future linguistic, cultural and possibly political internationalism.

Esquerra (Republican Left of Catalonia, ERC): Catalan Left separatist movement led by Francesc Macià and Lluís Companys in 1930s.

FAI (Iberian Anarchist Federation): founded 1927, closely allied with CNT; García Oliver and Durruti were leading militants.

Falange: leading Spanish fascist movement founded by José Antonio Primo de Rivera (the former dictator's son), in 1933, with its own distinctive theory of 'National Syndicalism.'

Generalitat: Catalonia's autonomous parliament, whose origins are in the medieval period.

Instituto Obrero: workers' educational institute founded by governments of the Second Republic in Valencia and Barcelona.

La Legión: founded in 1920, Spanish equivalent of the French Foreign Legion, though composed mainly of Spaniards.

Liberalism: political movement first founded in Spain in opposition to reactionary monarch Fernando VII.

Libertarian Atheneum: type of educational institute-cum-library for workers developed by Spanish anarcho-syndicalists, especially during the Second Republic.

Lliga (Catalana): Catalan League (known as Regionalist League until 1933), group of right-wing Catalan parties opposed to the Esquerra; its newspaper was *La Veu de Catalunya*.

Monarchy: Alfonso XII was the Bourbon king exiled in 1931 following his support of Primo de Rivera's dictatorship; his grandson Juan Carlos I became king in 1975.

Patriotic Union: founded by Primo de Rivera, 1924; included monarchists, conservatives, technocrats.

Popular Front: electoral alliance which governed Spain from February 1936 to the end of the Civil War, led by Manuel Azaña; included PSOE (though their leader Francisco Largo Caballero pulled them out of government), UGT, POUM, PCE and others; supported by Esquerra and CNT, though in practice most anarchists were opposed.

PSUC (Unified Socialist Party of Catalonia): Catalan equivalent of the PCE.

POUM (Workers' Party of Marxist Unification): Trotskyist-inspired anti-Stalinist communist party (not mentioned by Aub but central to George Orwell's *Homage to Catalonia*).

Radical Party (Partido Radical): Spanish anti-monarchical and anti-clerical party founded by Alejandro Lerroux in 1908 ('Young Barbarians' was a militant wing).

Republic (Second): the Second Republic, 1931–1939, was declared in April 1931 when King Alfonso XIII was exiled.

Servicio de la República: democratic republican organization founded by leading intellectual José Ortega y Gasset in February 1931.

Socialist Party (PSOE, Spanish Socialist Workers Party): founded 1833, leading socialist movement in Spain, became hegemonic under Felipe González in the 1980s.

UGT (General Workers' Union): the trade union organization closely associated with PSOE.

Historical Characters in Field Of Honour

Aranguren, José: Brigadier General in charge of 5th Zone of Civil Guard (Catalonia); helped put down the Nationalist uprising; executed by Franco in 1939.

Ascaso, Francisco: one of the three leading anarcho-syndicalist militants, together with Durruti and García Oliver; died on 20 July 1936 during the assault on rebel troops in the Atarazanas barracks.

Brotons Gómez, Francisco: Civil Guard colonel who remained loyal to the legally elected Republic; like his comrade, Colonel Escobar, he declined to escape from Spain at the end of the war and was executed by Franco.

Companys, Lluís: President of the Generalitat and leader of Esquerra Republicana; exiled after the war, he was returned to Spain by the Nazis and executed by Franco in October 1940.

Durruti, Buenaventura: perhaps the most legendary of all the anarchist revolutionaries; his mysterious death in Madrid on 19 November 1936 has never been definitively explained; buried at Montjuich, Barcelona.

Escobar Huertas, Antonio: colonel in the Civil Guard, Catholic and conservative, who nonetheless remained loyal to the Republic and helped suppress the Nationalist uprising in Barcelona; executed by Franco, February 1940.

Escofet, Federico: controversial soldier loyal to Companys, who put him in charge of public order in the Generalitat, and crucial in the defeat of the July 1936 insurrection in Barcelona; he escaped after the war and returned to Spain in 1978.

España, José María (Josep Maria Espanya): counselor, department of the Interior within the Generalitat of Catalonia; member of Esquerra; played a key role in the suppression of the July 1936 uprising.

García Oliver, Juan: leading figure in Spanish anarchism, advocate of paramilitary tactics, founding member of FAI and eventually its leader; minister of justice in Republican government during Civil War; escaped to Mexico in 1939.

Goded Llopis, Manuel: general in command of Mallorca at the time of the military uprising; moved to Barcelona to lead the rebellion there; executed at Montjuich on 12 August 1936.

Guarner Vivanco, Vicente: military head of public order services in Catalonia, remained loyal to Republic and helped suppress the military uprising; escaped to Mexico at the end of the war.

Llano de la Encomienda, Francisco: general in charge of the 4th Organic Division in Barcelona; loyal to the Republic and later exiled in Mexico.

López Varela, Luis: army captain stationed with the artillery regiment in Barcelona; active in linking rebel officers with the German Nazis, he was arrested on 20 July 1936 and shot in August.

Moxó, Manuel: colonel based in Captaincy-General of Barcelona; co-conspirator with Goded, though denied this.

Pérez Farrás, Enrique: military commander representing the Generalitat; it was he who arrested Goded; escaped into exile in Mexico.

Sanfeliz, Adalberto: lieutenant-colonel responsible to Moxó in the Captaincy-General.

Historical Characters with Fictional Names

González Cantos: the reader senses that this anarcho-syndicalist character was based on a historical personage, but there is no consensus about this. Several other characters give the same impression.

Lledó, José: based on well-known liberal Barcelona lawyer and journalist Josep Maria Lladó-Figueres (Barcelona, 1910–1996), exiled in France after the war before returning to Barcelona.

Morales, Federico: based on poet, critic and journalist José Jurado Morales (Linares, 1901–1991).

Salomar, Luis: based on Aub's friend the Falangist and writer Luys Santa Marina (Colindres, 1898–1980); worked on the literary magazine *Azor* with Aub and Jurado Morales.